To m[illegible]
C[illegible]

Christmas 1997

with love

from Alxxx

THE SEEKER

Also by this author, under the name of Josephine Cox

Queenie's Story
Her Father's Sins
Let Loose the Tigers

The Emma Grady Trilogy
Outcast
Alley Urchin
Vagabonds

Angels Cry Sometimes
Take This Woman
Whistledown Woman
Don't Cry Alone
Jessica's Girl
Nobody's Darling
Born to Serve
More than Riches
A Little Badness
Living a Lie
The Devil You Know
A Time For Us
Cradle of Thorns
Miss You Forever

THE SEEKER

Jane Brindle

First published in 1997 by
HEADLINE BOOK PUBLISHING

A HEADLINE FEATURE hardback

10 9 8 7 6 5 4 3 2 1

British Library Cataloguing in Publication Data

Brindle, Jane
The seeker
1.Ghost stories
I.Title
823.9'14[F]

ISBN 0 7472 1857 9

Typeset by
Letterpart Limited, Reigate, Surrey

Printed and bound in Great Britain by
Mackays of Chatham PLC, Chatham, Kent

HEADLINE BOOK PUBLISHING
A division of Hodder Headline PLC
338 Euston Road
London NW1 3BH

This story is for those who believe,
and those who don't.

CHAPTER ONE

Confused and afraid, Libby closed her eyes, convinced that when she opened them again, everything would be all right.

She was wrong.

A short time ago there had been the sound of laughter; the happy buzz of other diners talking, and the soft, lilting strains of music in the background. Now, suddenly, inexplicably, she felt horribly alone. But no! That wasn't right, because Dave was still there, smiling and talking across the table from her.

Yet even he seemed unreal. Almost as though if she were to lean forward and touch him, he would flow like vapour through her fingers.

Just now, she and Dave had been talking about how they had done the right thing in getting back together. They had talked about how the time apart had made them realise they belonged together. Tonight was a double celebration. After spending months apart, this was the first anniversary of their reunion; added to that, it was Libby's thirty-second birthday. Here, in this beautiful restaurant, amidst all the noise and bustle, they had been saying how their new-found relationship was strong enough to see them through anything. They both loved the new house. It was a brand-new start, and neither of them ever wanted to move again.

But that was before.

Unsettled, Libby glanced about the room. There was no laughter; no people; not even the sound of logs crackling in the fire. The air struck bitter-cold, making her teeth chatter, causing the skin all over her body to stand out in goose bumps.

Yet she could feel the heat from the fire warming her face. The sweat trickled down her back and the hair on her head stuck to her scalp as if it was larded down. Inside her head she thought she heard a stranger's voice whisper, 'He's mine . . . He's mine.'

For one awful minute, she thought she must be going mad.

Then, as suddenly as they had disappeared, they were back, the guests and the laughter, the buzz of talk and the clink of glasses. You're cracking up, my girl, she told herself wryly. Pull yourself together or they'll be carting you off in a straitjacket.

'Happy birthday, sweetheart.' Dave's voice gentled into her thoughts.

Raising her glass, Libby smiled. 'Here's to *us*.'

When he lifted the wine bottle to refill her glass, she shook her head. 'No more for me,' she said warily. The strange, fleeting experience still played on her senses. 'I think I've had more than enough wine for one night.'

Dave laughed. 'What? You've hardly had any at all. Two glasses at the most, and then only partway full.'

'Maybe. But you know how the wine plays tricks with me.' That was it, she thought. The wine was playing nasty little tricks with her mind.

Even so, she was unnerved. It had been the oddest thing, as though she was the last remaining soul on earth.

A chill swept through her. Shuddering, she closed her eyes.

'Are you all right?' Covering her hand with his, Dave was shocked. The room was suffocatingly warm yet her skin was ice-cold to the touch. 'My God, you're freezing.'

She laughed shakily. 'Time we went,' she said, 'before the wine plays havoc with my imagination again.'

He met her gaze with concern. 'What do you mean?'

'Nothing.' Her smile was bright now, the feeling of dread diminished. 'I'm fine. Really.'

Not quite reassured, he suggested, 'If you want to leave, sweetheart, we'll leave. The taxi I booked should be here by now.' He thought she looked ill. No. Not ill. She looked . . . scared.

What a strange idea. Why in God's name should she be scared? Feeling suddenly tired, he rubbed his knuckles into the hollows of his eyes. Maybe he was the one who'd drunk too much wine.

While Dave called for the bill, Libby forced herself to look across the room, to the far corner by the door. Caught unawares, the man quickly turned away. Anger raged through her. Damn him! All night he'd been watching her. Making her jittery.

'Ready when you are, my lovely.'

She answered with a smile. 'I'm ready now.'

'Tired?'

'A little, maybe.' She was lying. The truth was, for some inexplicable reason she felt totally exhausted.

'I'm not surprised.' Dave glanced at his watch. 'It's nearly two in the morning.' His dark eyes sparkled mischievously. 'Time I got you home to bed.'

'So you can have your wicked way with me?' She giggled, a flush of embarrassment colouring her face. After all this time, he could still do that to her. But then they were still young – though she didn't feel young at this particular moment.

Dave made no comment. Instead he cupped her hands in his, the light in his eyes communicating his love.

From the other side of the restaurant, the man continued to observe them, his dark, inquisitive eyes coveting their every move. Like Libby, he had sensed the weird, disturbing atmosphere. But he knew what it meant. At first he hadn't been certain. But now he knew.

Over the years, it had happened many times. It happened when *she* came. A tragic figure trapped in another time, another world. A beautiful, sad creature who wandered the highways and byways, searching, always searching.

The last time she made an appearance, a man died.

Others had seen her. He never had. He only knew when she was close, and she was close now. So close he could feel the silken brush of her hair on his face, the touch of her cold hand in his. He loathed her. He wanted her hurt as he and others had been hurt. But she was beyond his loathing. Though he would gladly give his life to be the one who punished her, he knew it could never be. He couldn't hurt her. Nobody could.

Maybe he was imagining it, willing her to appear. Maybe she wasn't here at all.

His instincts told him differently.

She was here all right. Outside. Waiting, in the shadows.

He glanced through the window. 'Be patient,' he muttered, as though talking to some unseen figure. 'They'll be leaving soon.' He was glad he didn't have to brave the darkness.

Curious, he returned his gaze to the couple. They were laughing and talking together, so much in love. He shifted his attention to the man in particular. It was this man who had unwittingly brought her back and, as sure as night followed day, he would live to regret it.

Outside, the wind screamed and sang, like a soul in torment. A human cry, yet not human.

Inside the restaurant, there was sudden laughter and he jerked his head towards the source. His customers. Ordinary people enjoying an evening out. He sniggered. Little did they know. Resentment uncurled inside him. If only she would choose him! Why was it always the others? Men of a certain kind. Men who could have her for the asking but were too afraid to follow. But then, fear was a powerful thing.

Aware of Libby and Dave approaching, he followed their progress across the room. 'You're too much in love,' he murmured with delight. '*She'll* make you pay the price.'

Smiling now, he moved forward to meet them. They made a handsome couple, he thought grudgingly. He guessed they were in their early thirties. The man was tall and dark-haired, with strong, handsome features. The woman was neither tall nor short; not pretty or plain. She was slim and feminine, with quick, bright ways and a warm, homely manner. He wanted to like her. He wanted to like them both.

For one brief moment, he pitied them.

A short time later, he opened the door and ushered them out into the night. He couldn't resist the warning, 'They say the lanes are haunted. Did you know?'

Buttoning up his coat, Dave shook his head. 'You don't need to invent ghosts to drum up trade,' he said politely. 'The food speaks for itself. Best meal I've had in years.'

Libby feigned indignation. 'Well, thank you, and here I was, imagining I'd fed you well all these years.'

Rolling his eyes to the sky, Dave groaned, 'Keep your mouth shut, Dave, before you put your foot in it.'

Libby laughed. 'I'll forgive you, but only because it's my birthday and you've done me proud.'

The man envied their closeness. 'They call her the Seeker,' he said.

Dave turned. 'I'm sorry, what did you say?'

'The one who haunts the lanes hereabouts – a lovely young thing. Some say she's bad, others that she's a figment of the imagination.' The rush of cold air made him shiver.

Libby didn't believe in ghosts. 'We've had such a lovely time.' That was no lie. 'I'm sure we'll be back.' That *was* a lie. Come back here? Not likely. The meal was wonderful, the restaurant charming, and the evening had been a dream, but for *him*. Watching. Making her feel uncomfortable.

In spite of herself, she was intrigued. Quietly regarding him, she thought what a strange little thing he was, with pale, quick hands, small, busy eyes and a slow, hollow smile that turned her stomach. And now here he was, sending them on their way with talk of lovely young ghosts and hauntings. Inwardly she cringed. It took all sorts, she mused, and he was one of the oddest.

Sensing her hostility, he turned to Dave. 'Tell the taxi driver to mind how he goes, sir. Everything else aside, the lanes round here can really be treacherous in the dark.'

'I can believe it,' Dave answered. The inn was far from the main road and the lanes were narrow and little used, with deep dark ditches either side. 'It's like no man's land out here.' Drawing the cool night air in through his nose, he blew it out in a long, noisy sigh. 'The countryside hereabouts is very beautiful. Too isolated for me, though.'

'It is off the beaten track,' the man agreed, 'but I'm used to it now, used to the quiet days and busy nights, and sharing my back garden with all manner of wild creatures.' A kind of childish wonder enveloped his shrewish features. 'All my life I lived in the city of London. Born and bred within the sound of Bow Bells. I thought I could never live anywhere else.'

Libby was astonished. He didn't seem like the type to set his roots deep in the countryside. She had him pegged as a man who might prefer to skulk around houses, peering in through the windows, hoping to catch some poor unsuspecting woman in a state of undress.

Suddenly embarrassed, he went on with a burst of pride, 'I've poured everything into this old place, and now it's all I have.' He put out his arms as though embracing his empire.

Over three hundred years old, with dark, timbered gables and warm, glowing lights in every leaded window, the inn made a charming sight. In its prime, it had attracted many a weary traveller looking for a place to sleep. Now they flocked here looking for cuisine second to none, and never went away disappointed.

An old black taxi turned into the inn's car park. 'Here's our chauffeur-driven limousine,' Libby joked. Relief flooded through her. She would be glad to see the back of this place.

'It really was a wonderful meal.' Dave shook the little man by the hand. Like Libby, he didn't much care for the fellow but it cost nothing to be polite. 'Time to go,' he said. 'We've a long drive ahead.'

'Of course.' Shifting his gaze to the waiting driver, the innkeeper added ominously, 'Go carefully now.' Stepping back, he watched them closely, like a cat eyeing a mouse at its mercy.

Feeling the night air sharp against his face, Dave glanced anxiously at the sombre sky. 'Looks like rain.' Even as he spoke, the raindrops spattered on to the porch roof, creating a weird and rhythmic melody. 'Better make a run for the car.'

The man's voice pursued them. 'They say she's lovely, with sad eyes and a smile you won't forget.'

Pretending not to have heard, Dave took Libby by the hand. Hurrying her towards the car, he muttered, 'For God's sake, let's get out of here. That fellow gives me the creeps.'

Libby was surprised. 'I thought it was just me,' she remarked. 'I didn't think you'd taken a dislike to him as well.'

'All this talk of girls and haunting. I don't want him spoiling your birthday treat, that's all.' But it was more than that. Deep down, he felt restless. Uneasy, as though someone was following him.

He swung round abruptly, half expecting to see a shadowy figure. 'Jesus!' A rise of warm sweat moistened the palms of his hands. 'I could have sworn there was someone there.'

Libby was startled. 'It's the wind in the trees.' She glanced nervously about. 'I expect there's a storm brewing.' It's this place, she thought, and that awful little man.

'You could be right, sweetheart.' His smile put her at ease, but it didn't quiet the turmoil in his guts. Somehow, that weirdo back there had got to him.

From the doorway, the 'weirdo' watched. With a rush of pleasure, he wondered how those two innocents would cope when the awful things began to happen. If experience had taught him right, they would happen soon. And without warning.

Lurking in the shadows, lost in disquieting thoughts, he didn't hear the woman sidle up. 'Who are they?' she asked, and he, startled, swung round.

'For God's sake, Ida, don't do that!' When he began trembling as he did now, it was hard to calm himself. 'Sneaking up like that, you frightened the bloody life out of me.' His glance flickered to the open door and beyond, into the dining room. Thank God, he thought. No one had heard. No one had seen. They were all too busy. 'All too wrapped up in their own pathetic little lives.'

The woman inclined her head to one side. 'What did you say?' It was so irritating when he mumbled.

'Never mind. I want to know what you're doing here.' He could hardly tear his eyes away from the diners. He hated their smiles and their laughter. He hated the way they took it all for granted; put a meal in front of them and they hardly noticed it. What did they know of the pain and effort that had gone into such creations? What did they care?

The woman's eyes followed his gaze. She had learned to read his every thought. 'You feed these people and you take their money,' she said. 'You smile and fawn over them, and yet you loathe them.' There was uncharacteristic kindness in her manner. 'You shouldn't hate them, Larry. It wasn't their fault. Any more than it was yours or mine.'

For one brief moment he felt ashamed. She knew him too well, damn her eyes, and she was right. Strangers they may be, but he resented them all the same. 'I asked you what you were doing here.'

Remaining in the shadows, the woman answered, her voice weary, 'I had to get out of the house, that's all.' She sighed. 'He's being difficult. He's always difficult before Eileen comes to visit.' Impatient, she lit a cigarette. To hell with him, she thought. To hell with them all.

'Sack her then. Get somebody else.'

'You know he won't tolerate anyone else. Have you forgotten? We've already had three. None of them lasted more than a week. Eileen makes him smile. She's good for him, and her rates don't cripple us – not like the others.' In the half-light she drew on the cigarette, blowing smoke rings with surprising skill. The smoke spiralled upwards, merged into a perfect sphere, then evaporated in the cold night air.

'You stink of tobacco!'

'And you stink of greasy chips.'

The look he gave her was murderous.

'I'm not getting rid of Eileen, so don't start on me,' she warned. 'If it wasn't for her, I'd go out of my mind.' Defiantly, she sucked on the cigarette, savouring the moment, before releasing the acrid blue smoke. 'You see, it isn't only your father who needs her. *I* need her too.'

Her whole life was a lie but her need for friendship was real. There was little comfort for her here. Tony Fellowes was a burden. Larry even more so. The past drove her on and the future was an empty, desolate place. Sometimes, in the night, in the dark when she couldn't sleep and memories played in her tortured mind, the fear was like a physical thing, weighing her down until she could hardly breathe. In the morning it began again, the purpose, the goal she had set herself. Sometimes, when it became too much, she was tempted to turn her back on them all and find a life of her own.

But then she would remember. And there was no going back.

Larry suddenly grabbed her by the wrist. 'I hope you're not getting too pally with her. After all, it wouldn't do if she was to worm her way into your confidence, would it now?'

Shaking herself free, Ida snapped at him, 'Don't worry. I'm always careful, you know that. I've never said a word out of turn, and I never will.'

'What about Father? Does she ever question him?'

'No! And even if she did, how could he tell her?' Besides, Tony knew nothing. That was a pity, she thought bitterly. *He* should be haunted by the awful things he had done. 'You know I love you both,' she lied. 'I've always done the best for you, haven't I?'

Regarding her for a moment, Larry felt a wave of compassion. 'I know,' he acknowledged, 'and I don't mean to be spiteful.' Laying his hands on her shoulders, he kissed her tenderly. 'You'd better get back. You shouldn't leave him alone with her.'

'I know. It's just that sometimes I wish . . . oh dear God, I wish . . .' She bowed her head, unable to go on. There it was again, that irrepressible urge to run away. But it was a foolish, treacherous notion. Besides, there was nowhere to run. If she knew anything with a degree of certainty, it was that when her task here was done, she would end her miserable life. That was as it should be. Since the day she had given herself to this man, her life had been dedicated to one purpose. Soon, her task would be accomplished. After that, there was nothing.

'Get back to him, Ida. Hurry, please.'

As always, she reassured him. 'You mustn't worry, my love.' The words stuck in her throat. She could still taste his kiss on her lips, like a poison, slowly killing her. Yet she continued to smile, her voice soft and caressing. 'I'll keep him safe,' she promised. 'Trust me.'

'He can *never* be safe. You said that.' Anger stiffened his voice. 'Not even when his time is over and he lies beneath the soil.'

'Don't punish yourself, my love.' She amazed herself at the sweetness of her voice. To anyone listening it would seem she idolised this man who was her husband. In truth, he was merely a means to an end. A single, destructive moment in her lonely life. A moment which seemed to go on for ever.

Throwing the cigarette to the ground, she stamped on it, grinding the soft, pliable mess beneath her heel. 'You didn't answer my question.'

'What question?'

'That couple.' Her gaze drew his attention to the spot where Dave and Libby had been. 'Who were they?'

'Just a young couple, celebrating a birthday.' He paused, his voice dropping to a sinister whisper. 'Strange though. Did you see?'

She took her time answering. 'Yes, I saw.'

When she had first seen Dave, she could hardly tear her gaze away. He was the key, she knew. The key to unlock the past and release the future. It didn't matter if he was lost. It didn't matter if they were all lost. All that mattered was that the bad ones should pay for what they had done. All these years she'd tried her mortal best. It was never enough. 'You didn't say anything, did you?'

He shook his head. 'Only that the lane might be haunted.'

'Nothing else?'

'No.'

'So he has no idea?'

He shook his head. 'None.'

'Hmm.' In the half-light, she discreetly observed him; his expression gave nothing away. She grunted again, her gaze shifting to the road and the direction in which the car had gone. 'It's just as well he doesn't know what's in store.'

'Poor devil.' His voice trembled with emotion.

She remained for a moment, her face looking up to his, her heart breaking. 'It's been a hard day. I'm really shattered. If your father falls asleep, I'll be in bed by the time you come home.' She touched him on the face, a soft, intimate touch that made him smile at her. The smile faded when she added gently, 'Try not to wake me.'

He watched her go, a tired, caring creature who had done nothing wrong, yet, like him, was being punished almost beyond endurance. He glanced up at the night sky, at the stars twinkling there, and for one magical moment he remembered how it had been before their whole lives had changed for ever. Still, it was not Ida's fault. 'I should remember that,' he murmured. 'I should treat her better than I do.'

Like his peace of mind, the moment of nostalgia was soon gone. Reality came rushing back and he turned, like an old man, his mind so weighed down he didn't at first hear the head waiter calling his name. 'Mr Fellowes, are you all right?'

'For heaven's sake, Carter! What is it now?'

'This.' Holding out a blue silk scarf, he said, 'I think it belongs to the lady who just left.' Carter was a slightly built man but as bright and fresh as the polished buttons on his jacket.

'What would you like me to do, run down the road after her?' Shaking his head impatiently, Larry took the scarf from him, crumpling it into his palm. It seemed to exude a natural, spring-like fragrance.

Suddenly he found it all too much. His mind slipped to another time, another place. Another younger, lovelier woman. The same woman who had left him only moments before, his own wife, now old and worn. Like him, she was chained by a love that grew stronger the more it was tested. 'She was quite pretty, don't you think?' he said absent-mindedly. He clutched the scarf, wanting to keep it for himself, to feel the nearness of beauty once more, before it was too late. 'The one who left this behind,' he murmured.

'I thought so, yes.'

Aware that Carter was regarding him with some slight amusement, Larry was suddenly repulsed by the feel of the scarf in his hand. Whipping it to the ground, he snapped angrily, 'Put it somewhere safe, where it can be easily found when they come back for it.'

Carter bent to pick it up, remarking with some surprise, 'Why? You don't think they'll be back for it, do you? I mean, it doesn't look expensive or anything.' He held it up to the light, showing how the silken fringe was frayed and worn. 'I reckon she's had the best out of it.'

Larry observed the scarf for a moment, then, with a small laugh, uttered softly, 'Put it somewhere safe, like I said. They'll be back. Or at least *he* will. Then get on with your work.' Squaring his shoulders, he took a moment to compose himself before striding into the restaurant.

'Bloody misery guts!' Carter grumbled. 'I could go anywhere and get a job.' But it wouldn't be so well paid, and so he stayed. One day, though, when he'd saved enough, he'd make his way in the world and have a place like this. Who knows, he thought with a burst of ambition that left him breathless, I might even buy *this* place. After all, Larry Fellowes is getting on a bit, and these days he seems to have his mind on other things. Miserable git!

In an instant Larry had shed his forlorn expression and

painted on a bright, benevolent smile. Entering the dining room with an air of authority, he proceeded to make sure his guests would look forward to coming back. Over the years he had perfected the art of making people feel at ease and welcome, and now he was a master at it.

Out of the corner of his eye he caught sight of the head waiter looking at him. Turning quickly he was gratified when Carter seemed uncomfortable and flustered. For the sake of appearances he smiled and nodded. Through his teeth he muttered, 'If you only knew.' He drew on such a long, hard sigh that his whole body trembled. 'Mark my words,' he whispered, 'we haven't seen the last of that unfortunate young man.' He knew.

He knew it was all part of a greater plan.

Dave had thoroughly enjoyed the evening. Now, with Libby curled up beside him, he felt immensely fulfilled. 'Good job we booked you,' he told the driver, a man of older years, with a kindly face. 'It seems we both drank a little too much wine tonight.' When Libby snuggled closer, he put his hand over her breast, thrilling at the small round curve nestling in his fingers. 'We're not used to the drink. Isn't that right, sweetheart?'

'If you say so.' She was incredibly tired, and glad to be on her way home.

'Sounds like you had a good time, though,' the driver remarked. 'A fine meal, good company and a bottle or two of wine on the wife's birthday – nothing wrong with that.' He sighed. 'My woman left me five years back. She took a fancy to my best mate and the two of them vanished from the face of the earth.' He laughed cynically. 'It's a lonely life for some, so you enjoy what you've got. You never know when it'll be snatched away.'

'I'm sorry about your wife.' Dave felt the warmth of Libby against him and his heart was full. The driver couldn't know how he and Libby had gone through a trial separation and almost lost each other. Thank God they had realised how much in love they were. Now, it would take wild horses to drive them apart.

'Don't be sorry, mate.' The driver looked both ways as they approached the junction. 'It was my own fault. She said I never took her anywhere, and she was right. Working all hours and thinking more of my mates than my wife, that's what cost me my marriage and serves me right.' He smiled into the mirror. 'It's good to see you're looking after *your* better half.' The driver glanced at Libby in the mirror. Pretty little thing, he thought enviously. Yet he was glad to see them so happy.

Dave might have said how it hadn't always been that way. He might have revealed how it had been the pressure of work that had almost cost him his family. That hard lesson had taught him to get his priorities right. Family and work were both important, but now, thanks to careful planning and some very motivated staff at the estate agency he owned, he had time enough for both. He might have explained all that, but he chose to say nothing.

'Tired, are you, sweetheart?' Bending his head, Dave brushed his lips along Libby's cheekbone.

Heavy-eyed, she snuggled closer.

'That's it,' he murmured. 'You have a sleep. It'll be a while before we're home.'

He couldn't sleep, though. He felt too restless. Unsettled somehow.

As the car left the inn further in the distance, Dave felt the urge to glance back through the car window. The road was dark behind them. Shadowy trees hung their great branches over the road, like monsters with outstretched arms. A wide, glowing shaft of moonlight threw a sinister glow over the landscape, and from somewhere in the forest came a shrill, unearthly cry.

'Jesus!' Glancing up into the mirror, the driver met Dave's gaze. 'What the devil was that?'

Dave shrugged. 'Just some night creature. Shouldn't worry about it.'

'I'm out of my depth in the country. I'm only here because the boss is setting up a new base and the manager hasn't recruited all his drivers yet. Six months, that's how long my contract runs. Once that's done, I'm back to the bright lights where the only screams and grunts you hear are two lovers having it off in a back alley.'

'Where are you from?' Dave felt he had to make conversation.

'Liverpool, and proud of it.'

'I've just sold a house to a man from Liverpool – retired, not short of money, by all accounts. He seems to have taken to the countryside like he was born to it.'

'Good luck to him then. Not me though.' He glanced sideways, out of the window. 'I don't mind telling you, mate, I've never heard the likes of that sound before. Fair put the wind up me, it did.' He laughed nervously. 'I expect you hear it all the time, eh? Get used to it, I suppose.'

'It's just animals. Fighting for territory or choosing a mate. Cats do it all the time. You must have heard cats yowling in the dead of night.'

'Not like that, I haven't.' He laughed, at the same time pressing his foot hard to the accelerator.

Turning slightly in his seat, Dave stared out of the window into the darkness. He couldn't rid himself of the uneasy feeling that they were being followed. He recalled what Libby had said about a storm brewing and the wind rustling the trees but this coal-black night and brooding atmosphere was like no storm he'd ever experienced.

As the driver accelerated and the car surged forward, Libby stirred out of a dreamy sleep. Half awake now, she looked up at Dave, her voice little more than a whisper. 'Except for that sweaty little man hovering over us all evening, it's been wonderful, Dave.' She sighed lazily. 'All the same, I'd like to choose where we go next time.'

His quick smile belied the anxiety inside him. 'Are you saying you don't like my choice?' he teased. 'That delightful inn? And that interesting little man, so attentive and all? Matter of fact, I think he took a real fancy to you.'

He wondered about the man in question. When they had walked away from the inn, he had felt the cold stare of his eyes in the back of his neck. The man was hostile, there was no doubt about it. But why? Before tonight, they had never set eyes on each other, hadn't exchanged a word. It was his secretary who had made the booking. It was odd. And yet he knew there were people like that; people who took a dislike to someone else for no apparent reason. In fact, he might have been guilty of it himself at one time or another.

Libby stretched her legs. 'How long before we're home?'

'Not long – half an hour.'

'Where are we now?' She felt too lazy to sit up; besides, it was comfortable having Dave hold her like this.

'A few miles out of Ampthill.'

While he concentrated on the road ahead, Libby chatted about this and that. He wasn't really listening. His eyes were scouring the way ahead; his mind up there, driving, overtaking; irritated and impatient.

'Hey!' He felt the tap of her hand on his arm. 'You're paying someone else to drive us home, remember? Relax. You're like a cat on hot bricks and you're making me nervous.'

'Sorry, sweetheart.' He kissed the top of her head. 'It's hard to relax when someone else is driving.' All the same, for her sake, he made the effort.

In the dim light she regarded the sapphire and diamond eternity ring on her finger. 'It's beautiful.' Reaching up, she gave him a fleeting kiss. 'Thank you.'

'I think you're right, sweetheart.' His attention caught by a swerving cyclist, he wasn't even aware she'd spoken.

'About what?' It peeved her when he didn't even glance at the ring.

'You said you thought there was a storm brewing. I think you're right.'

Opening the window a fraction, he let the night air bathe his face. Above them, the dark, seductive sky pressed so low, he could hardly breathe.

'You haven't heard a single word I've said,' Libby groaned.

'Sorry.'

Forgiving, she snuggled down again. 'Wake me when we're home.'

It was serenely quiet for a while. Too quiet, Dave thought. The driver evidently thought so too because he turned on the radio and began to hum along to the rich tones of Elton John.

The desultory rain suddenly became a fierce downpour, driven with such force it seemed the windscreen would shatter. Switching the wiper blades to full strength, the driver pressed his face closer to the windscreen, his eyes scanning the road ahead. The rain was drumming against the car so hard he couldn't hear himself think.

Libby sat up. 'I said there would be a storm,' she yelled. 'I was hoping I might be wrong.' Her mind soon turned to other things. 'I've left the washing out too. I hope the babysitter had the good sense to bring it in.'

Rain turned to hailstones and the noise was deafening. Just as Dave was about to suggest they ought to pull over until the storm had passed, the driver shouted from the front, 'I think I'll have to stop, mate. I can't see a bloody thing.' Looking for a suitable place to pull over, he kept his speed down. 'Sit tight,' he ordered. 'Looks like there are deep ditches all along here.' His head was stretched forward, his eyes skimming the road ahead. 'I'll need to find hard ground or we'll end up axle deep in mud.' He took a moment to glance at Dave who was also looking for a good place to stop. 'I don't mind telling you, I'd rather drive a hundred miles blindfolded than be stranded in this Godforsaken place.'

Dave knew what he meant. The road between Bedford and Ampthill was badly lit and flanked both sides by deep banks and ditches. On one side you could see for miles over the Bedford valley; on the other was a splendid view across the fields to the brickfield wastelands. This was not the best place in the world to be stranded.

'If I remember rightly, there's an opening just up here on our left,' Dave recalled. 'It's the entrance to a small factory. We handled the sale some time back. Slowly now, it's right on the bend. You could easily miss it.' Straining his neck, he peered into the darkness.

Was that a woman standing there?

At first he couldn't be sure, but then he saw her in the full glow of the car's headlights and knew he was not imagining it. Standing beneath the tree, she seemed almost a part of it, wet and bedraggled, long brown hair and big sad eyes looking at him. It was as though she had deliberately picked him out. With a shock he saw her raise her arms and open them wide, entreating him to come to her.

It seemed an age before he could cry out, but in fact it was no longer than it took to blink an eye. 'Look out!' he screamed. 'Don't run her over!'

Easing the car to a halt inside the factory entrance, the driver screwed round in his seat. 'Run who over?'

Flinging open the car door, Dave ran out into the road. 'There was a woman. She was sheltering under this tree,' he said, pointing to the big old oak. 'Soaked through, she was. No coat or umbrella.' He ran on, looking everywhere, frantic she might be hurt.

There was no sign of her.

Libby and the driver searched with him. 'There couldn't

have been anyone there,' Libby said. 'It's dark, and the rain was blinding. You probably saw a dog, or the branches of a tree moving.' She was wet through and growing more impatient by the minute.

So was the driver. Wishing he had never been given this particular fare, he was aching to get home. 'You said you'd had a bit too much to drink, and it looks like you were right.' At home he had a fire going, and a bottle of best whisky in his cupboard. With his feet up and a swig of that to warm his belly, he'd be a happy man.

As they walked back to the car, Libby commented on how quickly the rain had stopped.

'As quickly as it began,' the driver nodded, 'and the wind's dropped too. Just as if there was never a storm at all.' He winked at Libby. 'Like there was never a woman standing beneath that tree.'

They smiled at each other, but Dave wasn't smiling. He had seen her, and nothing they said would convince him otherwise.

Resuming their journey, the trio settled into their seats. The driver turned the music back on and Libby relaxed, wishing they were home, hoping the babysitter had brought the washing in.

Dave was beginning to wonder whether he really had imagined the woman when instinct urged him to turn and look again. Though it was growing ever distant, he could see the spot, the tree . . .

She was there! Just as before, she stood beneath the oak, long brown hair wet to her shoulders, big sad eyes following him.

Gently, he touched Libby, about to ask her to turn round and see for herself that he hadn't imagined it. But before he could speak, the woman was gone, vanished like the clouds had vanished from the sky. Gone as though she had never existed, like the rain had gone from the ground. The storm must have been real though, he reasoned, because all three had experienced it. But only he had seen the woman.

Alerted by his touch, Libby turned to him. 'What's wrong?'

Instinct again urged him, this time not to make an issue of it. 'Nothing,' he said, and held her close. For a moment he wondered if he was going out of his mind.

Letting the music invade his senses, he was surprised to find himself being lulled into a kind of sleepy trance. He closed his eyes, forcing himself to think of work and the big deal he hoped to pull off. He thought of Libby and his two children, Daisy, aged eight, and Jamie, four. A faint smile touched his features. Work was important, it had to be. The mortgage needed paying, there were everyday bills and unexpected ones, holidays and outings, and kids cost a fortune to raise. Yes, work was important. But the children and Libby were his life.

He gazed down on her. She was the best thing that had ever happened to him.

'Nearly home.' Libby sat up, straightening her hair, fastening the tie-belt on her coat. 'I hope the kids have been good.'

The roads were well lit now, and the cars were passing them both ways. Dave was relieved. Back there, it was like some kind of nightmare. Now, it seemed like something and nothing. He must have imagined the woman. What other explanation could there be?

His thoughts strayed to the owner of the restaurant. That man had put a notion into his mind and the storm had created confusion. That was it. Of course. The innkeeper was a bloody fool, and so was he. All the same, it pleased him to see the lights of oncoming cars. There were people walking on the pavement and over there a stray dog cocked its leg at a lamppost.

Everything seemed so normal.

Ida sat beside the old man, her hand in his, her gaze false with love. There were tears in her eyes, and a lifetime's agony too. Addressing the woman in nurse's uniform, she sighed forlornly. 'It doesn't seem fair, does it?' she said. 'A whole lifetime wasted. Why, Eileen? Why do these things have to happen?' She was asking about something else now. Something the nurse knew nothing at all about and, God willing, never would.

Small-boned and strong, with kind blue eyes and cropped fair hair, Eileen was an attractive woman in her late twenties. 'I don't have any answers, Ida.' She was tired, aching to go home and put her feet up. A mug of hot chocolate wouldn't go amiss either.

'If it wasn't for you, I don't know what I'd do. He likes you, you see. He trusts you.' That much was true at least.

'He trusts you too, Ida. You couldn't do more for him if you were his very own daughter and he loves you dearly. Anyone can see that by the way he follows you with his eyes. I know he can't speak or communicate in the same way we do, but he can still take immense pleasure from the simple, ordinary things in life – the song of a thrush perched on the windowsill, or the sunlight making patterns in the sky. It's hard, I know, but we must be grateful for even the smallest blessings.' She went to Ida and eased her out of the chair. 'Leave him now. You both need your rest.'

'You're a great comfort to us, especially to him.' Glancing at the old man's face, she noticed he was gazing at Eileen. 'See how his face lights up whenever he sees you.'

Eileen looked on him then, smiling when she saw his brown eyes twinkle. 'Go to sleep,' she chided and, like a child, he closed his eyes. 'When you hired me I wondered if I was up to it,' she told Ida. 'My first nursing job and all, but I'm glad to be of help, Ida, and I'll be here as long as he needs me.'

'*I* need you too.' Loneliness was a hard price to pay.

A few moments later, Eileen prepared to leave. 'You get some sleep, Ida. You've got my number. Ring me if you need anything.'

After the door closed behind Eileen, Ida went to her bedroom. Here, she opened the bedside drawer and took out a small photograph album. It was filled with yellowing photographs. Larry, through his baby years and into his youth. There were photographs of him as a teenager, then as a young man. Never handsome, but on the day they were married, he looked upright and proud. Beside him she seemed like a lost child.

There were pictures of his father before the tragedy. Unlike his son, Tony Fellowes had been a handsome man. The hair that was now grey and thinning had been a thick brown mane, and the dark eyes twinkled then as they did now. He was a fine looking fellow, with a strong athletic figure and a love of all things a young man of means might pursue: football; sailing; rally-driving. In fact, anything and everything that was foolhardy and dangerous.

'I know all about you, Tony Fellowes,' she muttered. 'I know all there is to know. More than your own son knows. More than *you* will ever know.' The soft, evil sound of her laughter was like a shock in the quietness of that house. The train of her thoughts more so.

Impatient, she flicked through the pages, searching for the one photograph that meant more to her than all the others. The one she looked at time and again, though it tore her apart inside. When she found it, she leaned back, her gaze roaming the picture and drawing comfort from it.

'You set me a terrible task,' she whispered, tears breaking from her sorry eyes. 'But I won't give up.' Kissing the photograph, she held it close to her heart. 'I'll make them pay for what they did to you. With all my heart and every breath in my body, I promise they'll be made to answer. *All* of them!'

Holding the picture away from her, she let her eyes take

in every tiny, fading detail. The woman was in a bridal gown, her small, pretty face crowned with a halo of rosebuds. She was smiling, but the smile was like a mask over her features, thin and transparent to those who knew and loved her.

On the day the picture was taken, her new husband had been standing proudly beside her. Now, though, only a jagged line remained where he had been torn out of existence.

A moment more to savour the memories of that sad, pretty young thing, and then, with the greatest care, Ida returned the cherished picture to its resting place.

Fired now by things of the past and with the need for sleep gone from her, she made her way back to his room. She sat beside him, her hand on his, her eyes boring into his sleeping face. 'Can you hear me, Tony?' she whispered. 'I've been looking at her picture again.'

Like an innocent, he slept on.

'I know you'd rather forget her, but I won't allow it. We both need to remember what you did to her.' Her voice shook with emotion. 'It's hard, every day pretending, living a wicked lie. But I have no choice, you must know that.'

She observed how deeply he slept and yet his sleep was not an easy one. 'What are you dreaming about, old man?' she persisted. 'Are you dreaming of her? Can you see her face as clearly as I can see it?' She wanted to end his life there and then. Grabbing the pillow from beneath his head, she pushed it hard over his face. 'It would be so easy,' she whispered, 'so easy.' Realisation dawned and she snatched away the pillow. The old man jerked, turned his head ever so slightly and began snoring.

'I almost lost control.' She was still shaking. 'That was unforgivable of me.' Leaning forward, she whispered, as though sharing a secret, '*She's* out there. The young man brought her back. But she won't have you. You know I can't allow that.' Lowering her gaze she watched with fascination as her fingernails dug into the soft flesh of his wrist. She watched the blood trickle on to the sheets and only then did she stop. 'Oh dear, I've hurt you.' She dabbed at the blood with her handkerchief. 'It's only what you deserve. You gave her no peace and now I can give *you* none.'

Returning to her own room, she undressed, bathed and got into bed. When Larry came home some time later, she was still awake. But she closed her eyes and pretended to be sleeping.

It was easier that way.

CHAPTER TWO

It was half past seven on Monday morning. As usual in the Walters' household, there was chaos and uproar.

'I can't find my PE kit!' yelled Daisy from the top of the stairs. 'I'm not going to school without it! Miss Lucas won't let me stay in the gymnasium. She'll send me to Frostie's class, and I hate it.'

In the middle of breaking eggs into the pan, Libby spun round. 'Look in the wardrobe,' she called out, swearing under her breath when she dropped an egg on the floor. The cat made a dash for it and Jamie made a dash for the cat. The result was a mess from one end of the kitchen to the other. 'Get up, Jamie!' she snapped. 'Leave the cat alone!'

Exasperated, Dave glanced up from the table where he'd been browsing through his schedule for the day. 'What's the problem here?' Aiming a disciplinary glare at his rebellious son, he waited for an answer.

'He's got a mood on, that's all,' Libby answered for him. 'The best thing to do when he gets like that is ignore him. He'll soon get fed up.' She spoke from bitter experience.

'Got a mood on, eh?' He was making light of the matter, but when Jamie put out his tongue, he took a more serious approach. Swinging Jamie up by the scruff of his neck, Dave sat him firmly in the chair. 'We've all got our problems, Jamie,' he said. 'Taking it out on others won't help, will it, eh?'

'I don't like that cat.'

'Maybe the cat doesn't like you, especially when you keep tormenting him.'

'I only tickled him.'

'Tickled nothing,' said Libby from behind the cupboard door. 'You pulled him across the floor by his ears. No wonder he bit you.'

Already out of his depth and thinking ahead to his first crucial appointment of the day, Dave gave some fatherly advice. 'Do as your mother says and leave the cat alone. That way he won't bite you.'

'I'm hungry.'

'We're *all* hungry.'

'I don't want eggs and soldiers.' Jamie's bottom lip began to tremble. 'I want beans.'

Libby was losing patience. 'We're out of beans until I go shopping.'

Now he was sulking, which was a small blessing, because at least he was quiet.

Not so Daisy, whose voice shattered the sudden quiet. 'I've looked in the wardrobe and it's not there!'

'Look in the drawer then!'

'I've looked there too.'

Engrossed in mopping up the egg, Libby appealed to Dave. 'If it's not in the wardrobe, it's definitely in the drawer,' she said.

Going up the stairs two at a time, Dave took Daisy by the hand. 'Let's look in the drawer again, eh?' And, after much arguing and protest, she led him to the pine chest. 'It's not there,' she insisted, 'I've already looked.'

'Well, for your mother's sake,' and for mine, he thought, 'it won't hurt to look again.'

The contents of the drawer had been turned upside down, with every carefully ironed article now hopelessly crumpled. Buried beneath it all was a small blue bag with the initials D. W. stitched on the front. 'One PE kit, I think.' Drawing out the bag, Dave dangled it before his daughter's wide, astonished face.

Delighted, she would have snatched it and made good her escape, but Dave pointed to the heap of clothes. 'I don't think you should leave it like this, do you?'

'No, Daddy.'

'Straighten the clothes and leave the drawer exactly as you found it. The bag will be downstairs in the kitchen when you've finished.'

'Aw, Dad. I'll be late for school.'

Adamant, he gave her a hug. 'You made the mess. You put it right. OK?'

She knew it was no use arguing. 'OK.'

Taking the bag, Dave made his way down to the kitchen.

In a surprisingly short time, Daisy burst into the room. 'I'm ready now.'

Libby's temper was sorely tried. 'Well, I'm not, and neither is your brother.'

'I can go to school on my own.' Eight years old, going on twenty, she was.

'You'll do no such thing, my girl.'

Horrified at how swiftly the time had flown, Dave grabbed his coat and car keys. 'I can drop her off if you like,' he suggested.

Libby would have none of it. 'I thought you had to meet an important client at nine o'clock.'

'So I have, but I'm sure he won't mind waiting a minute or two.'

'If you go out of your way to drop Daisy off at school, it will be more like half an hour,' she told him. 'Besides, you've been stuck with that old house long enough. This is the first real interest you've had in it for over a year.' She knew how important it was for him to be rid of that particular property. It was like an albatross round his neck. 'You go,' she told him, reaching up for a kiss. 'You can tell me the good news when we meet in the Boulevard.' Eyeing him suspiciously, she teased, 'You haven't forgotten, have you?'

'One o'clock,' he reminded himself. 'I expect you want me to buy you lunch.' His smile was wonderful.

'Of course.'

Daisy was frantic. 'If I have to go in Frostie's class, I'll run away!'

A quick goodbye and Dave was out of the door. Libby grabbed Jamie, and his coat. When he was ready for the outdoors, she put on her own coat, then her gloves and the pretty crocheted beret she'd bought at May Dexter's shop last year. 'Now, I can't find my scarf.' She hunted high and low but it was nowhere to be seen. 'Where the devil did I put it?' Another quick search in the pockets of her long woollen coat, then a frantic scramble in the bottom of the hall cupboard. 'It's not here.' The scarf was one of her prize possessions.

'You'll make me late!' Daisy cried, standing at the open door in the path of a force nine gale.

'I'm hungry.' Jamie's stomach was still his prime concern.

'Sorry.' Slamming shut the cupboard door, Libby ushered them both outside into the teeth of a biting wind. 'I'm lost without that scarf,' she groaned, packing them into the old red Escort. 'Besides, it was the first present your dad ever gave me.'

Daisy had the solution. 'Get him to buy you a new one.' Grinning from ear to ear, she revealed, 'Old Frostie's got a new scarf. It's red and green with yellow stripes, like the kilt she wore on open day. Simon Travers says it's her clan colours.'

Libby glared at her in the mirror. 'I've told you before, young lady,' she chided, 'it's rude to call your teacher by nickname.' Though when she was a child they did it all the time. She was a parent now, though, and parents should set an example. 'Damn these gears!' With an almighty heave she crunched into second gear.

Jamie piped up from the depths of a sunken seat, 'What's clan colours?'

'It's to do with Scotland and family tradition.' With a grinding screech the gear popped out again. 'Honest to God, one of these days I'll pay the scrap man to take this heap away.' With an angry thrust she crunched it back into third.

Jamie stared at her in horror. 'You can't give it to the scrap man,' he protested. 'It's *my* car. You said I could have it when I grow up.'

'And I meant it,' she lied, thinking how the old heap would have been transformed into a thousand tins of dog meat by the time Jamie grew up.

Woburn village school was only ten minutes away. After their reconciliation, the Walters had bought a house on the edge of the woods, far enough away from the beautiful historic village to avoid the rush of summer tourists, yet near enough to walk to the shops and post office, and beyond into the magnificent parks. The parks, like most of the village and surrounding area, belonged to the Duke of Bedford. With its old gabled houses and curiosity shops, it was a lovely place to live, and now that Dave had set up his own estate agency in the nearby town of Woburn Sands, the family had put down roots here. Now, Libby could not envisage living anywhere else. Even the house was a dream come true; large and rambling, surrounded by fields and woods and with panoramic views from every window, it was the most picturesque place.

It hadn't always been like that. When she and Dave first saw it, the house was dilapidated and the many outbuildings were falling down. She and Dave had bought it cheaply at auction. They lovingly planned its refurbishment and even rolled up their sleeves to help. It was a labour of love. The kitchen was the kind of spacious, country kitchen she'd always dreamed of, with old oak beams and a wide brick chimney above the cooker. On one wall she had asked for numerous deep shelves which she'd filled with blue plates and hung with copper pans. She had a big old pine table and a dresser to die for. The kids had a large playroom in the cellar, and Dave had the whole of the attic for his study. All in all, it was as if the building had been waiting for them all its life.

Twelve months after they first viewed it, the house was transformed into a wonderful, warm cosy home. A place to right all the wrongs of the past. A place to raise the family. Sometimes, Libby wondered if it would ever go wrong.

Daisy was still considering her mother's remark about the teacher. '*Everyone* calls her Frostie,' she retorted.

'Miss Frost,' Libby sighed, wondering how Peggy Blake always managed to stay so calm with six children, all boys. And she was always meticulously dressed and had a smile for everyone. I must be a lousy mother, Libby mused. I love my kids to bits, but I'm always in a rush; I never seem to do anything right, and these two little sods run rings round me. She glanced at them in the mirror; Jamie had his nose pressed to the window, his eyes big with pleasure as he watched a group of boys building a snowman. Daisy was so pretty, eager-faced and bubbly, much like she herself had been at that age. Her heart swelled with love, and she foolishly vowed never to show her temper in front of them again.

At that moment the car chose to splutter and cough, limping along one minute and jerking the next. 'Bugger it!' Banging a fist on the steering wheel, she suddenly remembered her silent vow. 'Oh sod it! I'll make a new start tomorrow,' she muttered, thankful they were at last turning into the courtyard of Daisy's school.

'Remember now,' she reminded her daughter, 'the teacher's name is Miss Frost.' Bringing the car to a halt, she groaned when the engine spluttered and died. 'Dammit!'

Daisy couldn't get away quickly enough. 'I can't call her Miss Frost when the others call her Frostie,' she said indignantly. 'Anyway, she's *not* my teacher.' Throwing her arms round Libby's neck, she hugged her hard. 'But I'm not late, so I won't be sent to her class, thank goodness.'

''Bye, sweetheart.' Libby was past arguing.

''Bye, Mum. 'Bye, Jamie.'

'I'm hungry.'

'You're *always* hungry.' With that Daisy ran to her friends and was soon lost in a sea of grey uniforms and bright, shiny faces.

With a sigh of relief, Libby watched her enter the building. 'Thank heavens I'm not a teacher,' she mumbled. 'I don't think I'm cut out to handle twenty-four Daisy Walters.' In an effort to start the car, she pumped the accelerator. When the pungent aroma of petrol wafted up, she realised with a sinking heart that she had flooded the engine.

'I don't want this old car,' Jamie declared with a sulk. 'It stinks.'

For one frightening, delicious moment Libby felt like strangling somebody – *anybody*! She scrambled out of her seat and, opening the back door, told Jamie with a carefree smile, 'Out you get.' Which he did, with a lip that dragged the ground.

'I'm hungry.'

In fact she could hear his stomach rumbling from where she stood. Compassion moved her, but she knew how difficult he could be and so remained stern. 'Serves you right for not eating your breakfast.' She hated Monday mornings. Oh, how she hated Monday mornings.

The school secretary must have had a bad start to the day too. Normally she was bright as a button with a smile that made you feel at ease. Today, however, she had a sour face and a mouth that resembled a puckered gash in newly-made bread. 'You can't leave that car in the gateway,' she declared stiffly. 'We have traffic coming and going all day. The school bus is due any minute, and the photographer's arriving at ten thirty.' It was etched on her brain, like every disaster waiting to happen.

'I really don't want to leave it there,' Libby explained patiently, 'but it won't start.'

'You'll have to get it moved then.'

'That's what I intend. If you'll let me use the phone, I'll get the garage to come and tow it away.' Under her breath she added viciously, 'With a bit of luck he might throw it in the nearest bloody tip!'

'Beg your pardon?'

'Nothing. Just let me use the phone.'

Jamie was still hungry and unforgiving. 'Mummy swore,' he told the astonished woman. 'She said bloody.'

Libby was ashamed but the woman laughed out loud. 'Come in and use the phone,' she said. 'It sounds like you've had a worse morning than I have.'

By the time the breakdown vehicle had taken away her car and the bus had delivered her and Jamie to the nursery, Libby was at screaming pitch. Mustering all her composure, she apologised for bringing Jamie late and was assured that it was perfectly all right. The nursery teacher even agreed that Jamie could have a biscuit and a glass of milk. 'In fact, we should all be stopping for a break in ten minutes,' she said, 'so we'll stop now. What's ten minutes between friends?'

The young woman's friendly smile and placid nature had a calming effect on Libby's shattered nerves. 'I can't tell you what a dreadful time we've had.' Libby's matter-of-fact voice belied her feeling of inadequacy. 'I'd better go or I'll be losing my job on top of everything else.'

Twenty minutes later, exhausted and tried to the limit, Libby almost fell through the door of the draper's shop where she worked. 'Oh, May, I'm sorry,' she said to the attractive, auburn-haired woman behind the counter. 'I'll work Saturday morning to make up.'

Large and kindly, May Dexter was normally easygoing. She had a heart of gold and was not given to bad temper. But this Monday morning seemed to be giving everyone a bad time; like the secretary at Daisy's school, May was not in the best of moods. She'd had to cope with a rush of customers as well as a very chatty plumber who had come to fix the burst pipe in the loft. 'I needed you this morning,' she snapped. Her mass of auburn hair was more unruly than ever and, much to Libby's astonishment, she was bare of make-up. 'I've been run off my feet. You know very well I should have been out buying first thing today. We're running short of twenties-style dresses, and there isn't a size fourteen of anything in the shop. I've already had two people asking for black cotton and I had to turn them away. I never thought I'd see the day when May Dexter turned away good customers. And did you know we were completely out of blue wool? Old Ma Hepworth wanted some to knit a matinee jacket for her new grandson. I had to disappoint her as well. It's bad for business. Why didn't you tell me we were running short? That's what I pay you for. Honestly, Libby! I can't be expected to keep track of everything.'

'I *did* tell you,' Libby protested. Throwing off her coat, she grabbed up the stock book and shoved it under May's nose. 'Look. It's all in here – blue wool, black cotton, and 1997 calendars. I did the stock list a week ago. I said we were running short of twenties-style dresses as well.' She pointed out the entry. 'I did my job, as you can see.' It had taken her nearly two hours to check the stock and make the entries, and now she was being held responsible for the shortfalls. 'I'm sorry, May, but it's not my fault if you don't look in the stock book. All the same, if you're not happy with my work, you only have to say.' So much had gone wrong this morning, she was past caring.

May was mortified. 'I'm sorry, you mustn't take it personally,' she apologised. 'I'm just an old fool. Take no notice, Libby. Of course I'm happy with you. What! I don't know what I'd ever do without you, and that's the truth.' She winked. 'Look, gal, we've made a bad start. How about if we started all over again and I make us both a nice cup of tea?' Checking the time on the wall clock, she declared, 'I'll get there when I get there, and to hell with it.'

Libby smiled at her, but before May could go and put the kettle on, the door opened to admit a customer. It was Miss Ledell. The moment she came through the door, the shop was filled with the sweet smell of newly crushed rose petals. Miss Ledell was in her late seventies, old yet not old. There was something very different about this particular old lady. Something inexplicable, a deep-down beauty that shone from her face. Coming from a time of graciousness, she was tall and elegant, with mesmerising dark eyes, and long, plaited grey hair.

She was always well dressed. On this cold winter's morning, she had on a long flowing black coat and ankle-length boots; over her head she wore a pale blue beret drawn down to one side and touching the curve of her high cheekbone.

Libby thought she was an example to every mature woman. 'What can I do for you, Miss Ledell?' Something about this woman urged a kind of reverence.

'Oh dear! Miss Ledell sounds so formal, especially when you've been neighbours for a long time now. Besides, your delightful daughter spends so much time with me, I've begun to feel like part of the family.'

Libby felt uncomfortable. 'I'm sorry, and yes, you're right. You're more than a neighbour to us. All the same, it doesn't seem right to call you by your first name.' Even if she knew what it was, which she didn't.

The old lady frowned. 'No doubt you were always taught to address your elders with respect.'

'Something like that,' Libby admitted sheepishly.

The old lady laughed. 'And they don't come much older than me.'

'I hadn't even thought about it like that.' The last thing she wanted was to offend.

'Age shouldn't be a barrier.' It was a wise remark, rooted in the pain of experience.

While Libby attended to the old lady, May scurried off to make the tea. When the door closed behind the regal customer, she came out, a cup in each hand, and a packet of biscuits gripped between her teeth. 'She's a strange old thing, isn't she?' Nodding towards the door, she almost dropped her tea when it opened again and Miss Ledell's face reappeared. 'Oh, and I'd appreciate it if you could keep two bright eyes for me. I won't need them yet, but I'd hate to find I didn't have any when the time comes.' She turned to go, but suddenly spun round, her long grey plait making a thud as it slapped against the window pane. 'Brown,' she said thoughtfully. 'They must be brown. And they *must* have a twinkle.'

'Of course. I'll look some out for you.'

'I mean to have it finished in time for Christmas.'

Libby had heard little else from Daisy for the past fortnight. 'It's very kind of you.'

The old lady smiled, a slow, whimsical smile. 'Good. Brown then. With a twinkle.'

When she finally departed, Libby commented thoughtfully, 'I wouldn't mind betting she's broken a few hearts in her time.'

'What's all this about brown, twinkling eyes?' May asked.

Libby chuckled. 'She's making Daisy a teddy bear.'

'I thought Daisy already had a teddy bear.'

'She has. In fact, she's got half a dozen, so I suppose one

more won't hurt. Apparently, it's a reward for being such a hard-working pupil. But if it's been well-earned, and it keeps an old lady happy, where's the harm?'

Perched on a stool, May sipped her tea. 'I wonder why she insists on teaching Daisy to play piano yet turns all other hopefuls away.'

Libby had asked the old lady the same question. 'She says she doesn't really have the time or energy to teach more than one child and, according to her, Daisy has a natural talent that cries out to be nurtured.'

'The next thing she'll be wanting is a piano to practise on at home.'

Libby had thought the same and she and Dave were prepared to go out and buy a piano, but, 'No, Daisy says she'd rather practise at Miss Ledell's. Anyway, you know what children are like. They get all excited about one thing or another, then weeks later they don't want to know. She might get fed up, so maybe it's as well we don't lay out money for a piano until she's absolutely sure. I mean, nobody else in the family plays.'

'Have you ever heard her play?'

'Just once.' It was only a few notes, but Libby would never forget it. 'I'd gone early to collect her. The window was open and I heard someone playing the piano. I was sure it couldn't be Daisy because it sounded so beautiful, too accomplished, if you know what I mean.' The memory was so vivid. 'I peeked in at the window and the two of them were seated on the long stool in front of the piano. The old lady had her eyes closed, listening. It was Daisy who was playing. Honestly, May, it was the most beautiful sound I've ever heard.' Just thinking about it made her flesh creep.

'I'd like to hear her play.'

'You'll have to wait in line.'

'Oh? Why's that?'

Libby laughed. 'Because my extrovert daughter, who

shines on stage in a school play and is first in the queue when teacher wants someone to read out loud, was horrified when she found out I'd been listening to her. I told her I thought it was beautiful and that her dad would love to hear her play, but she was adamant. "Miss Ledell says it will be some time before I'm good enough for other people to hear." That's what she said and there's no shifting her.'

'I always get the impression she comes from a long line of aristocrats.'

'Who? Daisy?'

'No, you silly arse! The old lady.'

Libby chuckled. 'I know what you mean.' The hot tea slithered smoothly down her throat, soothing her frayed nerves. 'She does have a certain grace, and such a soft, gentle voice. Being so tall and slender, she moves wonderfully well for her age.' In her mind's eye she could see the old lady in her youth. 'I bet she was gorgeous when she was young – those wonderful, dark eyes, and that long thick hair. I wonder what colour it was when she was in her prime.'

'Black, I imagine, or dark brown.' Dipping her biscuit into her tea, May cursed when the whole thing fell in. Fishing it out with her finger, she remarked, 'I'd love to see her hair hanging loose. I bet it's a sight to behold.'

'She never says much about herself, does she? I mean, nobody seems to know where she comes from, do they?'

'Hasn't she confided in Daisy? I should have thought if she was to tell anyone about her past, it would be your daughter. From what I can tell, she adores the girl.'

The faintest surge of envy touched Libby's heart. 'They are close, yes,' she admitted grudgingly. 'When Dave's mother passed away last year, the children were left with no grandparents. Jamie eventually accepted it, but Daisy was devastated. Dave and I couldn't seem to reach her, yet once the old lady took her under her wing, she was soon over it.' That had been a bad time for the family. 'We're immensely grateful and you can see for yourself how Daisy has given the old lady a new lease of life too.'

The tiniest smile crept over the older woman's brassy features. 'Aren't you just the teeniest bit jealous?'

Libby was honest. 'A little bit maybe.'

'You shouldn't be though. The old lady's nurturing the girl's musical talent, and taking the place of a grandmother into the bargain.'

'May?'

'Hmm?'

'Does anyone know where she comes from?'

May shook her auburn head. 'She's a mystery. I don't think anybody even knows her first name. Do you?'

'No, I don't.'

'She's lived in that farmhouse for more years than I can remember, and nobody knows any more about her now than they did the day she arrived.' After sucking in the remains of her biscuit into her mouth, she noisily slurped the last of her tea. 'All I do know is that she keeps herself to herself and never causes anybody any trouble, and you know yourself, she's as kind and generous as they come. She knits for the poor and needy, and every Christmas takes a sack of beautiful handmade toys to the children's ward at the hospital.'

'She's a special person, I'm not denying that.' Libby had a great deal of respect and liking for her. 'You know she won't take a penny for Daisy's music lessons? I've tried all ways to make her accept some kind of payment, but she won't hear of it.'

'Don't feel bad about it, Libby. From what I can tell, she's not short of a pound or two, and I expect she's glad of Daisy's company. I don't recall her ever mentioning any family of her own, and as far as I can tell she never goes anywhere, except to the village shops. It's no wonder she looks forward to Daisy's visits. The girl must be like a breath of spring to the poor old soul.'

'You're right. She does look forward to her visits. Whenever I drop Daisy off, she's waiting at the door, and when I pick her up, she waves us out of sight. Sad, really.' Libby didn't know what it was like to be lonely, and she didn't want to. She imagined there could be no worse feeling on God's earth than not having someone to care for; unless it was not being cared for yourself.

'There you are then.' May took her cup into the scullery. 'I'd best away and catch the train into Bedford,' she declared. 'Being late might have worked out in my favour because by the time I get there, the Monday morning rush should be over. With a bit of luck and a following wind, I should be back before you finish at three.'

'I know I shouldn't really ask, having made you late and all, but will it be all right if I close for lunch as usual?' Libby glanced at her wristwatch, amazed to see it was already twelve o'clock. 'Only I've arranged to meet Dave at the Bull Inn for a bite to eat. He's got a late business meeting so he probably won't be home until midnight.'

May grinned mischievously. 'Are you sure he hasn't got another woman?'

Libby was stunned into silence. But she couldn't blame May for her unthinking remark. She wasn't to know that it was Dave seeing another woman that had almost broken up their marriage.

'*I'm* the only woman in Dave's life.' She said it lightly but in truth she hadn't completely regained her trust in him although he had since proved himself time and again. Once a man cheated on you, it was hard to banish the knowledge. 'Where would he find someone else like me?' she asked with wide, innocent eyes. 'I'm a good cook, magnificent in bed and, though I say so myself, I'm not a bad looking bird – for my age.'

'Get away! You're only thirty-two. You haven't got the cradle marks off your arse yet.' May wished she was years younger, when the men chased her for her figure; now if they chased her it was because she had her own business and they were looking for a cushy life. 'Men! Who needs 'em?' She did, but would never admit it.

Libby gave no answer, but she knew in her heart that if she lost Dave for good, she would be devastated.

Sensing Libby's thoughts, May wondered if she'd said the wrong thing. 'It's different with you and Dave,' she said seriously. 'You only have to see the way he looks at you to know he's head over heels in love.' In truth, she envied Libby's relationship with Dave. From the rare snippets of information Libby let fall, she guessed they had been through a bad time but now, since getting back together, they were like Darby and Joan.

'So, is it all right then, if I meet him for lunch?'

'I don't see why not.' Her good mood reinstated, she was her usual kindly self. 'I think the initial rush is over now, and anyway you look as though you could do with a break. Yes. Go and meet your hubby as arranged, and if I'm not back by three, lock up and take yourself off. We can't have you being late to collect the children. Not with the world full of perverts and psychos.'

May had never married. She had never wanted the responsibility of family. Now, though, the older she got, the more she wondered if she had made the right decision.

Dave put down the receiver and leaned back in his chair. 'Another sale concluded,' he declared, winking at the girl across the desk. 'That was Lawson and Co. – Greg Harman's solicitor. Everything's signed, sealed and soon to be delivered.' With every new sale, he believed he and Libby were putting the troubles of the past behind them. 'What with four new viewings still to be done today, and three big sales in the pipeline, we seem to be going from strength to strength.' Even so, he crossed his fingers. So much had gone wrong in the past. He didn't want to tempt Fate.

Mandy's eyes lit up. 'Looks like you might have to take on another negotiator.' A pretty young thing, tall and slim, with cropped red hair, she was relatively new at the agency. But she was intelligent, smart and ambitious. Dave saw her as a candidate for promotion. Not yet, though. This was her first stab at this kind of work and she still had a lot to learn.

He saw the light of hope in her eyes and, as always, he didn't crush it. 'I've already told you, Mandy, if and when I'm ready to think about another negotiator, I'll bear you in mind.' The time would have to be right, though, he thought soberly. In this work there were peaks and troughs, and the market wasn't predictable. The old adage was still true: it didn't pay to run before you could walk.

As Mandy returned to her work at the outer desk, Jack Arnold swung open Dave's office door. For a while he stood there, arms folded, long, thin legs casually crossed, and a look on his face that said, 'I'm after something but I'm not sure I dare ask.'

'What is it this time?' Dave was used to his little ways.

'Aw, now, it's nothing for you to worry about.' His soft Irish voice sang across the room. 'Just a wee favour, that's all.'

'A favour, eh?' These days Dave regarded his friend and colleague with increasing respect. He looked at him now, and was impressed. Jack was meticulously dressed in dark suit and blue shirt, and wearing a tie, which in the old days was unheard of. Dave had known Jack since they were at school together. Two years ago, when he was down on his uppers after a particularly nasty divorce, Dave had given him a job at the estate agency. Jack had taken to it like a duck to water, and now he was earning the highest commission of all. It was well earned. Jack had an instinct for pairing the right buyer with the right property; his manner was charming and nothing was too much trouble. As a result, his sales portfolio was bulging, his bank balance was growing, and his confidence was at an all-time high.

Unfortunately, Jack still had a knack for choosing the wrong women. He'd walked twice down the aisle and each time it had been a disaster. The women took him for what he had, they broke his heart, then moved on to their next conquest. Jack never learned. Desperate to settle down and raise a family, he spent his life chasing women, yet wouldn't know a good one if he fell over her.

'All right, Jack.' Smiling to himself, Dave stood up, walked across the room and took his long coat from the peg. 'Who is she this time?'

Jack's face fell open with astonishment, his blue Irish eyes twinkling. 'Sure I never said it was a woman.'

'Are you saying it's not?'

He shuffled uncomfortably. 'No, I'm not saying that either.'

'So, who is she?' Dave had been through the same routine a hundred times with Jack. 'Come on, Jack, I haven't got time to play games. I'm meeting Libby in ten minutes.' Throwing on his coat, he strode across the room and stood face to face with Jack. 'Let's see now,' he mused, trying hard not to smile, 'you want the evening off, and you'll work two weekends to make up. There *is* a woman, but it's nothing romantic. She's just an old friend who's feeling lonely, and you believe that, as a friend, you should take her out and cheer her up.' He grinned. 'How am I doing?'

Jack laughed out loud. 'You're a mind-reader, sure yer are, and you're right. She is just an old friend, and I do owe her a favour.' He took the opportunity to remind Dave, 'And you owe me one, Dave, me laddo. Sure, haven't I just made my first six-figure sale? And doesn't that make me star of the month?' His chest swelled with pride.

Dave shook his head. 'Sorry to disappoint you, Jack, but I've just heard from Harman's solicitor.' He waited a moment to allow Jack to think on that. 'The sale's gone through, and the cheque's on its way.' Mimicking Jack's Irish accent he chuckled, 'Now then, me laddo, wouldn't yer say that makes *me* star of the month?' He always enjoyed their banter. Right now, the look on Jack's face was worth a fortune.

'You don't count,' Jack retaliated. 'You're the boss.'

Dave laughed. 'All right. But mind you juggle your workload to cover all eventualities.'

'Trust me.' He did a happy little jig on the spot. 'I've got an appointment with a client this afternoon, so I'll see yer tomorrow, yer old bugger.'

'Jack?'

'What?'

'Mind she doesn't have you for breakfast. Remember what happened last time?' He'd lost count of the scrapes Jack had got himself into.

Tapping the side of his nose, Jack quipped, 'No fear o' that. I'm a wiser man than I was before, sure I am.'

'Go on. Get out.' Since Jack had started taking life a little more seriously, it was a pleasure working with him. Now and then he would slip back into his old ways, but that was in his own time. As long as it didn't interfere with work, there was no harm done.

While Jack drove off, Dave stood for a moment outside his new offices. Originally the building had been a baker's shop and tearooms. Situated in the High Street of Woburn Sands, it was in a prime position. When he and Libby had first come to live in the nearby village, the baker's shop was being offered for sale. Dave saw the potential and snapped it up at a bargain price. He then did a deal with a local builder to refit and refurbish the place, and now it was one of the smartest properties on the street. Moreover, it had already grown in value to cover not only the purchase price but the cost of a new front and all the interior work. It was the start of Dave's new venture, and he had never looked back.

Pride shining in his face, he glanced up at the sign above the window: DAVE WALTERS – ESTATE AGENCY AND VALUERS.

Climbing into his Jaguar, he did up his seatbelt, his mind content but by no means complacent. 'You've been given a second chance and you're a lucky man, Dave Walters,' he murmured. 'Don't ever forget that.'

Libby had already ordered by the time he arrived. 'Quiche and salad for me,' she told him, 'chicken pie and boiled potatoes for you.'

The waitress had seen him come in. 'What would you like to drink, sir?'

'I'd like a beer, but I'm driving so I'll have a black coffee instead, with a jug of hot milk.' He used to drink coffee thick, black and strong, but that was before Libby weaned him off it. He didn't mind though. In fact he felt better for it. 'Tea for my wife, I think?' He glanced at Libby and she nodded.

'What kind of a morning have you had, sweetheart?' Leaning over the table he kissed her full on the mouth. She tasted good. One of Libby's finest assets was her skin; silky-soft and warm, it was, like a newborn babe's.

Libby was tempted to launch into the series of disasters that had marred the day. Instead, she shook her head decisively. 'Believe me, you don't want to know.'

The waitress brought the tray of drinks and set it down before them. With a nod and a smile she hurried away, leaving Libby pouring the tea. 'What about you, Dave?' she wanted to know. 'Did you make the sale?'

His face gave her the answer before he did. 'Not only did I sell that particular property, but I offloaded the old factory in Bedford as well.' Taking hold of her hand, he lowered his voice to a whisper. 'The market is really picking up, sweetheart. This morning's turnover alone was over a quarter of a million.'

Libby was delighted. 'A third for the taxman, a third for the business, and a third for you.' He had explained that much to her often enough.

'Not this time,' he said. 'We still have a few outstanding debts to clear. Once they're off our backs, we can start taking a more generous slice of the profits.'

She feigned misery. 'Oh God! So, I can't have a new car after all?'

'Give me a year, then you can have the car of your dreams. Until then, I'm afraid it's your trusty old Escort.'

Lunch arrived, and for a while they said little. It wasn't too long, however, before Dave became suspicious. 'What's all this about a new car anyway? I thought you told me you never wanted to part with that old Escort. If I remember rightly, you said you could never get rid of it – "I've grown too sentimental about it to let it go." That's what you said.'

'It's the Escort that wants to let *me* go,' she told him. Going on to detail the horrors of the morning, including the loss of her scarf, she concluded, 'So you see, I'm in the market for a new car, and to hell with sentiment.'

Dave promised to buy her another car if the Escort was beyond repair. 'But it won't be a new one, sweetheart. We can't stretch to that just yet.'

'Fair enough.' She knew the score.

'I'll buy you a new scarf instead,' he promised.

'I don't want another scarf, Dave.' Libby was adamant. 'I want *that* one. You bought me that soon after we first met. It's very special to me.' When they had been apart for all those awful months, the scarf had brought back so many memories. She recalled how Jamie had had an old piece of rag when he was a baby. Wherever he went, the rag went; he even took it to bed with him. The district nurse called it a 'comfort rag'. Jamie clung to it for three years and then one day he didn't need it any more. The silk scarf was

Libby's 'comfort rag' and she wanted it back.

'Oh, come on, Libby. It's just an old scarf. I'm sure we can find one almost identical.'

Ignoring his protest, Libby explained how she had already backtracked her moves since last wearing it. 'I had it on when we went to the inn. I don't remember having it in the taxi home, so I think I must have left it at the restaurant.'

Conceding defeat, Dave paid the bill and ushered her out. 'All right. I'll take a run out to the inn when I've concluded my business tonight. OK?'

'Not OK.' Linking her arm through his, she went with him to the car park. 'I'm not letting you go out there tonight when you're working late anyway.'

'I don't mind.' Easing the car on to the main road, he headed for Woburn.

'No, I don't want you to do that. Like you say, it's only an old scarf. You can buy me a new one.'

'You've soon changed your tune. Only a minute ago you were saying how it was special.'

'It doesn't matter,' she lied. 'It's time I had a new scarf anyway.'

At the shop, he would have gone in to phone the garage where her car was being repaired but she sent him on his way. 'I'm quite capable of doing that myself,' she protested, but kissed him all the same. 'Don't worry. I won't let them run rings round me. I can be a tiger when I'm put out.'

'Don't I know it.'

She waved him off then went inside. Locating the number of the garage, she dialled the number and waited, thinking how hard Dave was having to work. Until all their debts were cleared, they both had to work and earn. In her heart she hoped that, at the end of the day, it would all be worthwhile. 'Who knows?' she mused, a naughty smile lifting the curve of her mouth. 'I might even be awake when he gets home.' She felt incredibly happy.

A minute later she was shouting down the phone, 'What do you mean, I can't have my car back until tomorrow? I need it today!'

There was a short, impatient exchange of words, before she slammed down the phone.

She was still bristling with temper when May hobbled in. Red-faced and breathless, she threw herself into the nearest chair. 'I should never have got out of bed this morning!' she cried. 'I missed one train and the next was cancelled. My heel got caught in a grating when some lunatic in a car made me run for my life, and now I think I've broken my ankle. Honestly, gal, I don't know what the bleedin' world's coming to, I really don't.'

Trying her damnedest not to laugh, Libby went to put the kettle on. 'What a day!' she exclaimed, allowing herself the smallest chuckle. 'And it's not over yet.'

It was gone midnight when Dave got home. 'Are you asleep, sweetheart?' Sliding into bed, he kissed her softly on the forehead.

'Mmm.' She had been drifting in and out of sleep since eleven o'clock. Now, though, with his hard, cool body against hers, she was fully awake. 'I thought you were never coming home.' Wrapping herself round him, she ran her hands down his torso, her voice the softest whisper. 'I've been lonely.'

Astonished that she was stark naked under the sheets, he was instantly roused. '*How* lonely?'

Her answer was to fondle his hardening member.

It was all the encouragement he needed. With the tenderness of a man in love, he trickled his fingers down her body, letting them linger in the curves and crevices of her soft, warm skin. Easing her legs open he followed the shape of her inner thighs. He kissed and caressed her, bringing her to fever pitch, and then, with a rush of brute force, he entered her.

The mating was over all too soon, but the joining of hearts stayed long after he drew away from her.

Satisfied and content, she lay in his arms and for a while he held her there. After a time, when his arms began to ache and he saw that she was fast asleep, he eased over to his own side of the bed.

It had been a hard day and yet, tired though he was, sleep eluded him. He closed his eyes. He opened them. He stared at the ceiling and prayed for sleep. For a while he thought he might go down and get a beer, but dismissed the idea – that would wake Libby.

The sound began like a distant tapping at first. Soon it was raining with a vengeance. His gaze shifted to the window. Through the chink in the curtains he could see the rain pounding against the windowpane; relentless, invasive.

Like the rain itself, the image began faintly, a dark, vague thing in the shadows. *She* filled his mind. The young woman who had been standing beside the road. That sad, bedraggled figure who had mysteriously disappeared. Strange no one else had seen her.

Only him.

Only him!

Libby stirred.

'It's all right,' he murmured. 'It's only the rain.' But it wasn't only the rain, he thought. The room was so stifling, he could hardly breathe.

Suddenly he imagined he saw a shadow. There in the far corner of the room! But no, it couldn't be. There was no one here but himself and Libby, and she was right beside him, fast asleep.

He closed his eyes and smiled. 'Get some sleep, man,' he murmured. 'You're beginning to imagine things.' He looked again and the room was filled with moonlight. There on the window ledge was Libby's scarf.

He shook his head and blinked. Nothing was there. It

was only the light playing tricks.

He realised then. The rain had suddenly stopped. Just as it had on the night he saw the figure.

For a long time he lay still, his troubled gaze searching the shadows yet finding nothing untoward. After a while, sleep came over him like a dark, heavy blanket, smothering his senses. The weight on his eyelids became too much to bear and soon he was drifting into a restless sleep.

In his dreams *she* came to him. He was travelling along that same road. Lying beside him was Libby's blue silk scarf. He looked for Libby, but she was gone. Yet he wasn't alone. *She* was there. And he knew she would never leave. Not until she found what she was searching for.

CHAPTER THREE

It was Saturday, 21 November, a very important day on the Walters' calendar: today was Daisy's ninth birthday.

The first person to arrive was May Dexter. 'Am I glad to see you,' Libby told her. Since early morning she had been run ragged, putting the finishing touches on everything, checking she hadn't forgotten anything vital. 'Last night when I was lying in bed I ran through it all in my mind, you know the way you do?'

May didn't know, because she'd never planned a party in her life. All the parties she'd ever been to were other people's. 'You can tell me all about it while I make the coffee,' she suggested tactfully. 'And for heaven's sake, Libby, sit down before you fall down.'

Grateful for the time they had before the children poured through the door, Libby sank into a chair. 'Would you believe, I forgot the candles for the cake?' she groaned. 'I've been weeks making the cake. I've iced it, dressed it with ribbons, and then, at the last minute, found I hadn't bought any candles. I ask you, May, can you credit it? On top of that I'd forgotten to get a tin of strawberries for the trifle, and somehow or other I lost the wrapping for her present.'

Getting out the coffee cups, May gave her a sympathetic look. 'Sounds like you've had a harrowing morning, gal,' she chuckled.

'How is it some women are so well-organised they have

time to manicure their nails and visit the hairdresser twice a week? Me, I'm always chasing my own tail. My nails are always either broken or chewed, and my hair has a mind of its own.'

'I bet there isn't one woman we know who could bake a cake and organise a party like you've done. Besides, you can't be baking cakes and working in a draper's shop if you have long painted nails. What's more, you have natural, pretty hair, and you're a lovely, unselfish person. Unlike some of these prima donnas, you know how to enjoy life, you know how to have a good laugh. That's what matters most, my gal. Not looking like something that's just stepped out of the front cover of a magazine.'

Libby felt better already. 'You're a real tonic,' she said, and meant it.

'I won't have you keep putting yourself down.' Pouring the boiling water over the coffee granules, May took the milk jug from the fridge and brought the items one by one to the table. 'Any biscuits, gal?' She did like a biscuit with her coffee. 'Ginger nuts would go down a treat.'

'Help yourself. You know where they are.'

In less time than it took to eat one, May had retrieved the ginger nuts from the cupboard and was soon dipping one into her coffee. 'Everything's all right now though, ain't it?' she asked in her broad Cockney accent. 'The party, I mean.'

In answer, Libby went to the dresser and unveiled the prettiest of cakes; dressed with bright golden bows and nine white candles, it had the name Daisy written in pink through the centre. 'What do you think?' There had been a time when Libby would make a cake at the drop of a hat, but these days, what with work and everything, there never seemed to be any time. Today was special, though, and it was only right that she should bake Daisy's birthday cake.

May was suitably impressed. 'It looks good enough to

eat,' she grinned. 'The cake does you proud, gal.'

'It's the one thing I'm really good at,' Libby said. 'My mother was a great cook.' Nostalgia welled up inside her. 'It's been two years now, and I still miss her dreadfully.'

'It's only natural to miss her.' May had her own regrets. 'I lost my mum nearly twenty years back and it only seems like yesterday.' She blew out her cheeks in a sigh. 'Life goes on though, gal,' she said, wisely changing the subject. 'So, who else is helping at the party besides me?'

'It's just you, me and Miss Ledell. Daisy told her she was having a party and the old lady volunteered. Daisy's with her now. I've arranged to collect them later.'

May glanced about. 'Where's Jamie?'

'The little bugger was into everything this morning, so Dave took him into the office.'

'How many little monsters have you invited?'

'Ten in all.' With May here, Libby was beginning to get into the party spirit. 'Do you think you can cope?'

May had already swallowed a stiff brandy before she came out in the cold. Now, with a coffee and ginger nut, she was ready for anything. 'Just watch me, gal.'

Libby burst out laughing. She glanced at the pine clock above the door, horrified to see how swiftly the time was passing. 'Come on, there's a mountain of things still to do.'

At twenty minutes to three, everything was ready. The pine dresser was bedecked with balloons and streamers. On the shelf were ten little presents all lined up for the guests. 'You know what children are like,' Libby laughed. 'They all want a little present, even if it's not their birthday.'

The walls were festooned with birthday cards and garlands shouting 'HAPPY BIRTHDAY, DAISY', and the table was groaning with food – little sandwiches and dainty sausages, tiny pork pies bought at the supermarket that very morning, a huge plate of gingerbread men, and enough jelly and trifle to make them all sick for a week.

Set round the big kitchen table were ten chairs, with ten place mats and ten homemade crackers.

'The kids will love it,' May remarked approvingly.

At ten minutes past three, Libby got ready to collect Daisy and the old lady. 'The children shouldn't be arriving until half past,' she told May. 'If anybody turns up early, put them in the lounge. I've slipped a film of *Mary Poppins* into the video player. It's all set up. All you have to do is switch on and away you go.'

'I might want to entertain them myself.' Twirling round on the spot, May showed a rather chubby, black-stockinged leg. 'I've been to a few wild parties in my time and I've been known to do a good striptease.' When Libby swung round in amazement May looked indignant. 'What? You don't like the idea?'

Laughing, Libby shook her head. 'I'm just wondering who's going to give me the most trouble, you or the children.' With that she threw on her coat and headed for the front door. 'If Dave comes back, tell him I'll only be a few minutes.' He was so snowed under with work, she wasn't really expecting him until later, though he had promised to get back for Daisy's party.

The house where Miss Ledell lived was little more than a mile away from the Walters' place, but the lane was narrow and winding with potholes and cart tracks that made driving an uncomfortable business.

The trees were ancient, thick and broad, standing guard on the banks like old warriors of time. In summer the spreading mantles of foliage blocked out the sun, and even in wintertime, like now, the gnarled and twisted branches were woven in a pattern so tight and confused that little daylight was able to penetrate.

Libby drove carefully over the ruts and bumps, easing the old Escort higher up the bank, where the way was easier. She never failed to appreciate the solitude of this beautiful place. The house and grounds had a beauty all their own. Like the old lady herself, they exuded an air of grace and timelessness.

Approaching the house from the lane, Libby was forced to slow down in order to ease the car through the narrow gates. As she did so, she raised her eyes to the house, pleasure flowing through her. Low and rambling, with wide windows and thatched roof, it was a delightful sight. She well understood why Daisy loved to come here.

Inside the house, Daisy was seated at the piano, her small, fine fingers travelling lightly over the keyboard. Beside her sat the old lady, hands folded, eyes closed and a look of sheer pleasure on her face. As Daisy played on, the haunting strains of a love song filled the air. All too soon the melody ended, and for a moment the silence was overwhelming.

Turning to the old lady, Daisy looked for reassurance.

Her eyes opened, heavy with tears. 'Oh, Daisy, that was so beautiful.' Her voice trembled, her hands crushing against each other as though she suffered a terrible agony.

'Do you think I might have a piano like yours one day?' Daisy had come to love the old lady's piano. She had learned to make it talk and sing. Each time she left it, she counted the minutes until she could return to make it live again.

'You really love the piano, don't you, child?' Daisy always gave her so much pleasure. When the time came for her to leave, she would miss the girl.

She looked about the room, at the panelled walls and the gilt-framed paintings that hung there, the long floral curtains and the pretty patterned carpet, and her heart was alive with so many memories she could hardly bear it. This place, and the girl, had been the saving of her.

Her gaze fell on the wall above the fireplace, at the small painting there. It showed a young couple, so obviously in love. Above them the sun poured out of a blue, cloudless sky. The girl was smiling up at her man, a tall, dark-haired young fellow, with handsome looks and strong, capable frame. Holding her hands in his, he gazed down at her. In that split second when their love was captured, there remained between these two something uniquely wonderful; a bond so powerful that nothing and no one could ever break it. Not in this world, or the next.

The old lady gazed at the painting a while longer, remembering the moment as if it was yesterday. It was the most glorious summer's afternoon, and they had gone to the river for a picnic. Just as they were preparing to leave, an old man had begged them to stay so that he could sketch them. 'You look so happy,' he told them. 'Such a beautiful couple.'

Flattered, they stayed while he got to work, and in less than an hour he finished the sketch. When they asked to see it, he refused. 'If you're here next Sunday, I'll have something special for you,' he promised.

The following Sunday they returned to the same spot and so did the old man. What he gave them was a small, beautiful painting taken from the sketch, framed and signed. This was the painting that now hung over the old lady's fireplace, as fresh and vibrant as it had been on the day it was given. It was the old lady's most precious possession, filled with sunshine and love. The girl's crimson dress was picked out in painstaking detail – short, tapered sleeves and sweetheart neckline, with the warm breeze lifting the flared skirt and swirling it naughtily about her shapely ankles. The young man wore a blue blazer and light grey trousers, his thick dark hair tousled by the wind.

At first glance it seemed like any other picture of a young couple. Yet, if one looked deeper, there was something very strange about the painting. Something out of place and disturbing.

Daisy's voice brought the old lady back to the present.

'When I grow up, I want a red dress just like that.'

'And why not?' Miss Ledell smiled. 'You would look lovely in a dress like that.' Touching the girl's long hair, she felt a kindred spirit. Daisy was special. *Daisy was her only hope.*

Another longing glance at the painting. Bitter-sweet memories flooded through her. Yes. She would miss Daisy when the time came. A child's laughter; the music; this room. She would miss it all. Then she reminded herself how small a loss that would be compared to the loss she had already suffered.

Suppressing the painful emotions, Miss Ledell stood up, her attention drawn to the window. 'Your mother's here,' she said brightly. 'It's time to go.'

'What about my drawing?' Daisy asked excitedly. 'The one I finished last week. You said I could have it on my birthday.'

The old lady slowly shook her head. 'Tonight,' she answered thoughtfully. 'You may have the drawing when you come back . . . tonight.'

Frowning, Daisy reminded her, 'I'm not coming back until Monday.'

The old lady smiled knowingly. 'We'll see.'

'I can't wait to show my drawing to Mum and Dad,' Daisy gabbled on while the two of them made their way to the front door. 'I've never drawn anything like that before.' Again she sought reassurance. 'Do you really think it's lovely?' Daisy's words were spoken with the innocence of a child. She could not know how they tore the old woman apart.

'You will never know how lovely,' Miss Ledell answered softly.

'Will you let me draw some more?'

'Oh, yes.' That was the plan. 'There will be many more,' she promised, 'and each one will tell a story.'

'What kind of a story?'

'A love story.' Again the old eyes clouded over. 'Take your present.' Handing the girl a large, soft parcel from the hallway table, she urged, 'Go on now, my dear. Tell your mother I'll just be a minute.'

After Daisy had gone, the old lady stood quite still for a moment, a great sadness coming over her. 'I'm sorry, child,' she murmured. 'I wish there was another way.' She had come to love Daisy. The last thing she wanted was to use her. She had tried so hard, but it was too difficult a task for her alone. Too many forces stood between her and her destiny. Unforgiveness. Evil. These were powerful enemies.

With a heartfelt cry, she covered her face with the palms of her hands, the anguished eyes momentarily clouded by a terror that had long held her prisoner.

'Forgive me, child,' she whispered, 'but you and your father are the only way back for me.' After a moment she straightened her shoulders, a new determination flowing through her. 'You mustn't despair,' she told herself. 'The waiting is almost over.' Clenching her fist, she pressed it hard into her chest. 'I feel it in here.'

Hurriedly she put on her coat and hat, and then went into the kitchen. Here she transferred a number of scones from the tray to a wicker basket. She covered the scones with a square of gingham and retrieved two earthenware jars from the larder, one filled with cream, the other with homemade elderberry jam. She placed them in the basket beside the scones. 'That should fill a few small tums.' She hoped Libby would be pleased with her modest efforts.

Libby was delighted. 'But you really shouldn't have gone to all that trouble.'

'It was no trouble.' In fact she had forgotten what a pleasure it was to bake. Music was her food. Music and painting, and tending her ever-changing garden, these were things of the soul. Living alone, steeped in the past and obsessed with her thoughts, she found little joy in earthly matters.

The party was soon under way. Delivered in their party gear, with shining faces and Daisy's presents tucked under their arms, the children were bubbling with excitement. Their parents didn't linger. 'I should think they're glad to see the back of the little sods,' May declared with a laugh. 'I don't blame them either. The sight of ten monsters congregating is enough to send anyone scurrying for the nearest exit.'

All the same, she was thoroughly enjoying herself. Mopping up the spills and occasionally reprimanding the more unruly elements, she was soon in charge. 'She's like a sergeant major,' one cheeky lad remarked. 'I'm glad she's not my mum.'

'So am I!' Standing within earshot, May gave him the fright of his life. His silence lasted all of one minute, after which he took great delight in pinching Rosie Dunn's bottom. But Rosie was a big girl and able to look after herself. In the end, and much to May's satisfaction, the boy came off worse.

When Dave and Jamie arrived home, they could hear the sound of children's laughter emanating from the house. Jamie ran ahead. 'Come on, Dad!' he called. 'I hope they haven't eaten all the trifle.'

Libby came out to greet them. Sweeping Jamie into her arms, she asked, 'Have you been good for your daddy?'

'Ever so good.'

'Go on then. Into the kitchen with you, and don't worry, we've saved some of everything for you.'

While Jamie dashed to the kitchen, Dave gave Libby a hug. 'How's my best girl?'

'A bit ragged round the edges.'

'You don't look it.'

'Flatterer.'

He kissed her then, a long, lingering kiss that spoke volumes. 'You'll have to wait,' she said knowingly.

He laughed. 'You're a cruel woman.' Tightening his arm about her waist, he gently propelled her towards the kitchen. Screeches of laughter filled the house. 'Sounds like the kids are enjoying themselves.'

'You're just in time to see Daisy open her presents. After that we're all going into the lounge to play games.'

Before Dave could answer, Daisy came rushing out of the kitchen. 'Oh, Daddy, I'm so glad you're home!'

'Now, would I miss your party?' Stooping to kiss her, he whispered, 'If you've invited another boyfriend, I'm gonna be real jealous.'

Blushing to the roots of her long, blonde hair, Daisy protested, 'Don't be silly, Daddy! I'm too young to have a boyfriend.'

Deliberately raising his voice, Dave glanced up at Libby. 'Bet your mother had a boyfriend when she was your age.'

'Behave yourself, you.' Playfully cuffing him round the ear, Libby ushered Daisy into the kitchen. 'Present-opening time, then everyone into the lounge!' She could hardly make herself heard over the din.

Miss Ledell handed out the visitors' presents and there followed a few minutes of frenzied excitement.

'Cor!' one lad shrieked. 'A Luton Town football shirt.'

'Look what I've got!' someone else yelled.

Another boy was close to tears. 'Don't want this! Dolls are for *girls*!' It was all soon sorted out to everyone's satisfaction. 'It was an orange or an apple in my day,' May remarked. 'That's if you were lucky enough.'

'It's my turn now,' Daisy said. Going to the dresser, she collected her pile of presents and opened them one by one, with every face turned towards her, every eye eager to see what she'd got. Libby and Dave had bought her a complete set of Take That records; Jamie had raided his fat piggy bank to buy her a book token, and May had given her a blue, embroidered jewellery box. 'Next year I'll buy you something really special to put inside,' she promised.

While all this was going on, Dave stood at the back of the room drinking coffee, his gaze on Daisy and his expression one of pride. Libby had done well, he thought. He finished his coffee and absent-mindedly dipped into the biscuit barrel. He smiled wryly on discovering the barrel was empty. He thought about putting the kettle on for another coffee, but decided instead to have a cool drink. There was still some lemonade in the jug. He found a glass and poured himself a long drink, his dark eyes following the rush of cool, clear liquid as it ran into the glass.

Instantly his mind was filled with another image: the stark image of a young woman standing in the rain.

Imprinted deep in his subconscious, the memory continued to haunt him. Not because it had been a shock to see her suddenly appear, distressed and soaked to the skin; and not because she had just as quickly disappeared without trace. The image clung to him because, God help him, he had been oddly attracted to her. It was puzzling. The woman was a complete stranger to him and he had glimpsed her for only a moment and yet the memory was so vivid, so deeply woven into his mind that he was able to recall even the smallest detail.

Suddenly afraid, without knowing why, he mentally shook himself, deliberately concentrating on all that was going on around him. Things he understood. Normal things.

Just then Libby glanced up and smiled at him. Returning her smile, he sipped the lemonade, his face shining with love as he looked at the three most important people in his life. He loved them so much, it was like a physical ache inside him.

He was glad he'd managed to get back in time to see

Daisy open her presents. But he felt like a fish out of water. A children's party was no place for a man. Yesterday evening he'd spent hours blowing up balloons. He'd helped pin the decorations to the wall and carried whatever Libby thrust into his arms. But now, with everything done and the children engrossed in having fun, he felt out of place. As soon as he could slip away, he would retreat to the study and get down to some urgent paperwork.

While Dave watched his family, the old lady watched him. If Dave had seen her, he might have been shocked, so intent was her gaze. With her burning eyes locked on to him, she fed on his every feature, his every move and gesture. She let her mind wander back over the lonely emptiness of so many years and her tired old heart was close to breaking.

Without warning, Daisy ran across the room. In her arms was the old lady's present. She cradled it like a mother might cradle an infant at her breast, the limp, blood-red garment flowing over her arms. Her face soft with pleasure, she murmured, 'Oh, thank you. It's so beautiful!' It wasn't like a present at all. It was more a secret between her and the old lady.

'Thank you, my dear. I'm glad you like it.' She had feared Daisy might not care for her choice of present, but now, seeing that small, delighted face, she was filled with new hope.

Holding the garment before her, Daisy was enchanted. 'It's like the one in the picture, and you made it just for me.' The dress was soft to the touch, incredibly heavy, yet light as a feather. It seemed to pulsate against her skin.

'I made it because I knew how much you wanted a dress like that, and because you've worked so hard, you deserve something special.' The girl must never know the true reason she had made the dress.

A small voice called out, 'Put it on, Daisy. We want to

see you in it.' Other eager voices joined the chorus.

'All right then, I will,' Daisy agreed. 'But you mustn't look until I say.'

Libby told her to change upstairs. 'We'll be in the lounge when you come down.'

Thrilled, Daisy ran out of the room and up the stairs two at a time. 'I'm going to look like the girl in the picture,' she called back.

Libby was already occupied with the children. May was still clearing up. It seemed no one heard Daisy's comment. But the old one heard, and her heart leaped for joy.

As they ushered the children into the lounge, Libby thanked the old lady for Daisy's present. 'That was a lovely thing for you to do. It must have taken hours of work.'

'A labour of love,' Miss Ledell replied. 'Your daughter gives me many hours of pleasure with her music and her drawings. The dress is only a small thing to give in return.'

Libby was surprised. 'Drawings?' She stopped in her tracks, a small laugh escaping her. 'Don't tell me she's been wasting your time with her nonsensical pictures? I remember she drove me mad with her chicken sketches. All over the house they were, horrendous things, and I had to pretend they were beautiful.' She shrugged, moving on. 'I'll have a word with her,' she said. 'Daisy mustn't take advantage of your kindness.'

'No,' the old lady pleaded, 'please don't do that. I don't mind at all, really I don't.' She smiled and Libby was under her spell. 'Besides, she hasn't drawn any chickens yet.' In a bid to evade more questions about Daisy's painting, she went on, 'Daisy works very hard at her music lessons, you know. I'm amazed at how well she's coming along. But then she has a natural talent for the piano. It isn't the ear or the fingers that create music. It's the soul. That's what Daisy has, soul.'

'Why, that's wonderful!' Libby was so proud. 'We'd like to buy her a new piano so she can practise at home but

I'm afraid at the minute our finances won't run to it. Dave is keeping an eye out for a good second-hand one, though. If he finds one, we'd really appreciate it if you could see it, before we part with any money.'

'Of course.'

'I mean, we don't exactly know what to look for in a piano. Neither Dave nor I, or any of our family that we can think of, has ever played a musical instrument. That's why we're so surprised Daisy has a natural talent.'

'Sometimes it happens that way.'

Distracted by a fight between two boys, Libby was relieved when May dealt with it. Returning her attention to the old lady, she said, 'If you and May sit the children in the circle, I'll get the games from the other room.'

When the boys began arguing again, Dave took it on himself to step in. 'Time we had a little chat, you two,' he told them sternly and took them aside for a lecture.

May and the old lady watched with interest. 'They'll take no notice,' May said with a chuckle. 'They're a right pair o' little sods, an' no mistake!'

She was right. No sooner had they returned to their places than they were striking out at each other again. 'One word from me and they do as they like,' Dave laughed.

At that moment, when his eyes were alight with laughter, he met the old lady's gaze. Something in her expression shocked him and the laughter died on his lips. For a split second he felt he was back there, in the road where he had seen the young woman.

Warned by the look in his eyes, the old lady quickly turned away. 'I'd better go and help,' she said lightheartedly, 'before those two scoundrels kill each other.'

Libby returned with the games, but before they could get started, a small voice shouted, 'Oh! Look at Daisy!'

All eyes turned to the door.

As Daisy came into the room, the children gathered

round, a few giggling because she looked so grown up in the red dress, some admiring, wanting to touch it, and others remaining silent with envy as children do.

May murmured, 'That colour really suits Daisy. Oh, and doesn't the dress make her look different? Older, lovely as a picture.'

Daisy pushed through the children, did a twirl, then stood before her parents, seeking approval.

For a moment neither Dave nor Libby could say anything. A few minutes ago Daisy had been nine years old; now she showed the essence of womanhood; she had poise and grace, a certain look in the eye, a particular way of walking.

Libby was the first to speak. 'You look lovely, Daisy.' She had been shocked when Daisy walked into the room. For one very odd moment it was as though Daisy wasn't Daisy at all, but someone else. Like May had said, she seemed older, different somehow. But then, suddenly, Daisy was a child again, and everything was as before and Libby felt only a surge of pride.

Numbed by the sight of his nine-year-old daughter looking like a teenager ready for her first date, Dave didn't quite know how to react. He was intrigued. Inexplicably afraid. 'You look really grown up.' Smiling, he gave her a hug. 'And here was me, thinking you were still my baby.'

The old lady stood silent, her mind echoing with the words May had uttered when Daisy first walked into the room. It was exactly what she had planned. It was how *he* would see Daisy – 'Lovely as a picture.'

'Can I wear the dress until bedtime?' Daisy asked.

'I don't see why not,' Libby answered.

While the children got started on their games, Dave disappeared to the study. When he had gone, the old lady turned her attention to Daisy and the others, but her thoughts were elsewhere. Now that she had found hope, she grew more agitated by the day. 'Be patient,' she chided herself. 'It will all come right.' Now that she had come this far, it had to. The outcome was unthinkable if it didn't.

At half past five parents began arriving for their offspring, and by six o'clock the last of the party-goers had left. Daisy and Jamie carried a tray of goodies to Dave in the study, and the three women found sanctuary in the kitchen.

'Phew!' May fell into the nearest chair. 'I think we deserve a cup of tea before we start clearing up.'

Libby didn't agree. 'I think we deserve a glass of something much stronger.' She was thinking along the lines of white wine, or a measure of Irish cream.

'Not for me,' said Miss Ledell, 'but you two go ahead and I'll make a start in the living room.'

Closely regarding her, Libby became anxious. 'Are you all right?' she asked, thinking the old lady looked pale.

'It's them kids,' May retorted. 'They'd try the strength of a rhinoceros.'

Though she did feel worn, the old lady sought to reassure them. 'I'm fine,' she said. 'Really.' But then, as she rose from the chair, her senses reeled and she almost stumbled.

In an instant both women were at her side. 'Sit right where you are,' May ordered. 'I'll put the kettle on.' A cup of tea was her answer to everything.

'I'll get Dave to run you home,' Libby said kindly. 'May's right, those children are a real handful. You've been wonderful and I'm very grateful, but you've done far too much.'

The old lady chuckled. 'For my age, you mean?'

Libby had no idea how old Miss Ledell was, but now, as she looked into that ancient, lined face and those bright, beautiful eyes, she seemed no more than a girl. 'For *any* age,' she laughed.

A few moments later, Dave helped her into the car. 'I'll have you home in no time at all,' he said.

Libby asked Miss Ledell whether she would like her to come along and stay awhile, but her offer was graciously refused. 'If it's all the same to you, I think I'll settle for an early night.'

Daisy, however, was adamant. 'I'm going with them,' she informed a bemused Libby. 'I can help because I know where Miss Ledell keeps her front door key, and besides, if the cat's hungry, I can feed him.'

Dave and Libby looked at each other with amusement, while the old lady commented, 'I don't see how anyone can argue with that, do you?' Though she suspected Daisy was bluffing about knowing where the key was kept.

Daisy was right about the cat. As they drew up at the house, the big tabby was waiting on the step. 'See!' Daisy was triumphant. 'I told you so.' Running to the door, she retrieved the key from behind the door knocker.

The old lady was surprised. 'How did you know where I kept the key, Daisy?'

'Don't be surprised,' Dave said wryly. 'This young lady doesn't miss a trick.'

Daisy explained, 'I saw you put it here when Mummy collected me the other day and you were going for a walk.' Concerned that the old lady might think she would tell, she added in a whisper, 'Nobody else knows, only us three.'

'It doesn't matter,' came the answer. Earthly things were of no lasting value. There were other things beyond all that. Priceless, glorious things.

Dave insisted on escorting the old lady inside. 'You're to take it easy now,' he told her. 'Is there anything you want before we leave? Is there something we can do? Make you a bite to eat, a cup of tea, maybe?'

'No. I'm just tired, that's all.'

'It's no wonder, after all your help with the kids. Then there's all the time and energy you devote to Daisy, not to mention the beautiful dress you made for her.' He sensed the old lady's loneliness and it made him ashamed. There had been a time when he took all things for granted. Now he knew what it was like to be cut off from those you loved. This old woman had no one. No wonder she looked forward to Daisy's visits. 'I feel we owe you,' he said. 'Are you sure there's nothing more I can do?'

She shook her head. 'You've done more than enough.' She looked at the man, and then at the girl, and she was deeply grateful. These two were already repaying her more than they could ever know.

'Look!' Daisy pointed to the painting on the wall. 'My dress is the same.' Twirling on the spot, she laughed out loud. 'Don't you see, Daddy? I'm the girl in the picture.' As she twirled, the hem of her dress rippled and sang, until the girl in the picture and the girl in the room were indeed as one. 'We're the same.' Daisy was exhilarated. 'Isn't it wonderful?'

Dave was enchanted. He stared at the young woman in the painting and felt he knew her. 'She's very lovely,' he murmured. Turning to the old lady, he asked, 'Who is she?'

'Why do you ask?'

'I'm not sure but I feel I know her from somewhere.' He shook his head. 'But that's not possible. I mean, the picture looks fairly old, and the clothes belong to the thirties, I'd say.'

'That's right. The girl is . . .' She paused, checking herself. 'She's a relative. The young man is her fiancé.'

'Then I couldn't possibly have known her,' he said, somewhat relieved. 'That was way before my time.'

'Time is nothing.' Yet it was an eternity, she thought sadly. Strange how people believed that time was a passing of life itself, when in truth it was merely a stage in a journey.

Daisy was staring at the picture. 'I wish I could have a locket like the girl is wearing.' She spoke softly, as if to herself. 'Mummy's got a locket but it's not like that one. I've never seen a locket like that one.' The gold locket was in the shape of a flower, with a hinge at the top instead of the side, and a long golden stem beneath. The flower was yellow, with a dark centre.

A daisy.

Against his deeper instincts, Dave took a closer look. 'How did you know it was a locket?' he asked. 'It looks just like a necklace to me.'

Daisy shrugged her shoulders. 'I just know.'

The old lady was delighted. 'Your daughter is unusually perceptive.'

Daisy turned to her father. 'Why did you name me after the flower, Daddy?'

He felt out of his depth. The girl in the painting was getting to him. 'Enough questions,' he said impatiently. 'We're tiring Miss Ledell. She needs her rest.'

They said their goodbyes and just before she left, Daisy was given her drawing. Rolled up, it was small enough to slip into her pocket. Created with love and colour, it was a precious thing, to both Daisy and the old lady. 'Mind you take great care of it,' Miss Ledell said. 'It's very special.'

Anxious now, she bade them goodbye. 'Do it *now*,' she softly urged when they were out of earshot. 'Before it's too late.'

As they climbed into the car, Dave's mind was back in the house, with the girl in the picture. What had made him think he'd seen her before? It was such a strong feeling. He had been so sure, and yet it wasn't possible.

'Daddy!' Daisy sat forward in her seat. 'You've taken a wrong turning.'

Astonished, he realised she was right. Just then, an idea presented itself to him. Almost without realising it, he heard himself asking Daisy, 'How would you like to help me surprise Mummy?'

'How?'

Dave explained how Libby had left her scarf at the restaurant. 'Just like your drawing is special to you, Mummy's scarf is special to her,' he said. 'It was a present from me soon after we first met, and she doesn't want to lose it – though God knows why, it's old and frayed and I've promised her a new one. But I know she'd rather have the old one back.' He sighed. 'Women! Who can understand them?'

There was a pause while Daisy wondered whether she was supposed to comment on that or answer his first question. In the end something else took precedence. 'How will Mummy know where we've gone?'

'She's not supposed to know where we've gone. You see, she doesn't want me to go back there, not even to fetch her scarf.'

'Why not?'

He shrugged his shoulders and took a right turn, towards the lanes and Ampthill. 'Who knows, sweetheart? Women are hard to understand.'

'She'll be worried when we don't get home. She'll phone Miss Ledell and then she'll be even more worried, because we won't be there either.'

'You're right.' Drawing the car to a halt in a layby, Dave shifted the gear into neutral and pulled on the hand brake. 'Thoughtless of me.' He opened the glove compartment and took out a small, mobile telephone. 'Of course she'll be worried.' Removing the cigar lighter, he plugged in the lead from the phone. Then he pressed down the lock on his door and listened for all the door locks to click down.

Daisy heard them too. 'Why did you lock us in?'

'Because it's dark.'

'And because a bad man might jump into the back of the car?'

'Something like that, sweetheart.' Flipping open the phone, he began to key in numbers.

'Mummy said we live in a dangerous age.'

'Mummy's right, but it's OK if you're careful.'

The call connected and a woman's voice answered. 'Hello?' It wasn't Libby, so Dave assumed it was May, although she sounded different over the phone, but then most people did.

'It's Dave,' he said, instinctively raising his voice. 'Can you put Libby on, please?'

'She's in the bathroom. Jamie's being sick. He's eaten too much cake.'

'You're sure he's all right?'

'He's got a tummy ache, that's all.' She giggled. 'I expect he's not the only one either. The way them kids downed that food made *me* feel sick, I can tell you.'

Dave knew exactly what she meant. 'In that case, don't worry her,' he laughed. 'Just tell her I've got Daisy and we're going on a little errand.'

'Right then.'

'We shouldn't be too late.'

'Don't worry. I'll make sure she knows.'

'There.' Unplugging the phone from the cigar lighter, he replaced it in the glove compartment. 'Satisfied now?'

Daisy's silence meant she approved. The fact that she settled back in her seat and crossed her legs meant she was getting tired, but she would never admit it.

Before he'd gone three miles, Daisy was fast asleep. Tenderly, Dave looked at her. 'My little birthday girl,' he murmured. 'Looks like the day got the better of you in the end.'

The sound was familiar, a gentle tapping at first, then hard, resounding thuds. 'Here it comes,' he groaned, switching on the windscreen wipers. 'It never rains but it pours.'

And pour it did. It rained all the way to Ampthill before it stopped. 'Woke you up, did it, sweetheart?' He was glad when Daisy sat up, rubbing her eyes. It was one of those dark, empty nights, and he was beginning to feel lonely.

'Nearly there now.' The twists and turns of the road were comfortingly familiar.

The doctor put away his stethoscope and went with Larry into the front room. 'I'm sorry,' he said, 'there's no real change except, as you say, he does seem unduly restless. But then that's all part of his illness. Your father is very old. His mind has already given up, and there is damage to his internal organs. In fact I'm astonished that he's managed to hold on for so long.'

'We look after him, that's why. He knows we love him and he doesn't want to leave us.'

The doctor nodded. 'All the same, you should be prepared for the worst. He's an amazingly strong man, but age and the illness is taking its toll. No matter how well you care for him, you can't hold on to him for ever.'

'Thank you, doctor.'

'And get some sleep if you can.' He glanced across the room at Ida. She had her back to him and as yet had not acknowledged his presence. 'You both look exhausted.'

'Father's been very difficult. We've had no sleep for two nights, and it seems unfair to keep calling on Eileen.'

'Now that I've given him a sedative, he should rest easier.' Collecting his coat he put it on, laboriously buttoning it up against the night. 'Goodnight, Mr Fellowes, Mrs Fellowes.' He glanced across the room at the woman. She did not respond. He looked away, smiling at Larry as he walked with him to the door. 'Remember what I said now, we none of us can hold back the inevitable.'

'What do you mean?' Ida's voice shook with fear.

Both men stared at her. 'I mean your father-in-law has very little time left. I realise how much you both care for him, and I know how dedicated you are, but in the end it isn't up to us. One morning, or during the night maybe, he'll slip quietly away. With the best will in the world, with all the care and attention we can provide, I'm afraid there is nothing any of us can do to prevent that.'

He waited for her to answer. Instead, she glared at him for a moment, before turning away.

'I'm sorry,' he said. 'If you need me, you only have to call.'

At the door, Larry felt the need to apologise. 'My wife's devoted to him,' he explained. 'We both are.'

The doctor was already aware of that. In all his long experience he had never seen such love and attention given to an old man. 'I understand,' he said. 'She must be worn out. Hopefully, you should both be able to get some sleep tonight.'

Rolling his eyes, Larry groaned, 'Things to do before that, I'm afraid. Can't neglect our livelihood.'

'Ah yes. The restaurant. That fire was bad luck. Still, I'm sure it will all come right. These things usually do.'

While Larry showed the doctor out, Ida sat by the window, staring out at the night and thinking how *she* was out there. Well, let her stay out there, she brooded, let her stay in the dark and the cold where she belonged, for she would never get into this house. As long as it was in Ida's power, that sorry creature would never be allowed to rest, and neither would *he*.

Her soft laughter rippled through the air. Grimacing, she mimicked her husband's voice, 'My wife's devoted to him. We both are.' Again she laughed, soft, wicked laughter. 'Fools!' she hissed. 'Little do they know.'

She listened. They were still talking. Quickly now. Before he comes back!

Unfolding herself from the window seat, she ran across the room, up the stairs and into the old man's bedroom.

Standing beside the bed she stared down at his frail old face. Only her eyes moved, silently glittering, emitting a terrible hatred which seemed to taint the very air. 'We know, don't we?' she murmured. 'You and me. I've already paid the price, and now it's your turn, you cruel, heartless bastard.' A great sadness took hold of her. Small, reluctant tears ran down her face. 'My life is nothing to me. Even if, like *her*, I have to haunt the earth for the rest of eternity, it will be worth it, as long as I can make you suffer for what you did.'

Suddenly she leaned towards him and, with shocking cruelty, placed two fingers either side of his eyelids, prising each eyelid open until the bloodshot eyes were almost bulging out of his head.

Stepping aside, she left a clear view to the window. 'Look, old man,' she urged softly. 'It's dark outside. You can't see her, but she's out there. The young man brought her back, you see. And now she's waiting. You want to see her, don't you? You need to touch her, to talk to her. But I can't let that happen. I will never allow her to get past me. She knows that. She knows my hatred won't let her through.' Spitefully twisting away her fingers, she bent close to his face, telling him with immense satisfaction, 'You see, old man, hatred is always more powerful than love.'

Giggling like a schoolgirl, she eased herself into the chair beside him. 'The doctor was wrong,' she muttered. 'He said there was little time left for you, that you would "slip away". What does he know? We're the ones who have to decide, and you understand, I can't let you go until I know for sure.' She laughed again, stroking his gnarled hand and observing his face with keen interest. 'You're still handsome in a strange way,' she whispered. 'And we never did get to talk, did we? Now, I don't suppose we ever will.'

The hatred was subsiding. Spent and quiet, it retreated into her subconscious. In its place came an overwhelming sense of loneliness. She kept her gaze on his face, imagining the chiselled features buried beneath the layer of age.

While she gazed on him, the silence cocooned them, like a tangible presence. 'Pity it had to come to this,' she sighed. 'So many lives. Such a terrible waste.' Hatred bubbled, reminding her of a lifetime's purpose. Sitting up, she squared her shoulders and steeled her nerve. 'Can't forget.' Painful though it was, she had to keep reminding herself. There was a kind of insanity about her now. The kind that came with years of self-torture and memories that tore at her like a savage animal at her throat. 'Can't forgive.'

Slowly, deliberately, she laid her hand over his. Singling out the smallest, most crooked finger, she raised it from the others, bending it back until it became taut beneath her touch. Just a little more pressure, and it would go. There! Hearing it snap like a dry twig underfoot, she sighed with satisfaction.

When Larry came into the room, he found her, head bowed over the old man's bed, one hand placed lovingly over his and the other across his forehead as though she had fallen asleep while gently comforting him. It was a picture of devotion.

'Ida?' Softly he came across the carpet. 'Ida, are you asleep?'

She wasn't asleep. When she heard him coming, she had carefully staged the way she would look when he entered the room. Slowly, and groaning as if newly woken, she blinked her eyes. 'Oh, Larry. Your father seemed distressed. I'm sorry, I must have dozed off.' Silently she congratulated herself on her acting prowess. If things had been different she might have gone along that particular route. As it was, her life had been dominated by the need to carve a particular pound of flesh.

Larry was full of affection. 'It's me who should be sorry,' he said. 'In the few short years we've been married, you've shown nothing but compassion for my ailing father. You've refused me nothing, and yet there are times when I treat you like a stranger.' He came to her and, draping an arm round her shoulder, said fondly, 'I find it hard to cope, you see . . . with him.' He hardly dared look at the old man. 'There are things here that frighten me.' Instinctively he raised his eyes to the window. 'Are we doing right, Ida? Is she really evil?'

Again the doubts. Another battle for her to fight. 'You *know* she's evil. Hasn't she hounded your poor father all this time? Doesn't she blame him for what happened? She wants to punish him, to hurt him. We can't let it happen. We *have* to keep them apart.' Lowering her voice, she sidled up to him. 'Look how she caused the death of that poor young man, just because he reminded her of your father. If that isn't evil, I don't know what is.' In fact, she herself had caused the young man's death. Obsessed with unravelling the mystery of Bluebell Hill, he had come too close to the truth. That was why she had to kill him. Larry never knew. No one did. 'Trust me,' she entreated, 'your father is in great danger.'

Once more he was persuaded. 'You're right. What happened all those years ago was her fault and, yes, we must keep them apart. And if that means the life of one more young man, then so be it.'

'We have to be rid of her, don't we?'

'Yes.'

'Once she's gone, your father will be safe.'

'Then we can let him be. Let him have his rest.'

She nodded. 'It's clear what has to be done. We mustn't be afraid.'

Like a child he hung on to her, his eyes appealing. 'Before I met you, I didn't realise why she was here. I didn't even realise who she was.' He was like a little lost boy. 'I'm glad you found us, Ida. If you hadn't come along and seen what was happening . . .' He groaned, bowing his head into her breast.

She smiled sardonically, knowing there would be many times in the future, as there had been in the past, when he would doubt her again. As always she would outwit him. She was a past master at it.

'I'm not strong like you,' he confessed, 'and there are times when I treat you shamefully, but in my own way, I do love you.'

'I know.'

'I need you, Ida.' Reaching his forlorn gaze beyond her, he observed his father's quiet face. 'We *both* need you.'

'You look tired.' She could bear his touch for only so long before her skin began to creep. 'Go to bed. Sleep for a while.'

He appeared shocked. 'But the restaurant!'

'You know there's nothing you can do there. If you're needed, I'll wake you.'

'No. I can't trust them. I have to oversee the work.'

'Please yourself.' Her casual manner belied the irritation she felt inside. She wanted rid of him. She needed to get out. She had a rage to breathe in the clean cold air of the evening and clear her soul.

'Come with me then.' He was bending low, his warm, rancid breath fanning her face.

She drew back. 'What?'

'I said, come with me then. I'm sure I won't be missed for half an hour.'

It was painfully clear what he meant. If she went with him, maybe he would fall asleep afterwards. He often did. With him asleep, she could walk the lanes without fear of reprimand. If he was in the restaurant, she would have to stay here and be answerable. Often he would come back and forth a dozen times during the course of an evening. If he found his father left alone, there would be hell to pay. But the idea of him entering her, his groping hands all over her body and his nakedness writhing on top was deeply repugnant to her. Still, after all she had endured, it was only one more nightmare. Give in, she told herself.

Afterwards he'll sleep. Once asleep, he was like a man unconscious.

'We'll have to be quick,' she conceded, 'in case your father wakes.'

He took her by the hand and together they went upstairs. 'Father won't wake,' he promised. 'You heard what the doctor said.'

Upstairs in the back bedroom, he took off her clothes and fondled her breasts. 'You've a fine figure for a woman of your age,' he said callously.

She stood very still while he touched her all over, his probing fingers travelling sensuously across her shoulders and down the curve of her spine. He handled her breasts and played with her nipples, and when he grew too excited to contain himself, he got down on his knees and pushed his mouth into the crevice of her thighs. 'You're so warm,' he muttered, his face growing red with passion. 'Soft as down.'

In that moment when he looked up at her with admiration, she wanted to put her hands round his throat and squeeze. But she remained very still, letting him have his way. Allowing him to believe she wanted him as much as he wanted her.

With agonising slowness he undressed. 'Now,' he murmured and she followed him to the bed.

Lying on his back, he waited, his legs parted and his member erect, slightly bent, unduly thick at the shaft and narrowing to almost nothing at the point. It was grotesque. While she looked, the slightest dewdrop appeared at its mouth. Entranced, she watched it grow plump, rise up, then trickle down.

Hurriedly now, wanting it to be over, she climbed on to the bed and sat astride him, her arms reaching out, hands grasping the bedhead, her surprisingly firm breasts only inches from his long, searching tongue. Up and down she went. The rhythm was always the same. Up and down, increasing in ferocity, until he gave out a great moan and collapsed beneath her.

Like a mindless thing she went to the bathroom, doused herself inside and out, towelled off and returned to the bedroom, noting with satisfaction that he was fast asleep. If all went true to form, he would sleep for hours.

After dressing, she went downstairs, put on her coat and let herself out of the back door. She hated him; hated herself. 'You're nothing but a whore!' The words mingled with the wind, whipping back in her face, burning her skin. Wrapping her coat closer about her, she went on, pushing against the wind, her sharp eyes scouring the lanes, probing the darkness. 'Where are you?' Her voice was pitiful against the elements. 'You'll never have him, do you hear?'

Standing in the road, she raised her arms as if fending off a devil, her face a mask of loathing, her heart made hard by all she had seen, all she had suffered. The memories had made her mad, and the love stayed with her to keep the madness alive. The pity was, she too had been a victim.

The sin was not hers. It happened long before. And she never knew.

'How much further, Daddy?' Daisy was wide awake, her eager eyes scouring the lanes ahead. This was a rare treat for her, being out in the car with just her father, in the dark, going somewhere she had never been before. 'Why are there no lights down the road?'

'Because we're out in the country and these narrow lanes don't have lights.'

'Why not?'

'Who knows? Maybe the authorities think it's a waste of taxpayers' money. Maybe they think they should concentrate on roads that people use the most.'

'We've got lots of lights down our road.'

'Yes,' he said vaguely. His mind was on Libby, and her scarf, and other, strangely disturbing things. The deeper he travelled along this lane, the more restless he became.

They both saw it at the same time, a dark, shapeless figure that swooped out of nowhere.

'What the devil's that?' Slamming on the brakes, Dave yelled to Daisy, 'Hold on!' The car went into a sideways skid as he fought for control. He gave a sigh of relief when at last the car jerked to a halt. Shaking in every limb, he satisfied himself that Daisy was all right. 'Stay here, sweetheart, while I take a look,' he told her. He stopped the engine but left the lights on. 'You're not to get out. Lock the doors and keep them locked.'

Scrambling out of the car, he ran back down the road, frantically searching as he went. There was nothing. No one. Gasping for breath, he stopped, hands on his sides and body forward, letting the air into his bursting lungs. Out of the corner of his eye he saw a movement; then nothing. 'You stupid bastard!' he yelled. 'You almost had us in the ditch!' Silence. The darkness closed in around him, and he felt utterly alone.

Swearing under his breath, he made his way back to the car. Daisy was safe inside. 'It's me, sweetheart.' He pressed his face to the window. 'Unlock the door.'

'Daddy, I didn't let her in.' Unlocking the door, Daisy seemed highly nervous, glancing about almost as though she expected someone to leap out at them.

'What do you mean, sweetheart? Who didn't you let in?'

'The woman. The one who was in the road.' Clutching her rolled-up painting to her chest, she stared at him, her eyes big and frightened. 'She wasn't very nice, so I didn't let her in. I kept the doors locked, just like you said.'

In the glow from the headlights he regarded her anxiously. 'What was she like, this woman?' He hadn't seen anybody. How had she got past him to the car?

Daisy shuddered. 'Old, and sort of funny.' She wrinkled her nose. 'She stared in the window, but I didn't let her in.' A ripple ran through her body, catching her breath. 'She frightened me.'

'You're a good girl, and very brave.' Starting the engine, Dave put the car into gear. Who the hell could it have been? If she was old, then it obviously wasn't the same woman he'd seen before. Dark lanes, in the middle of nowhere. Thank God Daisy had done as he told her.

'Did that old woman want to hurt us?' Daisy asked shakily.

He tried to put her mind at rest. 'No, of course she didn't, sweetheart. I expect she was some poor old tramp who'd lost her way.'

'I expect she was cold too. Do you think I should have let her in?'

'No!' More quietly, he said, 'No, you did right to keep her out.'

'She asked me what I was hiding.' She was clutching the rolled-up drawing in her fist.

'Did she now?'

'I wasn't hiding anything, only my drawing. I took it out of my pocket to look at it but I didn't want her to see it.'

'It's all right, sweetheart. She's gone now.' Weird old bugger, he thought angrily. She'd have got a piece of his mind if he'd caught up with her. Funny, though, how she managed to get past him like that.

Behind them, Ida remained hidden in the undergrowth until the car was out of sight. 'He's back,' she chuckled. 'We knew he'd be back.'

Spinning round, she yelled at the night, 'Did you see? He's come back for you. Take him and leave the other one to me!'

As soon as Dave drew up outside the restaurant, he realised there was something wrong. When he had come here with Libby, the place had been blazing with light, soft music had been playing and at least half a dozen cars were parked in the forecourt. Now there was only a small light burning in the porch, and another shaft of light coming through one of the side windows. A faint tapping could be heard from inside the building. 'Strange,' he muttered. Turning his head, he peered through the back window. The car park behind was empty.

'What's wrong, Daddy?'

'Nothing for you to worry about,' he said thoughtfully. 'I imagined the restaurant would be busy, that's all.' Plugging the mobile phone into the cigar lighter, he dialled and waited. 'Better let your mother know how long we'll be.'

This time Libby answered. 'What are you up to?' she asked. 'What's all this about an errand?'

'Ah, that would be telling,' he teased. 'You'll soon know. We'll be home in about three-quarters of an hour.'

'Daisy all right?'

'Of course. What about Jamie? May said he'd over-indulged at the party.'

'He's fine now. He's watching telly.'

Dave chuckled.

'Be quick, the pair of you.'

'Quick as a wink.' And he did just that, much to Daisy's delight.

'Love you.'

'Love you too,' Dave said, then clicked off the phone and unplugged it.

'Are we going inside?' Daisy wanted to know.

Dave seemed not to hear her. He sat for a moment, drumming his fingers against the steering wheel. Lowering his gaze to the dashboard clock, he noted the time. It was almost seven thirty. And it was Saturday night. Why wasn't the restaurant lit up? Where were the patrons? The cars? The staff?

A man stepped out of the shadows. Tapping on the window, he asked loudly, 'Can I help you, sir? Is there something you want?'

Dave recognised him as the waiter who had served him and Libby. This time, though, he was dressed in casual clothes, over the top of which he was wearing what looked like a blue boiler suit.

Getting out of the car, Dave explained why he was here. 'It's not a valuable scarf, I hasten to say,' he added with some embarrassment. 'But you know what women are. Sentimental value and all that.'

'Of course!' In the dim light, Carter stared at him. 'I remember you now.' He quickly stubbed out the cigarette he'd been smoking. 'Nasty habit,' he apologised. 'I can't seem to give them up. Not allowed to smoke in the restaurant, of course, so it's a case of sneaking out here when the fancy takes.'

'You found the scarf then?'

'Yes. Blue silk with frayed edges, wasn't it?'

'That's the one.'

As Daisy got out of the car, Dave took her coat from the back seat. 'Better put this on, sweetheart.' He handed it to her. 'Don't want you catching cold.'

Reluctantly, Daisy put the coat over her shoulders. 'I don't catch cold,' she said, popping the drawing into her pocket. 'I've got a good constitution.'

A wide smile crinkled Dave's handsome features. 'A good constitution, eh?' he laughed. 'And who told you that?'

'Miss Ledell.'

'I see. Well, just in case she's wrong, put your coat on.'

Daisy did as she was told. When the drawing fell to the ground, she swiftly retrieved it.

'You can leave that in the car,' he told her. 'No need to carry it about with you.'

Daisy hadn't forgotten Ida's face peering at her through the car window. 'No,' she said firmly. 'I want to carry it.'

'You're as stubborn as your mother,' Dave chuckled. 'Come on then. Let's get the scarf and head back home.'

Carter led them towards the restaurant.

'My wife's had that scarf a long time,' Dave explained. 'I offered her a new one, but she said she'd rather have her old one back.'

'Women are like that. Sentimental creatures, bless their hearts.' As he swung open the door, the tapping grew louder.

Dave couldn't contain his curiosity any longer. 'Why aren't you open for business?'

'We had a fire.' The waiter gestured for them to keep walking. 'Started in the boiler room. Thankfully it didn't get beyond the kitchens, but it's caused enough damage to shut us for at least a month.' He gestured to his overalls. 'Some of us can't afford to be out of work for that length of time. A few have managed to get temporary work elsewhere, and others, like myself, have been given the chance to earn a wage here. We help out where we can – cleaning, scrubbing, scraping off the damaged paintwork ready for the skilled men to make a start. It saves the boss a bit of money and helps us into the bargain.'

Daisy's attention was elsewhere. 'Look, Daddy, a kitten!' Brushing round her ankles was the tiniest grey kitten.

The waiter shooed it away. 'Damned things,' he snarled. 'The mother was a stray Mrs Fellowes picked up. She let it stay in the shed at the back of their house and now the damned thing's had umpteen kittens. They all creep in here at every opportunity, looking for scraps. The boss is angry and rightly so. If the health authorities find out, we could be in real trouble.' He almost leaped out of his skin when a familiar voice addressed him from behind.

'It's *you* who'll be in trouble if you don't get back to your work.'

Startled, both men swung round. 'Oh, Mr Fellowes. I didn't hear you come in.'

Larry Fellowes was in a foul mood. First he'd woken to find his wife had gone out, and now here was one of his workers passing the time of day with a complete stranger when he should have been on his knees scrubbing the floor. 'What are you hanging about here for?' he demanded. 'I don't pay you to chit-chat with strangers.'

Carter hurriedly explained, 'This gentleman's come back for the scarf. Remember? You told me to put it aside. You were so sure he'd be back for it.'

Larry looked more closely at the visitor, only vaguely aware of the girl by his side. 'Ah, yes. Mr Walters, if I remember rightly.' A devious smile reshaped his peeved features. He prided himself on never forgetting a name, and in this particular instance he had not forgotten the face either. This was the young man who had brought *her* back. He had always known the lure of this place would be too strong for him to resist. 'I'm glad you came back,' he said sweetly. 'I knew you would.'

'In that case, you knew more than I did.' Dave felt sorry for the waiter who had gone scurrying away and was now scraping damaged paint from the walls. 'If I had my way, the scarf could stay here for ever,' he went on, 'but my wife is very fond of it, so here I am, doing my good husband bit.' He stretched out his arms as if surrendering.

'We'd better get it then. Thankfully the scarf was put into my office. The fire never reached there.' He began walking.

Dave made small talk. 'I understand the kitchen was badly damaged.'

'Gutted, I'm afraid.' Gratified that Dave had returned, just as he'd predicted, he began to feel benevolent. 'Perhaps you'd like to see.' Before Dave could answer, he veered away from the office and headed for the kitchen.

'Stay close, sweetheart.' Dave glanced at his daughter, who was lagging behind.

'No need to worry,' Larry assured him. 'Anything loose

or dangerous has already been stripped away.'

'Can't I stay here and play with the kitten?' Daisy wasn't interested in kitchens and dirty walls.

Larry's mood darkened. 'Don't tell me that kitten's in here again.'

'It's only a baby,' Daisy pleaded. 'I won't let it do anything naughty.'

Wanting to keep Dave here a while longer, Larry patronised her. 'All right, my dear, but we mustn't encourage it.'

Left to her own devices, Daisy threw off her coat and sat cross-legged on the ground, the kitten playing happily round her feet. 'We don't want to see the kitchen, do we?' she asked, stroking its soft, silky fur. 'You want me to stay here and play, don't you?' Holding out her drawing, she showed it to the inquisitive little creature. 'Look,' she said. 'It's mine. I painted it all by myself.' Shame suffused her. 'Well, Miss Ledell did help a little bit. She mixed the paint and told me what I should draw.' A bright smile lit her face. 'She said it was one of the loveliest drawings she had ever seen.'

The kitten rolled about, tapping playfully at Daisy's foot. Then, with surprising agility, it did a somersault and ran off. 'Hey! You come back when I'm talking to you.'

Keeping the kitten in sight, Daisy went after it; she saw it disappear into the foyer and then it was gone. 'Where are you?' Tiptoeing about, she looked in every nook and cranny. It was nowhere to be seen. She was disappointed but not disheartened. Wondering if somehow it had found its way outside, she opened the front door when, out of nowhere, the kitten dashed through her legs, running off into the night. 'You naughty thing!' Taking up the chase, she followed it across the lawn and down the path to the house. 'Don't run away,' she called out. 'I'll take you home with me if Daddy says it's all right.'

She followed the kitten round the back of the house

where it jumped on to a window ledge beside the back door and sat looking down on her. 'Don't you want to come home with me?' Daisy asked. 'That nasty man doesn't want you, but I do. If you're good, I'm sure Daddy will let me take you home.'

Reaching up to retrieve it, she cried out with dismay when the kitten evaded her and squeezed through the open window. There was a soft thud as it landed on the other side.

Undeterred, Daisy knocked on the door. 'Hello?' she called out, hoping someone would hear. 'My name's Daisy. Is it all right to get the kitten, please?'

There was no answer but she could hear the kitten scratching about inside. 'You silly thing,' she said. 'You've got in and now you can't get out, can you?'

Knowing her father would scold her but desperate to rescue the kitten, she tried the door. It opened at a touch.

Some way down the passage she could see a light. In the doorway she saw the kitten, scrabbling at the carpet. 'Come on, kitten.' She crept forward, afraid that at any minute she might be found and chased out. 'We shouldn't be in here,' she said, reaching down to snatch it up. 'You'll get us both in trouble.'

She almost had it safely in her grasp when the kitten leaped into the air, shot across the hallway and straight up the flight of stairs. At the top it sat on its haunches, leisurely washing its face.

Having come this far without detection, Daisy grew bolder. She went up the stairs and followed the kitten along the landing. The landing was wide and spacious, with thick, dark carpet underfoot and panelled doors on every side. The light shining up from the hallway below gave some comfort from the gloom, as did the softer shaft of light emanating from the bedroom at the end of the landing.

The kitten led Daisy into the room. Here it jumped up

on to the bed. 'Oh!' Daisy stopped, her troubled gaze falling on the sleeping figure in the bed. 'I have to go,' she whispered fearfully. 'You'd better come with me, before the man wakes up.'

When the kitten merely stretched out, unable to believe its good fortune, Daisy was in a dilemma. It had been wrong to come into the house, and now it was wrong to stay. But she did so want to take the kitten home with her. 'Please,' she murmured, her frightened gaze shifting to the man's sleeping face. 'We'll get into terrible trouble if we don't go now.'

Slowly she crept across the room, her heart in her mouth as she came close to the bed, arms out, hoping against hope that the kitten would not run away. 'I won't hurt you,' she whispered, 'I'm your friend.'

She was picking the kitten up when the old man opened his eyes. Aware that someone was beside his bed, he slowly turned his head towards her, his tired eyes struggling to focus.

'I'm sorry, Mr . . .' Frightened, Daisy stepped back a pace. 'It was the kitten, you see. I came to get the kitten.'

He looked at her for an age, his eyes pinning her there.

'We have to go now,' she said tremulously. 'I'm sorry we woke you.'

Slowly, he shook his head, every move an agony. His gaze roved her face. After a while he saw the dress; the crimson red dress that had been specially made for Daisy's birthday. He seemed startled, his whole face opening with astonishment.

Daisy wanted to go but she felt obliged to stay. He was such an old man, so sad looking. 'Do you want me to stay with you?' she asked boldly. 'I will if you like.' Now that she had the kitten safe in her arms, she didn't feel quite so frightened. 'But I can't stay long,' she apologised.

The old man's eyes were fixed on the dress. When he made unintelligible noises, Daisy realised he was trying to say something. He was so obviously taken by her dress, she stepped forward a pace and did a little twirl for him. 'It was a birthday present,' she said proudly. 'Miss Ledell made it for me. I'm like the girl in the picture now.' She held out the drawing. 'See?' When he grew agitated and tried to snatch the drawing, she stepped away. 'No! You can't have it,' she said sternly. 'It's mine.'

As she pointed out the young woman in the drawing, she didn't realise how affected the old man was. She didn't see the tears that rolled down his face, nor the way he grasped and tore at the blankets. She only saw what she had drawn in all innocence: a young woman, strolling through the woods, the sun in her hair and the light of happiness in her face. Pointing to the bunch of bluebells in the girl's arms, Daisy said, 'She's been collecting wild flowers. And look, by the oak tree, do you see? There's a long shadow.' Fired with enthusiasm, she held the drawing closer. 'There's someone waiting for her. But we can't see who it is.'

When at that moment the old man smiled into her eyes, immense joy softening his face, Daisy was momentarily humbled. Then she announced confidently, 'I expect we'll see who it is the next time I draw a picture.'

The old man stared at the drawing, his eyes raking over it, again and again, seeing but not daring to believe. He tried to reach out but fell back, his old bones weakened by the long, crippling years.

Daisy understood. 'You can touch it if you like, but you can't have it.' She held the drawing closer, waiting while, with much effort, he raised a gnarled old hand. With immense tenderness he let the tips of his fingers come to rest on the young woman in the drawing. For what seemed an age he traced her face, his old fingers trembling as they outlined every line, every dear, familiar feature. And, as he gazed on that lovely, wonderful face, he could hardly bear the emotions that swept through him.

At first Daisy wasn't sure where the sound came from. It began as a thin wall and then became increasingly stronger, as though something from a long way off was coming closer. Only when she looked at the old man did she realise it was him. He put both hands over his face and rocked from side to side, the strange, pitiful cries pushing through his fingers, echoing from the walls. Terrified, Daisy backed away. The kitten clawed at her, drawing blood, desperate to be free, and Daisy had to let it go.

Suddenly she was swept aside, a woman's voice, shrill and ugly, yelling at her, 'Get out! Get away from him! My husband will skin you alive when he gets back!'

When she saw it was the old woman who had peered through the car window, Daisy fled.

Careering down the stairs, she stumbled out of the house, straight into Dave's arms. 'Whoa! It's all right, sweetheart.' Anger marbled his voice. 'Where've you been? You had me worried sick.' Larry Fellowes had helped him search for Daisy but when they heard the old man's cries, they had gone straight to the house. Sweeping Daisy up, he looked at the open door. 'What were you doing in there? Who's that crying?'

'It's my father,' Larry answered quietly. 'He's very old, been ill for many years. I'll see to him. You get off.'

As they travelled home, Daisy confessed how she'd followed the kitten into the house. 'The old man was very sad,' she said. 'He was all alone in the house, and then the woman came in . . .' Her voice shook. 'That . . . woman . . .' She fell silent.

'What woman, sweetheart?'

'The one who stood in the road.'

He jerked his head round. 'Good God! The one who stared through the window at you?'

'She said I was to get out, get away from him.'

'She must be the old man's wife, Larry Fellowes' mother.'

'No.'

'What do you mean, no?'

'She said her husband was on his way back and he'd skin me alive.'

'Larry Fellowes, eh?' He took a deep breath. 'They seem a strange couple and no mistake. But you did wrong, my girl! You had no right to go into that house. *Anything* could have happened! You're never to do anything like that again, do you hear me, young lady?'

'Do you think the kitten will be all right?'

'I asked if you heard me!'

'Yes, Daddy.'

'Well then?'

'I won't do it again.'

They drove in silence. At the junction, Dave noticed that the street lamp was out. As he began to pull out, a car appeared from nowhere. Slamming on his brakes, he waited. At first the car had seemed to be going at some speed, but in fact it was only idling along. By the time it was close enough for him to realise this, it was too close for him to dive out. 'Come on! Come on!' He wanted to get home.

Peering in the mirror, he looked at Daisy. She was curled up on the back seat but her eyes were open. 'Thought you were tired.'

'I am.'

'Are you going to sleep?'

'Don't know now.'

He cursed when he saw the car still hadn't passed. 'Some old dodderer,' he grumbled. 'Shouldn't be on the road.' All the same, he had to chuckle. 'I expect I'll be an old dodderer myself one day, God willing.' The alternative was less attractive.

Eyes closed and starting to doze, Daisy didn't hear the

door open. When the young woman climbed in beside her, she was amazed, too shocked to cry out. 'Don't be frightened,' the young woman said. 'I mean you no harm. Besides, I can't stay if you don't want me to.'

Daisy stared at the visitor. Pulling out her drawing, she examined the face there. Shocked and thrilled, she stared again at the visitor. 'It's *you*!' she whispered. *'You're the same.'*

The visitor nodded. 'Will you let me stay?' she murmured. 'I can't stay unless you invite me.'

Daisy nodded. 'You can stay if you want to.'

Moving off at last, Dave called over his shoulder, 'Did you say something?'

Daisy leaned forward, eyes shining, her voice shrill with excitement. 'Daddy! Look! It's the lady in my drawing.'

He peered through the mirror, seeing only Daisy and the drawing in her hand. 'I thought you wanted to sleep.'

'I can't sleep *now*.' Turning, she smiled shyly at the visitor.

'Is your seatbelt done up?'

'Yes.'

'We'll soon be home now.'

Daisy settled back and studied the visitor. She was exactly like the girl in her drawing: slim and lovely, with long, flowing dark hair and soft, expressive eyes; her face was heart-shaped, with a wide brow and small, chiselled chin. Though the dark eyes smiled at Daisy, there was no happiness in the smile. 'Where do you live?' Daisy ached with curiosity.

'Everywhere.' The smile was mystical. 'And nowhere.'

'Do you want my daddy to take you home?'

The smile was soft as gossamer. 'Yes, Daisy. If he can.'

Daisy was taken aback. 'How do you know my name?'

'Because I'm a friend.'

'Are you Miss Ledell's friend too?'

Surprise flickered. 'What a strange thing for you to ask.'

There was something about the stranger that made Daisy think of Miss Ledell. 'Do you know everything?'

'Not everything.'

'Miss Ledell helped me to make this drawing.'

Dave could hear Daisy muttering. Smiling into the mirror he asked, 'Are you talking to yourself, or did you ask me something?'

Daisy couldn't understand why he hadn't heard the conversation. 'I'm talking to the lady in my drawing.'

'I see.' Wryly smiling, he looked away. After a moment he peered into the mirror again. Daisy was shrouded in darkness.

'Did you see the man, Daisy?' The voice was soft, lilting. 'The man upstairs. Did you see him?'

'Yes. He was very sad.'

'Did he see your dress? Did he see the colour, Daisy? Did he touch it?'

'Yes. He liked my drawing too. But it made him cry.'

The stranger was silent. There was a feeling of desolation, but then she sighed, her eyes shining, 'So. Now he knows.' Closing her eyes, she raised her head and, making a sound like a sob, spoke again. 'At long last he knows, and soon they won't be able to keep us apart.' When she looked at Daisy, her eyes were smiling, incredibly beautiful. 'Thank you, Daisy,' she murmured. 'You can't know what you've done, but it was a wonderful thing.' She touched Daisy on the hand. It was like the gentle brush of feathers. 'It isn't over yet,' she said. 'There is more to do yet. But it's all possible now. Thank you, Daisy.'

'When I went into the house, Daddy was very angry.'

'He doesn't understand. He will, soon.'

'Do you think Miss Ledell will be angry when I tell her?'

'Oh no.' A look of love crossed her features. 'She would never be angry with you.'

Daisy was glad about that. 'Miss Ledell teaches me to play the piano.' Raising the drawing from her lap, she pointed at the young woman there. 'Don't you think she's beautiful?' Suddenly a thought occurred to Daisy. 'That's funny.' Raising her gaze, she found herself looking straight into the stranger's dark, mesmerising eyes. 'You both look like Miss Ledell!'

'Cliona.'

'Pardon?'

'Miss Ledell. Her name is Cliona.'

Daisy would have asked how she knew the old lady, but in that moment Dave swung the car into the drive. When Daisy turned to the stranger, she was gone.

Libby was watching through the window. Seeing the car arrive, she rushed out to meet them. 'I thought you were never coming home,' she said, accepting Dave's kiss. 'Jamie's in bed. That's where you should be, my girl.'

In the kitchen she made them both a hot drink. 'Then it's upstairs for a wash and straight into bed,' she told Daisy. 'As for you, Dave Walters, you've got some explaining to do.' But there was a twinkle in her eye. May had speculated that Dave had gone out to bring her back a surprise. At first she had rejected the idea, but during the course of the evening she had come round to May's thinking.

Daisy took off her coat. 'My arms hurt,' she said, tenderly fingering the deep scores down both her arms. 'The kitten scratched me.'

Dave sprang out of his chair. 'Good God, Daisy! Why didn't you tell me at the restaurant?'

Libby stared at him with suspicion. 'What restaurant?' Visions of Larry Fellowes and that awful place rushed through her mind, as did the reason for Dave's 'little errand'. 'I told you not to bother about the scarf!' She was angry. Frightened. 'You know I didn't want you going back there.'

While Dave tried to explain that he'd gone out there

without thinking, 'a spur of the moment thing', and anyway he'd got the scarf now, so wasn't she pleased, Libby slammed about at the sink. After filling a small bowl with a measure of hot water from the kettle, she tempered it with a flow from the cold tap. 'Look at Daisy!' she shouted. 'What happened, Dave? Why weren't you watching her?'

Daisy took it on herself to explain. The words tumbled over each other as she launched into a breathless account of the evening's events. She began by outlining how Miss Ledell had given her the drawing and 'Daddy said we were going to surprise you, and we went to this place'. Then she explained how there'd been a fire and the restaurant was closed. 'The man took Daddy into the kitchen. It was horrible, all black and burned, so I played with the kitten and then the kitten ran away.' Pausing for breath, she winced when Libby dabbed at the scratch marks. 'Daddy told me not to go away, but I chased the kitten and we found this poor old man in bed. He liked the drawing, but it made him cry, and that made the kitten scratch me because he wanted to get down, and then the awful woman came in, the one who stared at me through the window when Daddy went searching the lane.'

Before either Dave or Libby could get a word in, she continued, 'It's been a real adventure, Mum. On the way home I sat in the back because I was tired, but I didn't go to sleep because I was talking to the woman in the drawing. She said I'd done a wonderful thing. She said there was a lot more to be done yet, and that Daddy would know soon enough.' She was about to reveal how the young woman had told her Miss Ledell's name was Cliona when Libby put a stop to it.

'That's enough.' Mentally dismissing part of Daisy's story as the product of a child's imagination, she still needed Dave's reassurance. 'Go to bed now. Your daddy and I need to talk.'

Kissing them both goodnight, Daisy took herself to bed. Downstairs, Dave enlightened Libby on the more worrying facets of Daisy's story. 'So you see, all's well that ends well.'

Calmer now, Libby snuggled up to him on the sofa. 'I still wish you hadn't gone,' she said. 'Promise you won't go there again.'

'Don't worry. I've no intention of going there again.' He kissed her long and tenderly, and all was right between them.

A short time later they went to bed. But they didn't make love, and for some reason they were too restless for sleep. For a long time they lay in each other's arms, until Dave drifted into uneasy slumber. After a while, Libby got out of bed and stood by the window, staring out at the night. The sky was fired with splashes of silver and gold where the moonshine spilled through the clouds, infiltrating the darkness below and highlighting nature's wintry colours. There was no breeze. No night creatures called.

It was a strange, magnificent night, and normally Libby would have taken pleasure in it. But not tonight. Tonight she was troubled.

She felt as though something, or someone, was threatening her happiness.

The old man was quiet now. Worn and broken, he had sobbed himself to sleep. The sedative in his blood took control and now, to the onlooker, he seemed peaceful enough. Inside, though, his mind was in turmoil. He had seen the girl in the red dress, and he had touched her face. For a lifetime he had carried her in his heart and now, at long last, she had come to see him. He should rest now, but he couldn't. Ida gave him no peace. She would not let him go. Her voice, her hands, her very presence kept him here, enduring the pain and the suffering she imposed on him.

She was a devilish creature, her wickedness cloaked in kindness to hide it from the world. They believed she cared for him, that she loved him, but the old man knew better. His bones ached where she had tortured him. Her voice invaded his dreams, and he felt her hatred in every fibre of his being.

He cried out for release from this world, from the agony of meaningless days and nightmares that never ended. His soul craved the freedom that he had been cheated of so long ago. Was there a reason? he wondered. Had he been so bad? Yes, he must have been. Somewhere in his life he must have committed a terrible wrong, or why was he now held prisoner in his own feeble body? His son was weak and the woman was powerful. Her hatred controlled and humiliated him, and only he could see. Yet he was not able to understand.

In the rare moments when his thoughts were lucid, he wondered about her. He felt he knew her from somewhere before. Either her, or someone like her. A child maybe? A woman he had known? Sometimes when he opened his eyes and she was there, his heart turned somersaults. The turn of her face; that certain way she looked at him.

He knew her from before, of that he was certain. But who was she? And why had she been sent to torment him?

Downstairs, the argument continued.

'What were you thinking of to leave him like that?' Larry Fellowes was beside himself. 'You know how strong he can be when he takes a mind to it.' Rocking backwards and forwards on the edge of the chair, he looked like a man defeated. 'Maybe we're wrong, Ida. How can we be so sure she means to harm him? Why can't we leave him alone, let him die in peace?'

Ida seemed not to hear. Instead she continued to pace the floor, her face a study in calculation. Suddenly she stopped and rounded on him. 'You know I'm right,' she snapped. 'She's getting closer. We have to be more vigilant.'

'I don't know. I'm not so sure. What if you're wrong? What if the thing that haunts the lanes is nothing to do with what happened all those years ago? What if my father isn't the reason for her being here? Maybe she doesn't mean to harm him.'

'Are you willing to take that chance?' Her heart was alive with malice but the eyes were masked with kindness.

Weary, he stared at the floor. 'All I know is this. Sometimes my father is in terrible pain. He can't talk or do for himself any more. He's little more than a cabbage and it's wicked, I tell you. What we're doing is wicked! Even the doctor says it's only your dedication and determination that has kept him alive all this time.'

'Have you forgotten *why* I won't let him die?' She had become a master at deception. Sometimes the weight of it all was too much to bear. But she had made a promise and, whatever the consequences, she must keep it.

Ashamed, he shook his head. 'No, I haven't forgotten. You believe *she's* waiting to take his soul, to punish him in a way no mortal can understand.'

'You must never underestimate the lengths *she* will go to.'

'Like that other young man, you mean?'

'That's right. He looked like your father as a young man, and he paid the price. Remember what she did to him, Larry! She used him, and when she couldn't get to your father through him, she haunted the poor creature until he leaped to his death.'

'I know.'

'She'll do the same to the young man who came here tonight.'

'Yes.'

'Do you really want her to get near your father?'

He was like putty in her hands. 'You won't let her hurt him, will you?'

'I'm his guardian. *She* knows that. She will never get to him through me.' Not until she herself had finished with him, she thought triumphantly. Keeping those two apart was the worst torture imaginable. Yet she had no compassion. Only memories that wouldn't leave her be.

'Maybe we're more evil than she is.'

'What?' Fear shot through her.

'We must be evil not to warn that man. He has a family.'

Seeing his weakness, she played on his love for his father. 'Think, Larry. Think what you're saying. That young man is only a distraction, to keep her from taking your father. We're buying time, that's all. She went away the last time. Maybe she'll go away this time and never come back. Isn't that what you want?'

'I just want my father to be at rest. I don't want him kept alive by drugs and artificial means. He's old. He deserves some dignity.' He shook with emotion. 'Oh, Ida! All these years. I can't begin to imagine what he's been through.'

She took a moment to enjoy his misery; the way his shoulders stooped and the outspread hands clutched at his temples. She saw how he had changed since she had come to his house, and it pleased her. Outside these four walls he was hard and ruthless, aloof to staff and customers alike, charming but unsure, a man of talents, an accomplished businessman. Inside, he was just a frightened child.

Sensing her gaze, he looked up. 'I don't know what I'd do without you,' he muttered. 'You're stronger than I am. You see things I don't.'

She smiled, pretending as always. 'You're not sorry you married me then?' She came and knelt at his feet, gazing up with adoring eyes.

'No, I'm not sorry.' Taking hold of her hands, he clung

to her. 'At thirty-two years of age, I was too set in my ways to think of marriage. And there was my father. He was getting worse, the illness was slowly eroding his mind.' He looked down, unable to go on.

'Don't be sad,' she murmured. 'I'll look after him for as long as he needs me.'

Life was cruelly unpredictable. For years she had searched for Tony Fellowes, and then, just as she began to give up hope of ever finding him, Fate delivered him into her hands. The only way she could be near the father was to marry the son. It was another small sacrifice.

'I'll go to him now,' she said. 'That girl. She really upset him.' Her face relaxed into a smile. 'No doubt she'll pay for it, as they all will.'

He looked up, sometimes loving her, sometimes fearing her. 'Where will it all end?' he groaned, wiping his hands over his face. 'What would Father say if he knew? He's never been an unkind man.'

Incensed, she opened her mouth to reply, but the words choked in her throat. She thought of the woman she had loved above all others; a woman who had suffered unspeakable cruelties; a miserable existence. And all because of that fiend lying upstairs.

'You'd better go,' she said, thinking that if he didn't, she might be tempted to kill him with her bare hands.

Straightening his shoulders, he went to the door. 'You're right,' he conceded. 'I'd better see what they're up to.'

Leaving the house, he made his way to the restaurant where he sat by the bar, his mind aimlessly wandering. He felt down at heart, driven into himself. He was a lonely man, a man who had it in him to be immensely cruel yet who had a core of softness deep inside where he hid in times of trouble.

He was hiding there now, cowering from the awesome powers that had been unleashed on them. If his father really was in jeopardy, then Ida was right and he was wrong. The signs were there – the accident, the sightings, the young man who was lured to his death. And what about the way his father stared out of the window, silent tears falling down his face, making unintelligible sounds as if calling to someone, or talking to something out there in the darkness? There *was* reason to be afraid, he was convinced. He himself had seen the ghostly apparition stalking the house, always staying at a distance as if kept there by an invisible wall. Never, until the day he died, would he believe the apparition was his own mother. The young woman had a magical beauty, but whenever she made her presence known, the air was charged with evil.

Only once had he felt that the evil was already here. It was on a storm-filled night, when the skies were raging and screaming, and the lightning cut through the night with long jagged blades. He woke to find Ida had gone. Drawn to the window, he saw her, out there in that devilish night, standing in the howling wind, shrouded in her nightgown. Only an arm's reach away was the young woman. For a long, terrifying moment they stood facing each other with hard, cold eyes. Then, just as he was about to run down and drag Ida away, the young woman looked up at his father's bedroom, then turned away dejected, to disappear into the woods beyond.

Triumphant, Ida returned to the house. He heard her climb the stairs. He heard her in the bathroom, and then, when she got into bed, he groaned and rolled, as if being woken from a deep sleep. He sensed that she was aching to boast about her experience. He felt her trembling with excitement but he kept his eyes closed and his face turned away. He couldn't talk about it. He didn't even want to think about what he had seen. He didn't sleep. His mind was throbbing with what he had witnessed. A scene so thrilling, so powerful, it was burned in his brain for all time.

That was the only time when he had felt the evil as though it was part of himself, part of Ida. But that was impossible. It was *her*, not them. *She* brought the evil with her. She wanted his father. If Ida was to be believed, she wanted his soul, to punish him for ending her life. But it wasn't his fault. She of all people should know that.

'Are you all right, Mr Fellowes?' Carter addressed him for the third time.

Absent-mindedly helping himself to a second glass of whisky, Larry looked round, a bemused expression on his face. 'Have you ever been haunted?' His voice was slurred, his reason softened by the alcohol.

'Haunted?' Carter was taken aback. 'Can't say I have.' This was the first time he'd seen the boss drinking. It was also the first time he'd addressed him man to man. It was a shock, even if the question was a bit odd.

'You're a liar then. One way or another, we're *all* haunted.'

Thinking this might be a good time to take advantage, Carter remarked boldly, 'I've finished the work. Is it all right if I go now?'

'That girl found her way into the house . . . frightened my father.'

'I heard.'

'What else did you hear?' He was suspicious. Always suspicious.

'Just the commotion.'

'You heard him crying?'

The other man nodded, embarrassed, afraid for his job. 'I think so.'

'In his youth, my father was a big, handsome man, did you know that?'

Carter shook his head. What did he know of the old man? Or of any of this family? He came to work, he was paid a wage, and then he went home. That was all he needed to know.

'He's a good man, my father.' All the old memories came flooding back, making Larry smile. 'When I was a boy, he was my hero. He talked to me as if I knew as much as he did. Mother would laugh and say he shouldn't expect me to understand, but he refused to talk down to me. He taught me all about catering – ordering, taking stock, preparing accounts, keeping a ledger, that sort of thing. I owe it all to him.' Flinging out his arms, he encompassed the room and everything in it. 'This restaurant is the result of what he taught me.'

'You're a lucky man.' Envy marbled Carter's voice, but Larry was too engrossed in himself to hear it.

'Sit down.'

'Beg pardon?'

'You've finished your work, you said.' He took another gulp of whisky, burped and laughed out loud. 'Unless you've got some big-busted woman waiting at home, you can keep me company.'

Carter couldn't believe his ears. 'Keep you company, Mr Fellowes?' Socialising now, was it? My, we were coming up in the world.

'Sit with me for a while, eh? It's bad for a man to drink alone.' Handing Carter the half-empty bottle, he said, 'Better get yourself a glass before I change my mind.'

'Well, thank you, I must say.' Carter took the bottle, fetched a glass and sat down beside his boss. 'This is all very nice.' He was growing bolder by the minute.

Inhibitions drowned by the booze, Larry went on, 'From as far back as I can remember, Father owned his own business. He started out with a small cafe by the beach at Weymouth and ended up with a fine hotel on the promenade. He was a busy man, but he always had time for his family. During the holidays, he'd take us inland. We'd picnic in the park and boat on the river, and oh, they were such good times.'

'I envy you, I do.' He wouldn't swap places though, thank you all the same. He envied Larry Fellowes his money and position, and that was all. He wouldn't want to be burdened with no old invalid, however much of a 'hero' he'd been when he was younger. Nor would he want to be lumbered with a woman like Ida. Pretty at a pass maybe, but dark-mooded and untouchable. He liked a woman that was red-blooded and accommodating, like the ones he paid on a Saturday night.

Still immersed in his own thoughts, Larry rambled on. 'I remember once the boat began to sink, and the man had to tow us back. We were soaked to the knees and Mother was worried we'd drown, but we laughed about it afterwards. We laughed a lot. Like children, we were, all three of us.'

'Sounds like your parents loved each other a lot.'

'Oh yes.' Just for a moment he couldn't go on. The harsh realisation of how it had all turned out was too real, too shocking. 'She was a lovely, warm-hearted creature, full of life, always smiling. My father adored her.' The suspicion of a sob broke his voice. 'No two people ever loved each other more than they did.'

'Then they were fortunate. That kind of love doesn't happen often.'

After considering this remark, Larry replied quietly, 'Sometimes a love like that can be dangerous too.'

'What do you mean?'

Larry declined to answer. Instead he took another soothing sip of whisky. It helped him forget. 'When he was young, my father was a rock of strength, and now look at him.' He wanted to smash his fist into the nearest thing. He needed to hurt someone like he was being hurt. Like his father was being hurt. Reduced to an empty shell, threatened by an unknown force that was way beyond his understanding – beyond *all* their understandings.

'I've never seen your father.' Carter wondered if he was treading on dangerous ground and would be held responsible tomorrow. 'I know nothing about him except that he's been bedridden these many years.'

'Bedridden. Senile. He can't talk and his hand shakes so much he can't even write. If he could, it wouldn't make too much sense.' Cut to the heart, he spat out the words. 'It's wicked! Half the time he sleeps and the other half he stares out of the window.' His voice dropped to a whisper, his eyes big and afraid as he turned them on Carter. 'Stares and stares, like he's waiting for someone. Do you know what I mean?'

'Can't say I do.'

'He can't tell us, you see. We never know what he's thinking.' Suffocating his sorrows, he took another gulp from his glass. 'I'll never be the man he was. I'm too much of a coward. I can't sit with him for too long. It's too painful, you see. But she's wonderful with him. Ida sits beside his bed for hours, never tires of talking to him. She knows all about these things.'

'My father ran off when I was a kid. It never bothered me, not really. I can't even remember what he looked like.'

'Oh yes, he was a handsome man, my father.' When Carter was slow to pour his drink, Larry took the bottle and did the job for him, then he half filled his own glass and sipped constantly at it, fuelling the need to empty his soul. 'When my mother died, he went to pieces. It took him years and years to recover.'

'That's understandable, when you lose someone you love, like you say he loved her.' Sadly, he had never known such love.

'When my father began failing, I devoted my life to him. It was the least I could do. I vowed never to marry but what with one thing and another, it just happened. My father was committed to hospital. Ida was there, taking care of him, and we got to strolling out, you know how you do.'

'Not really, no. I've never had a woman of my own. Don't particularly want one.'

'Ida took a real shine to my father. It was her who put the idea into my head that he should be brought home where he might be happier. She carried on nursing him, and it wasn't long before we got married.'

'Seems an ideal arrangement, I'd say.'

'Of course as she got older and Father got more difficult, I brought a nurse in to help.'

'Eileen?'

'She's good with him, it gives Ida a breather.' Hiccupping, he laughed out loud. 'I'm drunk!'

'What did she look like, your mother? Pretty, was she?'

This time Larry lapsed into a deep silence.

'Was she dark-haired? Blonde? Tall, short? What?' Feeling warm and merry now, Carter's curiosity was aroused.

The silence thickened.

Fearing he'd outstayed his welcome, Carter replaced his glass on the bar. 'I'd best be off, eh? See you tomorrow then, Mr Fellowes.' As he turned to slide off the stool, he felt the other man's fingers grip his wrist.

'Sit down!'

Doing as he was told, Carter apologised. 'Sorry if I were getting a bit too personal, Mr Fellowes.'

Silence descended as Larry glanced furtively round the room. 'Ssh! What was that?'

Carter shivered. 'I didn't hear nothing, Mr Fellowes.'

'Hmm.' Returning his gaze, he said softly, 'What makes evil?'

'Evil?' Fear was infectious. Carter began to tremble.

'I mean, why would someone who was always good suddenly become evil?'

'I dunno. Something bad would have to happen to make a good person become evil, I suppose.'

'Yes, you're right. That's just what happened, something bad.'

'In what way, Mr Fellowes?'

'Was your mother pretty, Carter?'

'Sort of.'

'My mother was like no other woman you've ever seen.' A smile filtered through the sadness. 'Long, dark hair, and eyes the colour of midnight. Small, she was, and slim. Her face was childlike, full of joy. She was fun-loving and so natural, everyone loved her.'

'No wonder your father adored her.'

Larry continued in a mutter, talking to himself. 'They were like two sides of the same coin. Inseparable.' He laughed, but it was a grim sound. 'That's the trouble, you see. He adores her, even now.'

'So? He's not so senile then?'

Surprised, Larry swung round. 'She gives him no peace.'

Out of his depth now, Carter wished he'd never sat down. 'I'm sorry. I'd better go.'

'There was a terrible accident, you see.' Larry stared at Carter, who visibly cringed. 'She was horribly injured and died soon after. My father was not expected to live but somehow he survived, in body if not in mind.' Impatient, he shoved his glass away, sobering a little as he recalled the event. 'He never really recovered. Never will.'

'Sounds to me like he's had more than his fair share of tragedy.' Not that he cared one way or the other. He had his own problems, and this pompous bugger was one of them.

'What would you know, you smarmy little bastard! Get out of here!' Grabbing the bottle, Larry threw it against the wall where it smashed. Carter made a hasty exit.

From the upstairs window of the house, Ida could see through the trees and into the bar. She had noticed the two of them sitting talking, and it made her smile. When later she saw Carter scurry from the building, she actually laughed out loud. 'I wish I could have heard what they were talking about,' she said, returning to the old man's bedside. 'I wouldn't mind betting they were talking about me, and you. I expect your son was asking how that little girl got to find her way into this house.'

The old man lay inert, face white as chalk and eyes tightly closed. His hands were clasped over the sheets; long, strong fingers which she couldn't help but touch. 'Such beautiful hands,' she murmured. 'What a pity they won't ever again stroke a woman's body.' Cradling one in her fists, she raised it to her face and held it there. 'So soft,' she whispered. 'Sensual.'

For one fleeting moment the hatred ebbed away and in its place came an irrepressible feeling of belonging. 'You've loved two women,' she whispered. 'One the mother of your son. The other the mother of your daughter.' She glanced at the window before returning her gaze to the old man. 'One waits out there. Not to harm you like I make him believe. She loves you too much for that. All she craves is for you and her to be together again. You want it too, don't you, old man? You sense her whenever she's near. I've seen you looking towards the window. I've seen the tears roll down your face.'

The rage wouldn't be held back any longer. 'But what about the other one? Do you ever think of her, old man?' There was such pain inside her she could hardly breathe. 'Why did you do it?' she pleaded. 'Why did you make her suffer when she loved you so much?'

Slowly turning back the sheets, she opened his pyjama top and roved her hands over his chest. The chest was deep and strong with small erect nipples on a bed of hair, the short thick hairs still surprisingly dark in places, and the chest muscles taut underneath.

His face was turned away and she looked at the once-virile features, the profile that still held a semblance of the looks that had made him stand out from others. 'I can see why they loved you,' she said. 'In a way I envy them.'

Taking hold of his pyjama bottoms, she slid them down until his nakedness was complete. The waist was thick, the hips narrow, the shape of the young man still embedded in the old. Though inactive for so long, the legs were surprisingly firm. Not so the penis, which lay sadly to one side, hidden in deep folds of skin which once were plump and full. 'Where is your dignity now, old man?'

When he made no move, she sighed long and deep. 'Don't blame me for hating you,' she whispered. 'Whatever I am, it's what you've made me.'

Folding her arms on the bed she laid her head against them. She was incredibly lonely, needing another soul to talk to, to laugh with, someone she might confide in. The nights were too long, the days too short, and always, *always*, she must stay on her guard. She knew no love, no comfort. She had no hope of a future. All she had was this old man, and her memories; memories that made nightmares and stalked her every waking minute.

She began to cry; soft racking sobs that gave her some release but brought no comfort. The sound of her crying stirred him from his slumber. When she peered over her arms, she found herself looking straight into his eyes.

Shaken, she sat bolt upright, seething with anger that he had seen her weakness. 'You old bastard!' she gasped. 'What are you staring at? What is it you want from me?'

His gaze didn't flinch, nor did he look away. Instead he seemed to smile. His lips parted as if he was trying to speak.

Like a cat she pounced on him. 'What is it you want to say?'

The smile slid away.

'Can't talk, can you? Cat got your tongue, has it?' Disgusted with herself, with him, she leaned away, but her eyes held his for what seemed an age. 'What are you thinking, old man?' she murmured. 'What would you say if you only had the strength?'

She paused, as if waiting for him to comment. The deep brown eyes held fast to hers, speaking volumes, searching her soul.

She had never seen him look at her like that before. Unnerved, she screamed at him, 'You know something, don't you? What? What do you know, old man? Was it the girl? Why was she here? What did she say that upset you so much?'

The eyes bored into hers, unafraid. Wonderfully dumb.

Incensed, she prodded him with sharp fingers. 'The girl brought something with her, didn't she? I saw her hide something when I spied on her in the car.' Taking him by the shoulders she shook him hard. 'I'm waiting, old man! What did she say to upset you like that?'

The eyes closed. But not the heart.

She covered him and moved away. 'Never mind, old man.' Holding the door open, she muttered angrily, 'I'll find out. There are ways and means, and I can be very clever when I need to be. After all, they believed that young man killed himself, didn't they?' She giggled like a girl, or a crazy thing. 'The fools thought he leaped to his death, but we know better, don't we, you and I?'

She returned to the bed and leaning over him said softly, 'The man who came here tonight, Dave Walters. A handsome man, like yourself when you were young. She'll use him, you'll see. And when she realises he can't help her any more than the other one, she'll be angry. Just like she was the last time.' She went quietly back across the room, pausing at the door. 'There is nothing you or I can do, old man. It's already written.'

On closing the door, her parting words echoed in the darkness of that small prison: 'Dave Walters is destined to go the same way as the other one.'

CHAPTER FOUR

It was Friday afternoon, a week before Christmas. The day was glorious, the sun poured down and it seemed as if everyone had a smile for their neighbours.

'Evening, Mr Walters.' The butcher's daughter had long fancied Dave, though always from a distance. 'You look pleased with yourself. Had a good day, have you?' She was on the other side of the street and had to raise her voice to make herself heard.

'I can't complain,' he called back. 'All the same, I'll be glad to get home.' Giving her a smile that made her weak at the knees, he swung away, heading at a smart pace down the street towards his offices, nodding and smiling as other locals greeted him. By the time he reached the office, he was whistling a merry tune.

'You look like the cat who's got the cream,' Mandy remarked. 'Did you get sole agency for the manor house?'

He kept her waiting for a second or two.

'You did, didn't you?'

'What do you think?'

She squealed with delight. 'I knew you'd do it,' she cried, planting a smacker on his mouth. 'How long for?'

'I tried for a year. The big man wanted to screw me down to three months. In the end I managed to persuade him to give us six months sole agency. After that it's wide open. So,' he leaned forward, 'do you reckon you could get it all off the ground before you swan off on your holiday and leave us stranded for a month?'

'Leave it all cushy for the new recruit, you mean?'

'Something like that, yes.'

'Have I ever let you down?'

'Not until now.' He saw her face fall at his remark and added quickly, 'Only joking. Of course you've never let me down. What's more, you deserve a month off.' He gave her a wide grin. 'Even if I could strangle you for it.'

'You won't even know I'm gone,' she said wryly. 'I'll leave everything so easy to follow, the temp will slip into my place like a hand in a glove.' Her expression became serious. 'As long as she doesn't slip into my shoes, so I don't have a job when I get back.'

'There's no fear of that, I can promise you.' He winked. 'Unless she's a stunner, then I can't promise anything.'

Shaking her head, she chided him, 'I'll never see the day when you have eyes for anyone but Libby. I mean, look at the queue of women who'd give their right arm for you. There's me for a start, then there's the butcher's daughter who can't take her eyes off you, and what about that other little girl who worked here for a while? She got all in a jitter every time you called her into the office. In the end she couldn't stand it.'

'Oh, so *that's* why she suddenly upped and left.'

They were still chuckling when the phone began ringing. Dave was nearest. Picking up the receiver he answered, 'Walters Estate Agency. Dave Walters speaking, what can I do for you?' The caller quoted an advert from the week before. 'Yes, that's right,' Dave confirmed. 'Ninety-five thousand, but we do have an offer on that property, I'm afraid.' A pause, then, 'Yes, you're quite right, I am obliged to put your offer to the vendor.'

A moment later, after making some notes, he thanked the caller, replaced the receiver and handed the notes to

Mandy. 'Drake's Close,' he said, satisfying her curiosity. 'Looks like we have two interested parties.'

'Right.' Sliding her rimless spectacles over her ears, she began tapping into the computer. 'Down to business.'

As Dave went into his inner office, she heard him yell, 'Feet off, you bugger!'

Mandy laughed out loud. 'Told you,' she called out. 'I knew you'd cop it when he found your big feet sprawled over his desk.'

Having spent the last few minutes on Dave's phone, Jack Arnold swiftly curtailed his conversation, slammed down the receiver and leaped out of the chair. 'Be Jaysus, here y'are! And I thought you wouldn't be back for ages yet.' He began an exaggerated bowing and scraping, a mischievous gleam in his eyes as he pleaded in lilting Irish tones, 'I'm sorry, Mr Walters, sir. Please don't sack me. Sure, I'll never do it again.'

Shaking his head, Dave put his briefcase on the desk and sat down. 'You're incorrigible,' he laughed. 'I should send you packing, but then who'd make the tea while Mandy's away?'

'Ah well, now yer talking because sure, don't I make the best pot of tea outside o' the Emerald Isle?'

Removing documents from his briefcase, Dave gestured for Jack to sit down. 'We've got the manor house,' he said. 'Now all we have to do is sell it.'

'For how much?'

'Half a million, and it's worth every penny.'

'Jaysus! Is that his price or yours?'

'Mine. Take a look at that.' He pushed his notepad across the desk. 'It's some property. Eight bedrooms, four bathrooms and enough space downstairs to entertain the whole of Woburn.'

'I see what you mean.' Flicking through the pages, Jack was amazed. 'Together with fifty acres of prime grazing land.' Handing back the notepad, he remarked thoughtfully, 'I see we've got sole agency. How in God's name did yer manage that?'

'With a bit of luck and a lot of sheer bloody nerve.'

Never able to stay serious for long, Jack stood up and began pacing the floor, his hands tucked into the lapels of his jacket. 'Well now, my good man, I suppose this means ye'll be wanting a rise.'

'Sit down, you bloody fool!' Dave laughed.

Throwing himself into the chair, Jack got himself into business mode. 'It's a good deal,' he acknowledged. 'No wonder the owner wanted the top man to value it. Sure the place should sell well enough. We've got a list as long as yer arm with people wanting land.'

'We need a hard advertising drive. I'll get working on the budget tonight at home. After we've seen the candidates for Mandy's job, I'm off. It's been a long day and I promised Libby we'd make an early start in the morning.' The idea of a whole day out was a real bonus.

'All right for some.'

'I haven't been fishing in ages.'

'You wouldn't catch me fishing. Sure, it's too soddin' cold. I'm surprised yer women are going along.'

'Ah, but they're not. That's why I chose Emmerson Park. Libby and Daisy drop me off at the river bank, then they go into Olney for the shopping. At twelve thirty, Libby collects me and we make our way to the Bull Inn for some lunch.'

'Yer crafty bugger.'

'Not crafty. Just sensible. I don't like shopping, and they don't like fishing, so I fish and they shop and everybody's happy. Which is why I want to be away as soon as we've done the interviews. So, being as you're the one who's been dealing with it all, what time do we start?'

Where women were concerned, Jack knew it all by heart. 'As you know, we've narrowed it down to three. We have Samantha Bowman, aged thirty-two, long legs and blonde hair, a proven expert on computer. Also, she worked as a telephonist for British Telecom.'

'Did Mandy follow up her references?'

'Of course. And they were impeccable.'

'Next?'

'The elegant Laura Morrison, redhead, small and curvy. She knows all there is to know about estate agency work. She was employed by one of our major rivals for some eight years, until the wanderlust took her off to travel the world. Apparently she got as far as Blackpool and decided it was too lonely out there.' An impish grin spread over his face. 'Sure, there'd have been no time to feel lonely if she'd taken me along.' Leaning forward confidentially, he began to amplify. 'In fact, if I had my way—'

'Later, Jack, or they'll be here before we've time to get our act together. The sooner it's done, the better I'll like it. I'm just not cut out for interviewing.'

Jack saw this as an ideal opportunity. 'Look now, it's a Saturday night and yer want to get away, so yer do. Leave the interviewing to me, why don't yer?'

'Not on your life! If I know you, it'll be the one with the longest legs and the brightest, most promising sparkle in her eye.'

'An' what's wrong with that, I'd like to know?'

'Nothing, in your own time. So, get on with it. Three, you said. Who's next?'

'Ah, well now, this one's a bit too quiet for my liking.'

Dave laughed. 'I see. Wasn't impressed by your line of chat, is that it?'

'Something like that. It's a shame, too, because she's a real beauty – dark moody eyes yer could die for, long hair to run yer hands through the morning after, and a smile to melt the icebergs in the northern hemisphere.' He sighed forlornly. 'She's too quiet, so she is. Seems to put up barriers, if yer know what I mean.'

'We're interviewing for a temporary secretary until Mandy gets back,' Dave reminded him. 'To hear you talk, anybody would think we were judging a beauty contest. Now, will you please put your mind to it, Jack.'

'Right yer are. Well, the young lady looks the part, so she does. She's twenty-eight, though if yer ask me she looks younger. Her name is Cliona Martin, and should she pass yer sharp, eagle eye, I'm sure she's more than capable of filling in for Mandy while she's away.'

'References?'

'This is where she falls behind the others. There were two references. One from her old employer who writes glowingly about her, though we couldn't follow that one up because apparently his business went belly up some two years ago and now he can't be traced.'

'What about the second reference?'

'Ah, well now, that was more personal than professional. From a lady of good standing, it claims the young woman is of exceptional character and able to fulfil every requirement mentioned in our advert.'

'Hmm.' Dave wasn't sure. 'We can't afford to take anyone on face value. Mandy has designed a small computer test which hopefully will sort the wheat from the chaff.' He rubbed his chin. The replacement had to be right. The business was really taking off now and with properties of the kind he was lately taking on his books, the wrong person sitting in Mandy's chair, for however short a time, could be disastrous. 'We'll see,' he murmured, glancing at the wall clock. 'It's quarter past six. That gives us fifteen minutes before they start arriving.'

A tap on the door admitted Mandy. 'While you two are discussing the candidates, the first one has already arrived.' The smug look on her face suggested she was obviously enjoying their discomfort. 'At this very moment, Samantha Bowman is sitting in the front office, long legs crossed and her battle paint on, ready to prove she is just what you need while I'm away.'

Dave said quietly, 'I take it you don't agree.'

'I'm saying nothing.'

Dave wouldn't leave it at that. 'Just say you'll postpone your holiday, then we won't need to interview anybody.'

With a disdainful glare, Mandy dropped a pile of paper on to the desk. 'I think it might help if you had these in front of you. Three files. One for each candidate.'

'Mandy?'

'Yes?'

'You wouldn't like to sit in on the interview, would you?'

'No.'

'Or take it on your own. I trust your judgement.'

'Absolutely not.'

'OK. As the proprietor of this establishment, I suppose it falls to me.'

'Exactly.'

'Right then.' Squaring his shoulders, Dave put on his 'face of authority', as Mandy called it. 'We're ready,' he said, glancing at Jack to make sure he wasn't about to do a runner.

For all his bravado, Jack was equally nervous. 'Don't look at me,' he said, bristling. 'I'm just here to watch and learn.'

'What a pair of cowards you are.' Mandy looked from one to the other. 'Just remember one thing.'

Relieved she was about to give them some good advice, they replied in unison, 'What's that?'

'You're interviewing for a *temp*. I shall be back in four weeks.'

Dave's quick smile was reassuring. 'I won't forget.'

'If you do give my job away permanently, I'll get employment with the opposition and slag you off from morning to night.'

'That settles it then,' said Dave with a grin. 'The job will definitely still be here when you get back.' He glanced at the note pinned to the top file. 'According to this, Samantha Bowman isn't due to be interviewed until seven. Laura Morrison is supposed to be the first at six thirty.'

'Some people like to arrive early,' Mandy informed him. 'They think it gives them the edge.'

'I see. Well, she'll just have to wait her turn.'

By six thirty all three had arrived. 'They're keen, I'll say that for them,' Mandy remarked. 'Are you ready for the first one?'

Dave nodded. 'Ready as we'll ever be.'

'Hope it won't take too long,' Jack said. 'I'm on a promise tonight.' He rolled his eyes towards the door. 'Though I could always be persuaded to change my plans.'

'Keep your mind on the job in hand, Jack. We can't afford to make any mistakes.'

Laura Morrison was everything Jack had said; she was also shrill-voiced and wore so much make-up you could have scraped it off with a builder's trowel. She played up to Jack unashamedly, mistakenly thinking it might get her the job. After the interview, Mandy escorted her to the outer office where she was put through the computer test. According to Mandy later, she passed it with flying colours. Her shrill manner, however, had already put her out of the running.

Samantha Bowman was intelligent and extremely attractive. She had a good grasp of business policy, and a pleasant attitude. Initially, she seemed a very likely candidate, until she laughed uproariously at one of Jack's remarks, after which her composure deteriorated until every other sentence was punctuated by a fit of giggles which left her breathless. Worse, she constantly crossed and uncrossed her legs until Dave felt dizzy watching her. The computer test proved to be a disaster, and she ran out in tears.

'Don't look at me,' Jack told Dave. 'Sure, I never said a word.'

'Nerves,' Mandy explained after she'd seen her out. 'Interviews take some people that way.'

'Miss Martin hasn't run off as well, has she?' Dave asked.

'Sorry to disappoint you,' Mandy answered cheekily, 'but I'm just about to show her in. Then if it's all right with you, I'd like to get off home.' It was now twenty past seven.

'Of course,' said Dave. 'And thanks for staying so late.'

Mandy disappeared into the outer office and returned a moment later. 'Miss Martin,' she announced crisply and placed a sheet of paper on Dave's desk.

Mandy lingered by the door to gauge their reaction. If it was up to her, she would give the job to this one straightaway.

Both men looked up, and both were mesmerised.

Dressed in a blue, smock-like dress that gathered softly at the waist, Cliona Martin looked almost childlike. Her long dark hair hung loosely plaited over one shoulder, and the dark eyes were incredibly striking against the paleness of her skin. Yet, for all that, she exuded a strength that belied her small, slim appearance. When she smiled, as she did now, the room seem bathed in a warm and wonderful glow.

As Mandy backed out of the office, she caught Dave's attention. She gestured to the young woman and gave the thumbs up. Her meaning was clear. She hoped Dave would bear it in mind.

'Do sit down,' Dave told the young woman, observing her curiously for a moment. 'We've met before, haven't we?'

'I don't think so.'

'I'm sorry,' he apologised, 'but you seem familiar. I really do have a feeling I've seen you somewhere.'

She shook her head. 'I don't think so,' she said again. Her voice was warm and silky, like the touch of velvet.

'You see, I've only recently come to the village.'

'How recently?'

'I arrived only two days ago. I'm staying with my aunt, but I don't expect to be here long. I saw your advert and thought it suited both our purposes.'

Dave was intrigued. 'Oh?'

She nodded, her wonderful dark eyes appraising his face as she spoke. 'I need to be occupied. To be doing something constructive.' There was purpose in her eye and steel in her voice. 'I know how important the work is, and I can do it so, like I said, we need each other.'

Jack was impressed. 'Yer believe in speaking yer mind an' that's a fact. If yer ask me, Dave, this is the one to do Mandy's job.' He was itching to be off to his date. If he'd been given any sign of encouragement by the young woman, he would have stayed, but she had eyes only for Dave. Either she knew Dave had the last word on whether she was given the job, or she fancied him. Jack hoped it wasn't the latter.

He went on, 'Everything in the office is computerised now, so you'll need to prove yer understand them.' He couldn't believe he was trying to dissuade this gorgeous young thing from working here. But there was something about her that made his skin creep. Jaysus, he thought. I must be getting old. 'Sure, yer can't do the job unless you understand computers,' he persisted.

She replied that Mandy had put her through a short programme while she waited in the outer office. Pointing to the documents on Dave's desk, she told him, 'I think you'll find your secretary's remarks among those papers. She told me there wasn't a problem.'

'If you get the job,' Jack asked, 'what will you do after the month is up?'

For a moment he thought she wasn't going to answer, but then she looked him straight in the eye. 'By that time,' she said quietly, 'I hope I'll have done what I set out to do.' Her dark, sad gaze fell. 'I hope by then I'll be able to go home.'

The two men looked at each other. Jack was about to say something when Dave told him, 'I know you have a pressing appointment, Jack, so you can go if you like. I think we can manage without you.' It was obvious the young woman had been through some kind of trauma, and for some reason he didn't understand, Jack was not helping matters here.

'Yer sure?' Curious now, Jack was half inclined to stay.

'I'm sure.'

A few moments later he was gone, and Dave found himself alone with the young woman.

'I know you must be wondering why I can't go home,' she said, 'and I don't really want to talk about it. All I can say is that for some long time now, I've been cut off from family and friends.'

Dave knew how that felt; he had gone through it himself when he and Libby were apart. 'That must be very lonely for you.' He felt an empathy with her.

'It's been unbearably lonely at times,' she admitted, 'but soon I hope everything will be resolved.' She had to convince him, but how could she explain the true reason for her being here? How could she tell him that she was here on a mission that had lasted for more years than he had been alive? Of course she couldn't say any of these things. 'It won't affect my work, I promise you.'

Dave could sense the tragedy in her voice. He could see it in her eyes, and he was momentarily at a loss. Was it wise to take her on? Was it wicked not to?

'Your personal life is no concern of ours,' he remarked kindly. He thumbed through the papers on his desk, seeing only what he wanted to see – what she wanted him to see. 'Mandy seems to think you're suitable, and so do I. As long as you can pick up where she leaves off, and you're happy to leave when she returns, I don't think we need to know much more.'

'Thank you.' Her voice was soft, marbled with joy. 'You can't know how happy you've made me.' Shining, dark eyes looked into his, probing his soul, stirring his senses.

Suddenly he knew. 'You're the girl in the rain!' he cried excitedly. '*That's* where I've seen you before.'

Alarmed, she shook her head. 'I don't think so.'

Feverishly racking his brains, he seemed not to have heard her denial. 'It was a month ago, maybe more. I was in a car heading towards Ampthill. You were standing by the side of the lane.' He had never forgotten. It still puzzled him. 'One minute you were there and then you weren't.'

'I just told you, Mr Walters, I only arrived here two days ago. I came here to stay with my aunt. Well, she's not really my aunt, but I've known her all my life.' For ever, she thought; she'd known her for ever. 'I know I said I've been cut off from friends and family, but she's the one person who's always looked out for me. Her name is Miss Ledell.'

Astonished, Dave momentarily forgot about the night in the rain – as she had intended. 'Miss Ledell?' His reaction was one of surprise and delight. 'She's our neighbour. She teaches our daughter piano.'

'I know. She's very fond of Daisy.'

'And Daisy's fond of her. In fact she seems to spend more time with Miss Ledell than she does at home. Still, it keeps her out of mischief.' He laughed. 'We're neighbours. Well, fancy that.'

'Have I got the job, Mr Walters?'

'Why not? Yes, of course. But you'll need to come in a few days before Mandy leaves, to ensure a smooth changeover, you understand.'

'When do you want me?'

'First thing Monday morning.'

'I'll be here.' She stood up. 'Thank you.'

Reaching his hand across the desk, he grinned amiably. 'Welcome to the madhouse.'

She hesitated, not yet wanting to make physical contact with him. But he was offering her the hand of friendship, and she couldn't refuse.

Slowly, nervously, she slid her hand into his. Their skin fused, warm and vibrant. There was a long moment during which he was filled with wonder, confused and afraid, and then, just as quickly, he was smiling again and she, standing on the other side of the desk, was smiling back.

'Goodnight, Miss Martin. We look forward to seeing you on Monday.' How cool he seemed, when all his senses were in turmoil.

In the outer office he handed her her coat and saw her to the door. The night was dark, bitter cold, and she seemed so vulnerable. 'Do you have a car?'

'I never learned to drive.'

'Then it's just as well you're not being taken on as a negotiator, because a car is essential.' He really liked her but she was a mystery. He felt he'd like to know her better. 'If you'll give me a minute to lock up, I'll take you home.'

Her smile enveloped him. 'I'd like that. Thank you.'

As they drove, talking and laughing, Dave felt as though he'd known her all his life. Some people were like that, he thought, you hardly knew them and yet they seemed to invade your heart and break down all inhibitions. Cliona was like that. He felt inexplicably close to her. Not in the same way he was with Libby. No one could ever make him feel like she did.

All the same, Cliona being here, so close and yet so far away, made him feel strange, almost as though he was somewhere else. It was odd. But not frightening. He felt the same as he'd felt that night when it was raining and she stood by the side of the road. He knew it was her, but didn't pursue the issue. She must have her reasons for denying it, he thought, and it was not for him to question her motives. Maybe she was just walking and when they stopped she panicked and ran, not wanting anyone near. He could understand that. She'd been lonely, that's what she said, cut off from family and friends. At times like that, you needed to get away, to be alone, where no one else could reach you.

When they arrived at Miss Ledell's house, Cliona leaned over and kissed him fleetingly on the face. 'You've been very kind,' she told him. 'I'd forgotten what it's like to have a friend.'

Taken aback, Dave didn't know quite what to say, so he said nothing. While she ran to the front door, waving like an excited child, he turned the car round. 'Poor kid.' He looked back in his driving mirror. She was still there. 'Sounds like she could do with a friend, but not me. I've got enough responsibilities without taking on stray kittens.'

He turned into the lane. 'She's nice enough though, but I shouldn't have let her kiss me like that.' Her kiss still tingled on his skin. It was a pleasant feeling. 'I hope she isn't getting the wrong idea about me,' he mused. 'No. She's just thrilled to be getting a job. If she's been out of it for a time, it must feel great getting back into the cut and thrust of the real world.'

Behind him, the door to Miss Ledell's house opened and the young woman entered.

Inside, the old lady turned the key, threw home the bolt and turned out the hallway light. Before making her way upstairs, she went to the window and drew back the curtains to look outside. 'He's gone,' she murmured. There was a moment of quiet contemplation before she closed the curtains and began her way upstairs; the light from the upper landing showing her the way, although she knew it with her eyes closed.

In her bedroom she undressed and got into her nightgown. After going to the bathroom, where she washed her hands and face, she returned to sit at the dressing-table. Taking the pins out of her hair, she undid the plaits and let her hair hang loose; it was magnificent, thick and shining, with glints of silver and deep, glorious waves. It fell about her face and shoulders like the hood of a cloak. Suddenly she was young again, and beautiful. She was in love, and happy, as she had never been before or since. Pain engulfed her. Pain, and excitement, and a feeling of betrayal.

She brushed her hair as she had done every night for the past eternity. Long, steady strokes, strong and deep, penetrating every strand, drawing out the light from the darkness. Stroking. From the top to the bottom. Again and again, until her arm ached and she yearned for sleep.

Presently she laid down the brush and sat, quiet for a time, eyes closed, hands together, wondering how far she had come this day.

'It's begun,' she sighed. 'Soon it will be over.' She gazed at herself in the mirror. The eyes were sad, tears brimming but not falling. Joy was tinged with agony. 'At last he knows you. He's touched you, and his heart is open.'

There was hope, but not contentment. Happiness, but not for them. 'Try not to hurt them,' she told herself. 'These are good people.' She gazed long at the face in the mirror. It was a lovely face, incredibly young and beautiful; hair black as night; skin smooth and soft as velvet. 'He likes you.' The old lady spoke softly. 'You did well, Cliona.'

After a time she got into bed and closed her eyes. Sleep did not come. It never did.

The house was sleeping, though. Only the whispered groans of ancient wood disturbed the solitude. There was no one else in the house. Only her. Only the old lady and her tortured dreams.

CHAPTER FIVE

Rolling over in bed, Dave stretched out his legs and yawned. Opening one eye he peeped at the bedside clock. When he saw it was eight in the morning, he couldn't believe it; he felt so tired, as if he'd never been to sleep at all. It had taken him a while to relax after getting into bed, and he was still awake long after Libby had fallen asleep. For some reason, he had been troubled, yet strangely excited.

He put it all down to pressure of business. Even after he fell asleep, his mind was alive with all manner of weird and wonderful dreams; there was no real pattern to the dreams, but *she* was there. The woman in the rain. Cliona Martin.

Finally the dreams had gone and he slept peacefully. Now he was half awake, with a hard on, and a deep yearning to make love to his wife.

He glanced at the window. The curtains were half drawn, the room bathed in a soft, shadowy light. He reached out, his need for her raging like a fever inside him. 'Libby?' The sheets were cold. He groaned, disappointed. 'Sweetheart?' He rolled closer, his arms longing to hold her. Suddenly, she was there, soft, cool beneath his fingers. 'I thought you'd deserted me,' he murmured, nuzzling her hair. 'Mmm! You smell like a newborn baby.' A sense of laziness spread through his body. He closed his eyes, drawing her close.

She didn't speak, or move, or yield to him. Instead she whispered, so softly he could hardly hear, 'Help me. Please help me.' Her voice faded and he was alone.

At first he thought he was still dreaming. Through the half-light his frantic eyes scoured the bed; it was just as before, the sheets cold, the pillow indented where her head had lain. Rigid with shock, he sat bolt upright. At that moment the door was flung open and Libby came in. She was carrying a tray. 'Oh! You're awake.' She seemed disappointed. In an instant the frown was gone and a bright smile lit her features. 'It's been a long time since we had breakfast in bed,' she laughed. 'I thought I'd surprise you.'

Setting the tray down on the bedside cabinet, she crossed to the window and threw back the curtains. Instantly, the room was flooded with light. 'It looks cold out,' she said, feigning a shiver. 'But the sun's shining so it's bound to warm up.' She turned to smile at him. 'I'm really looking forward to our day out.'

Dave was wide awake now, his mind stark with the sound of her voice – '*Help me. Please help me.*' The horror returned. The same cold horror that penetrated his dreams.

Unaware of the turmoil inside him, Libby busied herself. She poured the tea, then set out the boiled eggs and toast, and all the while he watched her, wondering if he was going mad.

Passing him the tray, she climbed into bed. 'I've done them exactly as you like – yolks soft enough to dip your soldiers in.' She grinned. 'Men are all boys at heart. Don't think I'm doing it too often, though. Today is special. It's the first full day you've had off work in a month.' She covered herself with the duvet and set the tray between them. 'Mind you don't knock it over with your long legs,' she quipped, 'or it'll be all spoiled.'

'Libby?'

'Mmm?' She raised the teacup to her mouth, wincing. 'Ooh! It's hot!' Licking her lips, she took up the milk jug and tipped a measure of the cold liquid into her cup. 'I'll have a blister on my lips now,' she moaned, 'you see if I don't.' Realising he wasn't listening, she nudged his arm. 'Well?'

It was a moment before he was aware of her. 'Well what?'

Smiling, she tutted. 'Just now, what did you want to ask me?'

He focused his mind. 'How long have you been downstairs?'

'I don't know.' She looked at the clock. 'A good hour, I suppose. Why?'

He didn't understand. Only a few moments ago he had held her in his arms. Or at least he *thought* he had. Maybe he was dreaming after all.

'Dave?'

'Yes, sweetheart?' But he had been so sure. He had felt her skin against his. He had run his hands through her hair. How could he have imagined that?

'Dave!'

Startled, he took hold of Libby's hand and held it fiercely in his own. 'Sorry, sweetheart. I was miles away.'

'I can see that.' She felt his hand tremble. 'What's the matter with you?' Replacing her cup on the tray, she saw how pale he was, and how preoccupied he seemed. 'Dave, what's wrong?'

He forced himself to shake off the memory of what he thought had happened. 'Not a thing.' Seeing Libby beside him, talking to her, and feeling the warmth of her flesh on his was immensely reassuring. 'I had a dream and it shook me, that's all.' Saying it out loud almost made him believe that it really had been a figment of his imagination.

She took a moment to observe him. She couldn't remember ever seeing him so disturbed – except for that night when they drove back from the restaurant. Fleetingly, his fear touched her, too. 'What kind of dream?'

He shrugged. 'Just a dream.'

Convinced there was more to it, she asked cautiously, 'Do you want to talk about it?'

'Nothing to talk about. It's already forgotten.' It would never be forgotten, he knew. The girl in the rain, the woman in his bed. One and the same.

'OK. Whatever you say.' She knew Dave too well. If he didn't want to discuss it, wild horses wouldn't make him, and anyway, why should she doubt him when he said it was nothing. 'Eat your eggs, before they congeal.'

'Congeal?' Making a face, he pushed them away. 'You've put me off now.'

'Eat your toast then.'

'I'd rather have you.' Sliding his arm round her waist, he kissed her on the neck.

Twisting round, she looked him in the eye. 'Aren't you hungry?'

He whispered against her mouth, 'Ravenous.' His hand slid beneath the bedclothes and lifted her nightgown. Long sensuous fingers probed the moist area between her legs. 'What about you?' he asked. 'Are you hungry?'

With a heart full of love and her body crying out for him, how could she say no?

Some short time later, Libby got out of bed and threw her robe round her body. Her voice rose in a wail as she saw the teastains on the duvet cover. 'Look at that,' she cried. 'It's all your fault, Dave Walters.'

He winked over the bedclothes. 'It takes two,' he grinned. 'And if you want me out of this bed, you'll have to carry me out.'

She dragged the offending duvet across the bed, leaving his naked body exposed to the chilly air. 'Don't think I can't,' she warned, fighting him for the duvet.

Mercilessly tickling his toes until he screamed aloud, she tugged hard with her other hand until he was precariously balanced on the edge of the bed. 'Come on, get out,' she persisted. 'The kids are up. I heard them just now.'

'Liar!' Laughing, he grabbed her by the wrist and hauled her easily on to the bed, crushing her in an iron grip when she struggled to be free. 'Whose fault is it if I'm still in bed?' he demanded, refusing to let her go. 'How can I help it if some shameless hussy got into bed and seduced me when all I wanted to do was sleep?'

'Get off, the kids are awake.' She was giggling like a schoolgirl. 'Let me go, you great bully.'

'Never.' He flicked her to his side of the bed where the two of them rolled over and landed with an almighty crash on the floor.

When Daisy and Jamie came running in, they were amused to see their parents wrapped round each other, arms and legs flailing and Libby desperately trying to cover her husband's nakedness. Helpless with laughter, she spluttered, 'Take Jamie down, Daisy. Me and Daddy will be down in a minute.'

But it seemed they were having so much fun, the kids wanted to join in. Grinning from ear to ear, they looked at each other and in a minute were running across the room making Indian war cries. With a yell of delight, they flung themselves into the affray.

The mood of happiness carried them through breakfast and beyond that to the beautiful village of Olney. The route to Olney took them through some of Bedfordshire's finest countryside. By the time they set off, it was a fine December day. There was no wind at all and, surprisingly for the time of year, there was real warmth in the sun's rays. 'We picked the right day for fishing,' Dave said.

'*You* picked the right day for fishing,' Libby reminded him. 'Me and the kids mean to spend the day mooching round the lovely old shops in Olney.'

Jamie piped up, 'I'd rather stay and fish with Daddy.'

'Well, you're not going to.' Libby was adamant. 'Daddy

will have his hands full without keeping an eye on you.'

'I won't go near the water, I promise.'

'No, you won't,' she agreed, 'because you'll be in town with me and Daisy, shopping.'

'I hate shopping!'

'Oh, what a shame,' she winked at Dave, 'and I meant to buy you a new pair of trainers.'

'With blue stripes and yellow laces?'

'That's what I had in mind.' She'd never seen any like that, but these days nothing surprised her.

'I expect I will come shopping with you and Daisy.'

Smiling, Dave leaned over to Libby. 'Shame on you,' he whispered. 'Resorting to bribery with a four-year-old.'

'Whatever it takes,' she said, though in fact she was always careful not to let the children think money grew on trees.

For the remainder of the journey, the children played 'I Spy' in the back; there were a few squabbles but nothing Dave couldn't quell with a firm warning.

From a good fishing spot along the River Ouse, it was a ten-minute drive into the town of Olney. 'Don't go falling in,' Libby said as she settled herself into the driving seat. 'It looks dangerous to me.' Her troubled gaze travelled down to the flat area where Dave would set up his fishing gear. The water was lapping high up the bank there.

Dave was in buoyant mood. 'Don't worry, woman,' he said, grinning. 'Here you see a man who swam for the county.'

'In your schooldays, maybe.'

He slung his fishing bag over his shoulder and tucked an umbrella under his arm. 'Once a swimmer, always a swimmer.' With that he kissed them cheerio and set off down the river bank.

'Daddy won't drown, will he?' Jamie asked, close to tears.

Daisy dug him in the ribs. 'Don't be daft,' she retorted.

'How can he drown when he's got his waders on?'

Dave watched them drive off, with all three waving, until they were out of sight. He looked around, satisfied that he was all alone in this small wilderness. The idea was inspiring. His face grew a broad smile as he stood there, arms folded, eyes closed and head held high, breathing in the smell of the open air.

Dave's parents had been farmers, so he knew the countryside like an old friend. Now, as he set about making a place from which to fish, he thought fondly about the two people who had shaped his earlier life, and his heart grew warm. They were good, ordinary people, and he would never stop missing them.

'This is just what the doctor ordered.' Feeling as though he'd just been let out of prison, he laughed out loud, the echo of his voice bouncing back from the woods across the river. 'When I retire,' he announced, carefully casting his line, 'I'll fish every day, and in time maybe Libby will learn to love it too. Out here, in the open air, with the song of the birds and Nature's beauty all around you, there's nothing more satisfying.' Though right at that moment there was little birdsong. In fact the atmosphere was heavy. Brooding. Like the calm before the storm.

Dave looked up at the sky. 'Hope it doesn't rain,' he muttered, but the sky was clear and bright. There were no cloud shadows, no rumbling of distant thunder, and yet the air was so heavy he could hardly breathe. 'Stop fussing,' he told himself. 'Time's wasting.'

While he indulged in a hobby taught him by his grandfather, Libby parked the car in the old market square. On Wednesdays and Saturdays there was a colourful market here, with stalls of every size and description, carrying all manner of goods and chattels. But today, a Sunday, it was a car park, and the High Street was filled with tourists strolling the streets where many others had strolled over the years, searching for a bargain in the antique shops and gazing through the windows, marvelling at the curios that were crammed there, displayed on shelves or hanging from the ceilings, and even piled one above the other on trestles behind. Olney was a magical place, ancient as the world itself, and just as mysterious.

Libby was in her element. She went in and out of the shops, looking at this, touching that, and wanting everything she saw. But money had the last word, and her purse had many demands made on it. Jamie's trainers for one. 'Come on, you two,' she said. 'It's already eleven o'clock and we have to be back for your dad in an hour.' Her voice was lost in thin air as the children ran forward to press their noses against the window of a shoe shop. 'Look!' Jamie was ecstatic. 'There they are!'

Libby looked through the window and sure enough, there on the shelf was a pair of trainers with blue stripes and yellow laces. 'Go on then.' She ushered them inside. 'No harm in taking a look, I suppose.'

What she had in mind for Jamie was a pair of black leather school shoes, with black soles and black laces, and at least a year's worth of wear in them. Ah well, she thought wryly. He might decide the trainers are not what he wants after all. But judging by the look on his face when the assistant got them down, there wasn't much hope of that.

Glancing at his watch, Dave moaned. 'Half an hour before they fetch me and I haven't had a single bite!' Digging into the wicker basket he took out a fresh handful of bait and, raising his arm, scattered it across the water. 'Can't go back without having caught anything at all.' There was something humiliating about a man returning empty-handed from a fishing trip. He supposed it must hark back to the times when man was hunter, and if he didn't bring home the bacon, so to speak, his family would starve.

Another ten minutes and still nothing. 'Not my day,' he

grunted. Then suddenly it seemed he'd got a bite after all. 'Jesus! Must be a big bugger!' The line was bending and straining as he tried desperately to reel in. Just as he thought he had it home, there was a frantic flurry, the line stretched to breaking point, then bounced up and snapped. 'Damn!' His quarry was gone.

As it was almost time for lunch, he continued to reel the line in. When he stooped to take up the broken line, he felt as though someone was watching. He looked up, his eyes roving both banks. There was nothing there. No one. 'You'd better watch it, Dave old son,' he chuckled, 'or they'll be taking you off to the funny farm.'

Ten minutes later he had packed away his gear. With still some fifteen minutes before Libby came to collect him for lunch, he sat on the wicker basket, his dreamy gaze drawn to the water. Mesmerised by the gentle rippling tide made by a lone mallard which paddled by, he felt immensely content. His eyes followed the mallard's trail past him, then on to the reeds before it made a gentle swinging turn towards the opposite bank. As it went on its way, its small beady eyes kept vigil on him, wary of his every move, for the man was a stranger here, and strangers meant danger.

'I don't mean you any harm,' he murmured, instinctively smiling. 'Though I mean to do you out of a fish dinner if I have my way.' The mallard's eyes glittered in the watery sunshine. It was incredibly beautiful; long proud head, its body sleek with iridescent colours. But it was the eyes that held Dave's attention; bright and shiny, like two new buttons, they continued to stare at him, seeming to suck him in, draining him of the will to move his gaze away.

Suddenly he felt an impulse to look up at the opposite bank. *And there she was!* Curled up on the far bank, she smiled at him, holding his gaze. Like the bird, she was amazingly beautiful, sylph-like, her long hair dripping as though she had been in the water, and in her eyes a dark, pained expression.

For one inexplicable moment he felt he could reach out and touch her. But she stayed only for a moment and in that moment the breeze carried her voice to him: 'Help me,' the words floated towards him. 'The lane. The old man. The truth is there.'

The light shifted, causing him to blink. When he could see again, she was gone and he was alone in that desolate place. And the silence was awesome.

With his mind drifting and his eyes straining to seek her out, he didn't hear the footsteps. When she called out, his heart lurched. 'Daddy!' The silence was broken. All was as before.

'God Almighty!' White and shocked, he clutched at his throat, the image of the woman burning in his brain.

Daisy swung herself into his arms. In the distance he could see Libby and his son making their way over. Quickly, he composed himself. 'Did you see her, Daisy?' He needed to believe it was not a figment of his imagination. Sitting her beside him on the basket, he put his arm round her shoulders, drawing her gaze to the far side of the river. 'Just now, the young woman.' He pointed to the spot where she had been. 'Did you see her?' There was panic in his voice.

Daisy looked across the river, then at her father, a frown creasing her forehead. Slowly shaking her head, she answered, 'No, Daddy. I didn't see anyone.'

'A woman,' he insisted. 'Older than you, younger than Mummy, with long dark hair and . . .' he hesitated. What was happening to him? 'She had the most beautiful, dark eyes,' he finished lamely. Into his mind came the other young woman, Cliona Martin. Was it her?

Daisy knew, and her eyes lit up. 'You mean the lady in the painting,' she cried. 'Was she here? Oh, Daddy, was she really here?'

For a while he couldn't think straight, he couldn't even move his mouth to talk. He was so shocked he just froze.

'Daisy?' Gently turning her round to face him, he asked softly, 'That night, when we were in the car and you said you were talking to the woman in the painting, did you mean the one you had drawn or was she really there, in the car with us?' He felt as if he was crazy. What was he doing? What was he thinking of, for Christ's sake!

Astonished that he should think anything else, Daisy answered indignantly, 'Oh, Daddy, I already told you. She was sitting next to me.'

His mind was spinning. Dropping his head to his hands, he mumbled, 'She was really there?' But how could that be? Suddenly he grabbed Daisy by the shoulders. 'I want you to be sure about this, Daisy,' he begged. 'The lady I just described to you, did she really get into our car and sit beside you?'

'Yes, Daddy.' Daisy sighed. 'She's very pretty.'

'When did she get into the car? How could she do that, without me knowing?'

'You stopped at the junction and had to wait for that slow car to go by. She opened the door and got in. She said she wouldn't do me any harm.' Impatient now, Daisy said, 'I told you, Daddy. You *knew* she was there.'

He glanced up. Libby was only a few feet away. 'Daisy, I want you to keep this a secret between the two of us. Will you do that?' He loathed putting such a burden on her but he was out of his depth. He needed time to think, to decide what to do.

It didn't seem to bother Daisy as much as it bothered him, but then children were so deep, so much more knowledgeable about these things. 'All right.' She ran off to meet her mother and seemed to forget all about it.

As they walked to the car, he looked back to the river bank. She wasn't there. But she had been there, he was certain of it.

★ ★ ★

The Bull Inn was very old, with low ceilings held up by gnarled oak beams, and dressed with brass artefacts which hung like souvenirs of old. Lunch was delicious: baked chicken and fat, crispy French fries, with apple pie and custard for dessert. Afterwards the children had strawberry milkshakes, while Libby and Dave settled for a pot of herb tea, served in front of a huge inglenook fireplace where a cheery wood fire burned in the hearth.

'We'll have to do this more often.' Libby had really enjoyed herself, wandering in and out of the shops. Jamie had got his trainers and Daisy a new dress. As for herself, she had indulged in a pair of black, wedge-heeled shoes and a darling cream jacket which would pair with her black trousers and at least half a dozen of her skirts.

Out of the corner of her eye she looked at Dave. She was concerned, as she had been all through lunch. He was too quiet, too thoughtful, and every now and then he would go into himself, seeming miles away. 'Why don't you want to go fishing this afternoon?' she asked. 'I thought you planned to make a day of it?'

He shrugged his shoulders. 'No reason.' Every reason, he thought, only he couldn't tell.

'You don't feel ill, do you?'

He knew she was concerned. The trouble was, Libby knew him too well. In spite of his trying to behave as though nothing had happened, she had seen how on edge he was. 'I'm perfectly all right,' he answered with an easy smile. 'But I didn't get a bite all morning, and from what you tell me, you've finished shopping. So we might as well take a leisurely drive home.'

Daisy saved the situation with her excited cry of, 'Can we go back through the park?'

'I don't see why not.' Dave was glad of the opportunity to change the subject. 'As long as that's OK with Mummy.' He looked at Libby.

She nodded. 'We haven't gone that way in a long while. And it's such a lovely drive.'

A short time later, they all made their way back to the car.

During the journey home, the children chattered about their day, and Jamie unsuccessfully tried to put on his trainers, getting irate when he didn't have the room to do it properly. Daisy tried to help and they ended up arguing, until Libby told him to take off the trainers and put his shoes back on. After that, peace reigned again.

Libby and Dave chatted about this and that, and he tried hard not to think about what he had seen and what Daisy had told him. He found it difficult to believe that he was actually being visited by a *ghost*. But if she really was a ghost, what was her purpose here? Who was she? And why had she chosen him?

Mentally he shook himself. There were no such things as ghosts. There was this world and the next; life and death, with nothing between. He was a simple man. He believed what he could see, and he had seen a young woman, beautiful yes, and somehow different from every other woman he had ever encountered, but a ghost? No.

'Look, Dave.' Libby pointed at a notice at the edge of the park. 'Nineteen deer were killed along this road last year. Drive carefully, sweetheart. They're all around us.'

For a moment he took his eyes off the road and looked at the meadows beyond where a herd of deer stood grazing.

'Aren't they wonderful?' Libby was like a child.

Daisy screeched, 'Look there! Look at its horns.' The stag was magnificent, with large black eyes and tall twisting horns.

Jamie took fright. 'Hurry up, Daddy, in case he charges.'

Daisy laughed at him, and he started to cry. Like a mother hen, she cuddled him until he dried his eyes. Dave put his foot down. He wanted to get home. He needed some time to himself.

He thought about Cliona Martin. He didn't understand. At first he'd imagined that she and the woman in the lane had been one and the same, but how could that be? Especially after what had happened today. Twice he had seen the young woman, and each time she seemed to have vanished into thin air. If she really was a ghost, Cliona Martin couldn't possibly be the same woman. She was flesh and blood. He had felt the touch of her hand. For God's sake, she'd even kissed him. Involuntarily he felt his face where her lips had touched him.

Libby's voice broke his train of thought. 'Dave?'

'Hmm?' He daren't glance at her in case she saw the truth in his eyes. 'What's wrong, sweetheart?'

'Nothing. You're just so quiet. I wondered if something was troubling you. Work maybe.'

'Nothing's troubling me,' he lied.

'Are you sure? You know what they say, a trouble shared is a trouble halved.'

Reaching out, he squeezed her hand. 'I have a bit of a headache,' he said truthfully. 'Apart from that, the only thing on my mind is whether I've made the right decision over Mandy's replacement. After all, we don't know all that much about her.'

'I thought you said Mandy had put her through the test and gave her the thumbs up?'

'Well yes, she did.'

'Mandy is a good judge of character, isn't she? Besides, you said yourself that this new woman seems right for the job, and after all, it is only temporary.'

'You're right, and Cliona Martin was by far and away the best candidate.'

Daisy leaned forward. 'Cliona? That's Miss Ledell's name,' she squealed. 'The woman in the painting told me.'

Dave felt the colour drain from his face.

'Honestly, Daisy,' Libby laughed, 'you talk about the woman in the painting as though she was real. She's only a drawing on a piece of paper.' She rolled her eyes at Dave. 'Kids!' she exclaimed, and it was just as well she couldn't see his face in the growing darkness.

In his mind, Dave tried to sort out the jigsaw. Each time he'd seen the young woman, she had pleaded with him. In the rain that night, she had pleaded with her eyes; in bed this morning, she had spoken to him, her voice reaching him as though in a dream. *'Help me,'* she whispered. *'Please help me.'* And on the river he had heard the same voice, desperate, immeasurably sad. *'The lane. The old man. The truth is there.'* And again she had asked for his help. What did it all mean? Was 'the old man' the same bedridden old man in the house where Daisy had followed the kitten?

Daisy was involved. She had seen things too. *She knew.* If he was going mad, then so was Daisy.

As he turned into the driveway of the house, Dave was sure of only one thing. He had two choices. Either he had to put the whole thing right out of his mind and pretend it had never happened. Or he must try, by some means, to get to the bottom of it and root it out of his life once and for all.

He thought of Daisy, and his own sanity, and he realised there was no choice at all.

Eileen had nursed the old man for so long now, she had come to love him like her own father. 'He's sleeping, now,' she told Ida. 'Come downstairs with me. I'll make us a sandwich.'

Curled in the chair, her bony legs tucked under her and her eyes stricken with tiredness, Ida shook her head. 'You go down,' she muttered. 'I'll stay here with him.'

She dared not leave him. All night she'd sat here, forcing herself to stay awake so she could keep a wary eye open. Things were beginning to happen, she knew. She could feel it in her bones. All her well-laid plans were not turning out as she had expected. There was danger all around. She must keep watch or he would win, and that must not be allowed to happen.

She looked up at Eileen, and as always was struck by the woman's prettiness. Whatever time of day, and even when she was called out during the night to tend the old man, Eileen was always bright and fresh, with a smile and a word to lift your heart. 'You're a good friend,' she said softly. 'I don't know what I'd do without you.'

'You'd probably starve.'

'You go on down. I'll be all right.' Eileen's gaze met hers and there was such kindness in her face that Ida felt close to tears.

Moving forward, Eileen laid a friendly hand on her shoulders. 'Oh, Ida. You really shouldn't punish yourself like this. He's sleeping peacefully now. Come downstairs with me.'

Ida shook her head.

'Please, Ida. It's not good for you to stay in this room all the time.' She was concerned for Ida's health; she had noticed these past few days how frail and preoccupied the older woman had been. 'We'll have something to eat, then if you like I'll stay with him while you go to your own room and have a lie-down.'

Ida hesitated.

'Come on. He'll be fine, I promise.'

Ida stared at the old man, at his worn face and the gnarled hands lying over the bedclothes, and for a moment she wanted to hold him, to tell him how utterly lonely and unloved she felt. She wanted to explain again why she must go on hating, and how the hating was draining her, killing her. When he was awake, she would let him know how he had only himself to blame.

Suddenly she was crying, long, shivering sobs racking

her weary body. 'Oh, Eileen!' she said brokenly. 'I can't let him die.'

Mistaking revenge for love, Eileen embraced her, like a mother might embrace a child. 'Ssh now,' she murmured, raising her gently from the chair. 'You're tired, that's all, and look, Tony is asleep. He wouldn't want you to spend your days watching him like this. You'll make yourself ill.' Tenderly, she propelled Ida across the room.

'You will stay with him, won't you?' Ida asked nervously. 'You'll let me know if anything happens, if anyone tries to disturb him.' Her eyes swerved to the window. 'No one must be allowed in. You do understand?'

Eileen promised she would come straight back up after they'd eaten. 'I'll stay with him until you wake.'

Ida seemed content. For a time.

Downstairs, Eileen sat Ida at the table while she busied herself preparing a plate of cheese and pickle sandwiches, and a pot of tea. 'Here. This will make you feel better.' Sitting opposite the older woman, she laid out two plates, poured out two mugs of tea and put one before Ida. 'Drink it while it's hot,' she urged. 'And eat the sandwiches. I want to see you polish off at least two.' She chose a firm, crusty one, with pickle oozing from the side, and laid it on her plate. 'Ida?'

Ida looked up.

'I want you to eat.'

'The voice of authority, eh?'

'Don't forget I was trained to be tough when the occasion demands.'

Bending forward, her shoulders hunched, Ida laughed. 'You couldn't be tough if you tried.'

Smiling, Eileen shook her head. 'You may think I'm an old softie, but for your sake I mean to be firm, and if you can't think about yourself, then think about me.'

Serious now, Ida sat back in her chair. 'What do you mean?'

Taking a bite of her sandwich, Eileen chewed and quickly swallowed. 'I mean, if you make yourself ill, I'll have two to nurse, won't I?' She really was worried. The way Ida punished herself, it was beginning to tell. The poor thing was near to breaking point, anyone could see that.

There was a quiet, tense moment, before Ida took a sandwich and began nibbling it. She didn't speak. Instead she kept glancing at the door, her eyes large and deep, staring but not really seeing. *Like the eyes of a mad woman.*

For twenty minutes Eileen kept her there, gently coaxing her to eat and drink. Afterwards she returned to the old man's room with her. 'See,' she pointed to the bed, 'he's still fast asleep.'

Ida nodded, a nervous smile playing round the corners of her mouth. 'No one's been in here, have they?'

Humouring her, Eileen answered patiently, 'You know they haven't. We were right downstairs. We would have heard.' Brushing back a lock of hair from Ida's face, she said firmly, 'Now you go and get some sleep.'

Feeling refreshed after the food and knowing that she must sleep in order to fuel the crucial barrier of hatred that kept him under her control, Ida reluctantly agreed, saying, 'I can sleep in the chair beside him.' She moved forward.

Restraining her with a gentle touch on the arm, Eileen was adamant. 'No. You can't sleep doubled up in a chair, Ida. Go to bed. I'll stay here.'

Ida smiled. 'You're a bully.'

'And you're the most stubborn woman I've ever come across.' She was relieved that Ida seemed in brighter mood. The refreshment had done her good, but she still needed to sleep. 'If you like, I'll wake you in an hour.'

'And you won't leave him? Not even for a minute?'

'No, I won't leave him.'

'Promise?'

'I promise.'

When Ida had departed, Eileen dug deep in her shopping bag and took out a tattered old book entitled *Goings On At Pimple Pond.* It was a hilarious reflection of life in a village community and, hoping to have a good hour's reading before being disturbed, she carried it to the bed.

After checking that the old man was still sleeping, she sat down in the chair and opened the book. After a few minutes she looked up. The old man was still sleeping. For some reason, she felt restless. 'I can't settle,' she sighed. 'I just want to get home, have a bath, and put my feet up.'

Closing the book she returned it to her bag and for a while sat there, watching the old man. 'I bet you were a handsome fellow once,' she smiled. 'Kind too. You can always tell if a person is kind by looking into their eyes.' Sitting forward on the edge of the chair, she gazed at him. 'I wonder if you know how much she loves you. How much they both love you. But then why shouldn't they? You have a way of creeping into people's hearts – even mine, you old rascal.' Feeling his hands to make sure they weren't cold, she tucked them inside the blanket.

She then went about on tiptoe, tidying the room to help pass the time. After a while, she sat in the chair again, leaned back and closed her eyes.

It seemed only a minute before she opened them again, when in fact it had been almost half an hour. During that time, Larry had entered the house, peeped in to see her asleep, then gone in search of his wife. It was his raised voice, coming from the bedroom next door, that woke Eileen. Glancing at her watch, she was shocked to find she had slept while on duty. But then it had been a long day and now evening was drawing in, and the night before, she'd been awake with toothache. All the same, she felt embarrassed and guilty. 'Some nurse I am.' Checking the old man was still comfortable, she tut-tutted, 'Sleeping on duty. Isn't that shameful?'

Next door, Ida and her husband were engaged in a fierce argument. 'For pity's sake, Ida, can't you see, my heart isn't in it any more.'

'What does that matter?' Ida's voice trembled. She sounded afraid, close to tears.

'Damn and bugger it, Ida! It matters to *me*! Since the restaurant's been damaged, I don't feel I belong here. The business will never be the same. Besides, there are other reasons why I want us to move away. You know that. You've always known it. Oh, Ida, can't you see? I've had enough. My nerves are shattered.'

'For God's sake, Larry, think. What about *him?* Your father can't leave. The risks are too great. He belongs here. *I* belong here, and so do you.'

Pacing the floor, Larry wrung his hands. 'How do we know he's in danger? We could be wrong. For all we know, the best thing for my father is to take him away from here.' He grew excited. 'Think of it, Ida! We can go anywhere that takes our fancy. We'll make a new start. We've done it before, we can do it again.'

'I say no!'

'Be sensible, Ida. Being here has brought us nothing but heartache, can't you see that? We have to move away, for his sake as well as ours. The restaurant will be up and running in a week. We can put it on the market. It's sure to fetch a tidy sum. *Please,* Ida.'

'No! I can't leave, and neither can he. He's too old. It would kill him if you moved him now. You can't do it, Larry. I won't let you.'

'How can you stop me?' His voice grew hard, unyielding. 'You forget, Ida. This is *my* house, and *my* restaurant.'

'If you move him, you'll kill him!'

There was a long silence, then in a trembling voice he answered, 'I wonder if that would be so bad. Since we came here, he hasn't had a minute's peace. None of us has.'

Beside herself with rage, she flew at him. 'You're mad even to think of moving from here. I won't go, and I won't let you take him.'

'I need you, Ida, but be warned. I might be tempted to go without you.'

She stared at him, momentarily dumbstruck.

'I mean it.'

'What about your father?' She gave a little smug smile. 'You'd never cope without me.'

He regarded her for a while, his mind working, searching for an answer that might convince her, even if it was a lie. 'I could always put him in a home.' In his heart, he asked his father to forgive him. The idea of committing his father to strangers sickened him to his stomach. He loved his father, otherwise he would never have listened to Ida and brought him back here in the first place. 'He needs to confront it,' that's what she'd said, and he had believed her. Lately, though, his doubts had grown.

The row continued.

Next door, Eileen wasn't sure what she should do. She toyed with the idea of sneaking out and leaving them to it, but just now, when Larry had yelled how he'd consider putting his father in a home, the old man had opened his eyes and looked straight at her. For one brief second, there was fire in his eyes and she imagined he would speak. Her heart soared, but then she recalled the doctor's words: Tony Fellowes would never speak again. Just now, though, he seemed so alive, so vital. Somewhere in that frail old body was a young man, virile and strong, and the mind was still alert, whatever the doctor believed.

Larry's voice invaded the room. 'Tomorrow morning I mean to call in an agent and have the business valued. The house too.'

'Please, Larry, don't do anything rash,' Ida begged,

changing tack. 'Let me think on it. Give me until tomorrow night and we'll talk again.'

He was pleased at that, showing it by crossing the room and kissing her soundly on the forehead. 'Now you're being sensible. You won't regret it, I'll see to that. We have to stop being afraid and start living for ourselves. Father will be better off too once we're away from here.' He strode to the door. 'Oh, and don't worry about having him moved. He's as strong as a lion, or he wouldn't have lasted this long.'

'He's lasted this long because I've fought to keep him alive.' Inside she was seething.

'You can't love him more than I do,' he argued. 'And yes, I'm well aware of the care and devotion you've given him. But look what it's done to you.' He observed her with pity. 'He's made you look far older than your years.'

'Maybe you're right about moving away.' It took every ounce of her self-control to say that, but she had to keep him sweet until she could decide what must be done. She didn't care whether he himself went or stayed, but the house was his. She could take him through the courts and fight for her share, but that would take time and energy. Meanwhile, she would lose control, and that was unthinkable.

Next door, Eileen tried hard not to listen. Over the years she had learned to distance herself from other people's domestic upheavals. 'It's over now,' she told the old man, who was lying very still, seemingly untroubled. 'He didn't mean what he said, don't worry.' She never could tell whether he was able to understand. But just now, when Larry had made his threat about putting him away . . . In all the time she had been nursing the old man, she had never seen that look in his eyes. It made her spine tingle.

Lost in thought, she was startled when she felt a hand on her shoulder. 'Did you hear all that?' Ida was pale, visibly trembling. 'Did you hear what he said about selling up and moving the old man away from here?' Her features hardened, her eyes flat and dark, as she glared at the old man. 'I won't let him do it. I can't.' She was not thinking of herself. It was someone else she spoke for; a woman from her past, a woman she had loved so much it hurt even to think of her. As she looked at the old man, a solitary tear rolled down her face.

Eileen saw it and comforted her. She didn't know what to say. A shoulder to cry on, that's all she could give.

After a while she felt Ida was quiet enough for her to leave. 'I know it's difficult,' she said, 'but you must try and get a good night's sleep.'

Ida promised she would, but she was lying. As soon as Eileen closed the front door, Ida grabbed the old man by the hair. 'Don't think you've won,' she hissed. 'I've come too far to let him ruin it all now. *She's* out there, thinking I'll weaken and she can take you, but she can't. I've built a wall of hatred all round this house and she can't get through.' She tugged at his hair until he moaned, his tired old eyes opening to look on her madness.

She cackled with delight. 'So you know what I'm saying? You old bastard, I always suspected you understood every word I said.' Bending closer, she almost touched his face with hers. 'You'll stay here and rot before I let *her* take you away from me, and even when you draw your last breath, I'll be here, cursing you all the way to hell!' When he half-closed his eyes as if in a smile, loathing oozed from her every pore. 'You haven't suffered enough. You're not afraid enough.' Unpredictable as ever, she let go of his hair and smoothed it down, whispering in the soft, intimate tones of a lover, 'Before I'm done with you, you'll be begging me to put an end to it.'

The hours grew longer, and still she paced the floor, up and down, back and forth, muttering and cursing, wondering what to do. She was frantic, gripped by a fever that burned like a physical pain.

From his bed, the old man watched. And slept. And watched again. He made no noise, only a deep, agonised rasping as her antics excited and disturbed him.

Unable to rest, Larry had gone to the study. Here he settled down to deal with a pile of urgent and overdue bills. 'Money going out, nothing coming in,' he moaned, thumbing through them. 'First thing in the morning I'll have the agent round to value. Now I've made the decision, I can't get rid of this place quickly enough.' Engrossed in his work, he didn't hear the soft footsteps outside his door, nor did he see the handle turn and the door open.

Softly, the footsteps travelled across the carpet; two gloved hands picked up the heavy marble paperweight, raised it high into the air and then down, speeding towards its target.

In that awful moment before impact, he looked round, his eyes stricken with horror, the scream frozen in his throat.

The footsteps retreated, and all was as before. Save for the spreading crimson pool on the carpet, and the constant 'drip, drip' that sounded oddly comforting in that quiet, still room.

CHAPTER SIX

Libby was frantic. It was Christmas Eve and there was still so much to do. She hadn't even wrapped the children's presents, and this year, because she'd been foolish enough to insist on a real tree, she had to keep running the Hoover round to suck up the falling needles.

The children were unusually boisterous and wouldn't sit still. Just now when she sent them up to their rooms, they were so excited that Dave had to address them sternly before they settled. On top of all that, her hair was an absolute mess and she had the beginnings of a toothache.

Prodding the joint with a skewer, she didn't hear Dave come into the kitchen.

'Penny for them,' he murmured, sliding his arm round her waist.

'Believe me, they're not worth a farthing.' After a busy, tiring day, she was feeling sorry for herself.

Dave sniffed the air. 'Something smells delicious. Makes me hungry.'

'You'd better be hungry,' she warned. 'Only Jack and his woman are coming but I've cooked enough for an army.' Basting the joint, she returned it to the oven for browning. 'What time is it?'

'Quarter to eight, I think.' He frowned, glancing at the clock on the wall. According to that, it was still two thirty. The strange clicking noises were a dead giveaway. 'Sounds like the battery's running out.'

Libby wiped the sweat from her forehead. 'I know just how it feels.'

Taking the clock off the wall, he regarded her. 'Are you OK?'

'They'll be here in an hour and I haven't even finished in the kitchen. I need a bath, and you know what my hair's like if I try and dry it with a hairdryer, I always look like I've had a fright.'

'There must be something I can do. After all, it was my idea to ask Jack and his new girlfriend to Christmas supper.'

'I'll survive.' In fact Libby was really looking forward to Jack's company, though she had no idea what to expect of his new girlfriend. 'I might accept your offer of help,' she said, 'if you weren't a bigger disaster in the kitchen than I am.'

Feigning indignation, he retorted, 'Do you think I could manage to lay the dining table without too much damage?'

'Good idea! You'll find everything in the cabinet.' As he walked away, she asked, 'Are the kids asleep yet?'

'They were when I peeped in on them a few minutes ago. Want me to go and check again?'

'By rights they should be unconscious after the hectic day they've had. We did a morning's shopping, Jamie skipped everywhere, and Daisy had him running round in circles. When we got home they stuffed their faces with jelly and ice cream, before helping me dress the Christmas tree.'

He felt guilty. 'I'm sorry I had to go in today, sweetheart, but the buyer was going abroad and it was the only time I could get to see him.' He winked. 'Looks like a solid sale though. He's paid his deposit and everything.'

She was delighted. 'That's good. And anyway, you were better off out of the way today. It was woman's work. Besides, I had to get your present, didn't I?'

'What did you get for me?' His dark eyes shone with mischief.

'What did you get for *me?*'

His handsome face broke into a grin. 'All right, point taken.'

'I'm really pleased things are going so well at the agency,' she said. 'You always did believe it would do well, even when I had my doubts.'

'It *has* to do well,' he replied jovially. 'I've got a family to support, not to mention Christmas trees and trainers with blue stripes and yellow laces.'

Blowing a hair out of her eyes, she regarded him with a thoughtful look. 'Who else was in today?'

'Just me. Why do you ask?'

'Oh, I just wondered. I thought maybe your new recruit might have been called in too.' It was hard to keep the jealousy out of her voice. Next to that young lady, she felt positively dowdy.

'No. Just me.' In fact he had been tempted to call Cliona in but thought better of it.

'Dave?'

'I thought you wanted me to set the table?'

'Do you think we could go away for a romantic weekend in a few weeks maybe?'

He laughed. 'What? With the kids?'

'May has always said she'll stay over and take care of them if we fancy getting away for a day or two.'

'OK.' His lazy smile reached her heart. 'If you're happy, I'm happy.' He had reservations about leaving the kids with anyone, even May. But if Libby said it was all right, then it was all right. He trusted her judgement. 'She'd have her hands full though, and no mistake.' Whistling, he departed to lay the table.

Libby smiled to herself, humming along with the tune she could hear him whistling. When she was a girl her father would never allow whistling in the house. 'It's bad luck,' he used to say. It didn't matter to her though, because she never could whistle properly.

At quarter to nine, and in spite of her earlier anxieties, Libby had everything under control. The vegetables were cooked to perfection; the joint stood draining in the roaster, and the wine was cooling in the fridge. Dave had set the table, and with the serving hatch open to the dining room, the warm, delicious aroma of dinner filled the air.

Dave had been ready for a while now. Libby was bathed and dressed, and putting the finishing touches to her auburn hair, which went just where she put it, with not a curl out of place. She stood in front of the long mirror, looking to see whether she had forgotten anything. She twirled with satisfaction and even gave a little joyful whoop. 'Well, after all the fussing, you made it in time,' she told herself. 'So now you can relax.' Glancing at the bedside clock, she saw that it was still only five minutes to nine. 'There might even be time for a glass of wine before they arrive.' With that thought in mind, she went downstairs.

Dave was in the kitchen, sneaking a taste of the joint. On hearing her come in, he snatched round guiltily, his face lighting with admiration as she walked in. 'You look stunning.' The blue dress suited her colouring, and with her wild auburn hair drawn into a mass of curls, she was as pretty as a picture.

'Thank you, my good man.' She blushed like a schoolgirl.

Taking the wine out of the fridge, he said, 'I feel like celebrating. How about it?'

She nodded. 'I was thinking the very same. But it will have to be a quick one. They'll be here soon and I haven't dished out the vegetables yet.'

Dave poured the drinks and they linked arms. 'To my beautiful wife,' Dave whispered, sipping out of her glass.

Taking a sip from his, Libby toasted, 'To all of us.' She looked at him then, her eyes bathed in a smile and her love spilling over. 'I adore you, Dave Walters.'

He ran his finger over her lips, his gaze drinking her in, wanting her, loving her as he had never loved anyone before.

The sharp peal of the front door bell made Libby jump. 'It's them!' she cried, breaking away. 'Let them in, Dave. I'll follow you in a minute.'

While Dave went to the front door, Libby put the vegetables in the serving dishes. She could hear Jack's lilting Irish voice, 'Ah, that's a wonderful smell, so it is. Sure, I'm hungry as a horse, so I am.' There was a pause, before he spoke again, this time sounding nearer. 'Where is she then, eh? Where's the lovely Libby?'

Libby was still scooping vegetables out of the pan when he grabbed her by the waist. 'Hello, me little darling,' he said, kissing her soundly. 'Sure, you're a sight for sore eyes, that's what yer are. Ah, just smell the air in here.' Raising his face, he drew in a long, slow breath. 'A man could die for that, so he could.'

As Dave led him away, he pinched a roast potato out of the dish. 'I'm a peasant, that's what I am,' he told his girlfriend, a tiny thing with saucer eyes and blonde hair. 'I like me food and I like to be pampered, so don't say you weren't warned.' It was obvious he'd had a nip of the good stuff before arriving, but he wasn't drunk. Jack never got drunk. He had hollow legs.

When Libby joined them in the sitting room, she thought how smart and handsome Jack looked in a pair of dark trousers and navy jacket, while his girlfriend Patsy was prim and neat in a smock dress and indigo silk blouse. Her blonde hair was loose to her shoulders, and she had a friendly, outgoing disposition. 'Lovely to meet you, Mrs Walters,' she greeted Libby with a smile. 'Jack's told me so much about you and your husband, I feel I know you both already.'

Libby liked her straightaway. 'Been talking about us, has he?' she joked. 'You'd better tell me what he's been saying, so I can defend myself.'

The saucer eyes grew even larger. 'Oh no! Nothing like that. He thinks the world of you. He'd never say anything bad about you and Mr Walters.'

Libby put her at ease. 'I was only joking,' she said. 'Besides, I never take any notice of what Jack says at the best of times. He talks a lot of ol' blarney, so he does.' She always could mimic him to perfection. 'Oh, and call us Libby and Dave,' she entreated. 'Mr and Mrs Walters sounds so formal, especially when I hope we're going to be friends.'

'Oh, yes. I hope so too . . . Libby.'

When Libby returned to the kitchen to put out the food, Patsy insisted on accompanying her. While Libby carried the dishes to the serving hatch, Patsy waited on the other side, putting them down on the dresser. When that was done, Libby came round to set out the table, and what a sight it was. There were sprouts and broccoli, fluffy potatoes mashed in milk and butter, chunky parsnips and small crispy roast potatoes, all displayed in Libby's best china serving dishes. In the centre of the table, on a plate with miniature chef's hats, stood the huge meat joint dressed with herbs and running with hot, golden juices.

The evening was a wonderful success. Patsy proved to be a real conversationalist, though she did have a tendency to dwell on the more morbid of subjects. 'Did you hear about that awful murder? Near Ampthill, it was,' she began. 'The poor man was sitting in his own house when the killer struck. Dreadful! Nobody's safe any more these days.'

Jack took up the story. 'Yer right, so yer are. The poor divil had his head caved in, and for what?' He looked round the table, wondering if any of the others had the answer. When he realised they hadn't, he went on, 'Sure, it's a funny ol' business, if yer ask me. There's more to it than meets the eye.'

Having thought about little else but the murder since it happened, Dave was curious at Jack's remark. 'Why do you say that?'

'Well now, think about it.' Leaning forward, Jack grew excited. 'According to the newspaper reports, it was a particularly vicious attack, so it was. The intruder meant to kill him, that's for sure, or why would he have gone for him in such a terrible way? But why? There was nothing taken. No money. Nothing.'

Against her instincts, Libby was drawn into the debate, and what she had to say shocked them all. 'I'm not surprised he's been murdered.'

Patsy looked up, big-eyed and curious. 'What a thing to say, Libby.'

'No, I mean it. I'm not a bit surprised. Dave took me to his restaurant for my birthday treat. The owner of the restaurant, the man who was murdered, was the oddest, most hostile little man I've ever met.' Involuntarily shivering, she confessed, 'He really made me feel uncomfortable. I've never been back there, but Dave has. I left my silk scarf and he went to fetch it. Even then, there was a problem. Daisy came home in a terrible state. She apparently followed a kitten into the house and some dreadful old woman chased her out. Mrs Fellowes, no doubt, so it sounds as if she's every bit as nasty as her husband.'

Patsy was all ears. 'Goodness me!' Ramming a potato in her mouth, she almost choked on it.

'What do you think of it all, Dave?' Jack asked.

'I think it's a terrible way for any man to die but, like Libby said, he was an obnoxious little man. He was also in a cutthroat business. I dare say he had more enemies than you or I put together.'

Libby sent the parsnip dish round the table. 'What about that tramp they took in for questioning? Have they charged him yet?'

'No, not yet.' Forking out a couple of parsnips, Dave dropped them carefully on to his plate. 'They haven't been able to check out his story, but the man still protests his innocence.'

'Because he *is* innocent, that's why!' Jack was convinced. Settling back in his chair, he spread his hands and smacked them on the table. 'Remember what I said? Nothing was taken. No money. Nothing. If that tramp had killed him, what was his reason? Why would he leave empty-handed? He wouldn't, would he? So it wasn't a burglary. And if that's the case, the killer wanted that man dead for some other reason.'

Libby was beginning to enjoy the debate. Wrangling round the dinner table with good company was a favourite way to pass an evening. 'Unless someone *paid* him to kill Mr Fellowes,' she suggested, helping herself to another slice of meat.

Dave nodded. 'You've got a point there, sweetheart,' he said, and wondered why he hadn't thought of it.

Patsy opened her mouth to speak but Jack put up his hand. 'Wait a while, me darling, I haven't finished yet.' By this time the wine was doing the talking for him. 'What do you make of this then. Mrs Fellowes was in the house, and so was her father-in-law, who we're told is bedridden. But is he? And why didn't the pair of them hear anything? A murderer entered the house, killed the husband and left again, and not a sound was heard. I call that very unlikely.'

Libby had other ideas. 'What makes you think the old man might not be bedridden? From what I understood, he's been lying in that bed ever since they moved to the house, and long before that he was very ill. It said in the paper that he'd been in a medical institution for a long time, recovering from a bad accident. It wasn't only his body that suffered, it was his mind too, and from what I can gather, he never really recovered.'

Stubborn to the end, Jack argued, 'You should never believe all you read in the papers.'

Patsy piped up, 'It's possible that the old man and the wife wouldn't have heard anybody come in. I mean, if they were in another part of the house and the killer was really quiet, he could have come and gone and no one be any the wiser.'

Dave had thought of that. 'They've already questioned his wife and let her go, so they obviously don't believe she's guilty.'

Getting into full gear now, Jack persisted, 'All right, let's say the two of them didn't hear anything that night. But there's something else that bothers me, and if they're doing their job right, it should bother the police too, so it should.'

'Oh, and what's that?' Libby began gathering the dinner plates.

'Why didn't she go looking for him, eh? Jaysus! The man wasn't found until eleven o'clock the next morning, an' even then it wasn't the wife who found him. It was the nurse. So, where was the wife? When he didn't come to bed, why didn't she wonder where he was?'

Libby had an answer. 'Sometimes Dave stays downstairs doing the books until the early hours. I'm often asleep when he comes to bed and I don't hear a sound. Maybe that's what happened with the Fellowes. Maybe he stayed down and she knew exactly where he was and that's why she didn't worry.'

Smiling confidently, Jack shook his head. 'As far as I'm concerned, that's not enough.'

'What do you mean?'

Dave had been preoccupied with his own disturbing thoughts, but now he intervened. 'I think I know what Jack's trying to say.' He knew exactly what Jack meant because the very same thought had occurred to him. 'Accepting what you say, Libby, that they heard nothing, and the wife wasn't suspicious, because she thought he stayed down doing the books, there is still one question that begs an answer. Why didn't she go looking for him when she woke up the following morning? I mean, if you woke up at eight or nine in the morning and I still hadn't come to bed, wouldn't you come looking for me?'

Libby laughed. 'Probably with a shotgun!' Her wry comment lightened the atmosphere and another bottle of wine was opened. 'You'd better stay the night,' she told Jack and Patsy. 'I don't want you driving home and neither Dave nor I can run you back because we've all been drinking.' In fact, after only two glasses of wine, she was feeling uncomfortably light-headed.

Jack was grateful for her concern but he had other ideas about where to spend the night, with Patsy, and not to sleep if he had his way, which he usually did. 'Yer not to worry about us. Sure we're foine,' he protested. 'We'll get a taxi, so we will.'

Dave was still mulling over the death of Larry Fellowes.

Amused, Libby clicked her fingers. 'Excuse me, are you with us?' When there was still no answer, she nudged him playfully. 'Hey!'

'Huh?' Jolted out of his reverie, he stared at her. 'Oh, I'm sorry, sweetheart. What did you say?'

'Where were you? On another planet?' Not for the first time, little alarm bells were going off in her mind.

'I was just thinking.'

'About what in particular?'

'About that fellow who was murdered.'

'What about him?'

With everyone waiting for an answer, he gathered his thoughts. 'I think it would be a mistake if the police completely ruled out Mrs Fellowes as the murderer. One report said there was no love lost between him and his wife, and judging by the way she put the fear of God into our Daisy, she might well be capable of extreme violence.'

Libby was astonished. 'I didn't know you were taking such a close interest.'

He shrugged his shoulders, his dark gaze shifting uneasily round the table. 'I'm not,' he lied. 'It's just that everyone's talking about it wherever I go.'

'I still say there's more to it than meets the eye.' Jack was feeling raunchy, eager to get Patsy home and into bed. Under the tablecloth his hands began to wander. 'But when all's said and done, I imagine the police know what they're doing. If they say his wife's innocent, who are we to argue?' His hand wriggled up Patsy's skirt.

'You're right.' Dave feigned indifference. 'What do we know anyway?'

It was midnight when Jack and Patsy left. As they walked to the taxi, Jack shouted, laughing, 'Happy Christmas, you two. Get off to bed and don't do anything I wouldn't do.'

With his arm round Libby, Dave called back, 'That means we're free to do as we please, eh?'

Luckily the children were still fast asleep when they went upstairs. 'God, I hope they don't come bounding into our room too early in the morning.' Libby felt shattered. After dinner everyone had insisted on helping with the clearing up, but the dishes were still piled high in the sink. Dave promised he'd give a helping hand in the morning, and Libby didn't need too much persuading to leave them until then.

When they both fell into bed, there was a bit of foreplay, and the light-hearted promise of lovemaking. But it came to nothing when Libby rolled over and fell asleep. 'Just as well,' Dave muttered. 'I never believed in brewer's droop until now.' He softly chuckled, turned out the light, and before he even had time to draw the clothes up over himself, he was asleep.

★ ★ ★

Just as dawn was breaking over the skies, Dave was awake again. Daisy was standing at the foot of the bed, rubbing her eyes and softly crying.

'What's the matter, sweetheart?' he asked as Libby leaped out of bed.

'I don't want her to go,' Daisy sobbed. 'Please tell her not to go.'

Libby hugged and soothed her. 'Ssh now, it's only a dream.'

But Daisy was inconsolable. 'Please, Daddy,' she begged, entreating Dave who was pulling on his dressing-gown. 'Please don't let her go away.'

Taking her in his arms, he asked gently, 'Who are you talking about, sweetheart? Who is it you don't want to go away?'

'Miss Ledell. She was in my room just now and she said she would be going away soon. I don't want her to go. Please, Daddy. You have to stop her.'

Momentarily stunned, he felt the chill run up and down his back like icy fingers playing on his skin. 'She wasn't in your room just now, Daisy,' he said a little more sternly. 'Mummy's right, you've had a bad dream, that's all. Look, you climb into bed with Mummy while I go downstairs for a drink.' He couldn't think straight. He felt strangely vulnerable, as though someone somewhere was reading his mind, urging him in a certain direction.

'Don't be down there too long,' Libby said, settling Daisy in their bed. 'You need your sleep.' Lately he had begun to look haunted. This evening, for instance, there were times when he didn't even hear what they were saying, as if his mind was elsewhere. That had happened a lot lately, and it was beginning to worry her.

Downstairs in the kitchen, Dave sat at the table, lost in thought. He didn't know what to do or where to turn. 'How could Miss Ledell be in Daisy's room?' he muttered.

'Of course she wasn't in her room. What am I thinking of? Daisy had a dream, that's all. She obviously went to sleep thinking of the old dear, and it played on her mind. There's nothing more to it than that.'

But what if there *was* more to it?

He carried on talking to himself, unaware that his voice was trembling with fear. 'Bad things are beginning to happen. It's like a game of chess. They make a move, then I make a move. The only difference is I can't see my opponent.' He was certain now that something was expected of him; the girl at the river had pleaded with him: *'The old man. The lane. The answer is there.'*

It was a strange thing but he felt different somehow, sadder, older, but not wiser. There were times when he felt lost, and yet there was a curious sense of belonging, as though he was never alone, almost as though he was sharing his body and soul with another. At other times he was filled with despair, yet he could find no reason for it. Thinking of it now, a crippling fear took hold of him.

Raising his face to the window, to the lightening skies beyond, he called out, 'Who are you? What do you want of me?' Suddenly aware that he might sound like a madman, he laughed softly. 'You're losing it, Walters,' he told himself. 'One minute you're imagining things, and the next you're talking to thin air.' Feeling foolish, he rubbed his hands over his face and wondered if he, like Daisy, was having a nightmare.

His heart nearly stopped when Libby spoke. 'She's asleep. I thought I'd come down and see if you were all right.'

'Of course I'm all right.' Anger tinged his voice. 'Why wouldn't I be?'

Sitting opposite him now, she laid her hand over his. 'No reason.' She thought she'd heard him laughing and muttering to himself, but couldn't be certain. 'No reason that I know of anyway,' she said pointedly.

'What's that supposed to mean?' He hated the way he was snapping at her but he couldn't help it. *The other one* was in the back of his mind, firing the rage within him.

Libby made no reply. Instead she went to the sink and filled the kettle with water. She switched it on, prepared the teapot with two mugs, and then came and sat down again. Now she regarded him carefully, the way he was slumped over the table, his shoulders drooped as though he carried a great weight, and every now and again he would close his eyes as if he was in some terrible anguish. She had her suspicions, and his erratic behaviour convinced her she was right.

Wondering how she might broach the subject, her heart quailed. The only way was to ask him. 'Dave, if I ask you something, will you answer me truthfully?'

He looked up, surprised. Something in her voice, in the softness of her eyes, as though the tears were just beneath the surface, made him feel ashamed. 'You know I would never want to tell you a lie,' he answered warily. 'If there's something worrying you, I want to know about it.'

Consumed with guilt, Libby hesitated. How could she tell him what was on her mind? How could she ask him such a thing? Right now she couldn't even look him in the eye. Losing courage, she answered nervously, 'Nothing. It doesn't matter.' But it did. It mattered like hell.

Getting out of his chair, he came to where she sat. Taking her in his arms, he bent his head to hers. 'I know I've been preoccupied lately and I'm sorry. It's just that I have a few things on my mind.'

She didn't look up. Instead she hung on to him, keeping him there, not daring to look at his face. 'Dave?'

'What is it, sweetheart?' He bent his head closer, but she was determined not to let him see her face either.

She took a deep breath. When she released it, the words fell out in a rush. 'Are you having an affair?'

She felt him reel with shock. For a moment the silence

was overpowering, and then gently he put his fingers beneath her chin and made her turn to look at him; his face was chalk white, his eyes wide with disbelief. 'Is that what you think?' he gasped. 'That I'm having an affair?'

She paused, hating herself, hating him. 'I don't know what to think,' she said. 'These days you seem so far away, sometimes you don't even know when I'm talking to you.' A sob caught in her throat. 'I forgave you once because I was just as much to blame for what happened. But we've been through all that, and I don't want us to lose each other again.' Her voice hardened. 'But I swear to God, if you're cheating on me—'

'You have my word, Libby. I'm not cheating on you.'

She gazed up at him, wanting to believe he was telling the truth but not yet convinced. 'If you're not cheating, what's wrong? Why are we drifting apart?'

'Are we?' That surprised and worried him, but then his mind had been on other things.

'You tell me.'

'OK. Maybe I have been neglecting you lately, but it's not for the reason you think.' He wished there was something more he could do to ease her mind, but he couldn't tell her what troubled him. What would he say? I'm preoccupied because this ghost keeps bothering me? She'd think he was nuts. 'I'll tell you what. Why don't we take that romantic weekend you were talking about? We could take the kids if you want, or ask May to stay over, I don't mind.' He was still uneasy about that. 'We could go in a fortnight or so. What do you say?'

'I don't know.' She was smarting. Unsure.

'I thought it was what you wanted?'

'Not if it's just to keep the peace.' She nearly said, 'Ease your conscience,' but her instincts warned her not to.

'Come on, sweetheart, you have to trust me or there's nothing left.'

Libby knew he was right. Besides, it would be good for

the two of them to be alone for a time. They hadn't enjoyed any privacy since the kids were born, and a couple of days wouldn't hurt. 'Can you spare the time away from the agency?'

'I'll *make* time.' And he would. For Libby he would do anything.

'When?' She felt the need to punish him even though she didn't know what he'd done to deserve it.

'Whenever you say.'

'Let me think about it.' Standing up, she turned to leave.

'Libby?'

Without a word she swung round and stared at him.

His dark eyes spoke volumes. Reaching out with his heart, he told her softly, 'I'm not cheating on you.'

She remained silent, her gaze unfaltering, her arms falling to her sides. Suddenly she came back, letting him hold her, half believing him yet afraid to trust him completely.

Crooking his fingers under her chin, he raised her face and kissed her full on the mouth. 'You're everything to me,' he murmured, and she knew he meant it.

Disentangling herself from him, she smiled up at him. 'I think we'd better try and get some sleep, don't you?'

He wasn't ready for sleep. 'You go up,' he said. 'I'll be there in a while.' He sensed that was not the answer she wanted, but right now he needed to stay down here and try to fathom things out, rather than lie in bed not daring to move in case he disturbed her or Daisy.

'All right, but don't be too long, or you'll be fit for nothing in the morning.' She kissed him then, aching with love, needing to believe him.

Upstairs she stood by the window, arms folded, heart aching. 'Don't throw it all away, Dave,' she whispered. 'Not now I've come to love you more than ever.'

In the kitchen, Dave couldn't rest. 'It's beginning to

destroy us already,' he muttered. 'But it won't. Not if I can help it!'

Since the murder of Larry Fellowes, he had wondered more and more about that odd couple, and the more he thought, the more he believed they had something to hide. And he was certain that somehow they were also tied in with the disturbing sequence of events that plagued him. *'The old man. The lane. The answer is there.'*

He had no way of knowing what it all meant, but one thing he did know, it all led back to that night. To that house.

CHAPTER SEVEN

Christmas came and went and soon it was as though it had never been. Much to Dave's relief, he and Libby settled back into a more relaxed relationship, and the question of him being unfaithful didn't arise again.

On New Year's Eve, he asked May if she'd stay with the children while he took Libby to a dinner and dance at a local hotel. Being all alone after spending Christmas with an old friend in London, she was only too pleased to accept. She stayed the night and for a time was part of the family.

Dave would always remember that night as being one of the best times he and Libby had ever shared. It was a wonderful evening. They danced the night away and toasted champagne to the New Year. When they arrived home, it was to find May and the children tucked up in bed and out to the world. 'They looked exhausted,' Libby laughed. 'I expect they've been playing games the whole night long.'

They crept in and kissed the children goodnight. 'She probably let them stay up and see the New Year in too,' Dave remarked. But it didn't matter.

'I hope they did see the New Year in,' Libby said as they went down to the sitting room, 'Why shouldn't they, after all?'

Downstairs they relaxed in front of a cheery fire. Dave thought Libby looked lovely, and told her so. Her eyes were sparkling and her cheeks tinged pink with the after-effects of the champagne. The flickering light from the fire gave her auburn hair a warm, golden glow, and now, when she kissed him, he thought he must be the luckiest man on earth.

They made love right there on the rug, drank a little wine and afterwards fell asleep in each other's arms. Before he closed his eyes, he thought how tonight had been very, very special.

So why did he feel like the prisoner enjoying his last meal?

In the morning Dave woke feeling surprisingly refreshed and optimistic. He showered and sang and even gave a little skip as he came into the bedroom to get dressed. 'It looks like a perfect day for walking,' he commented, sneaking a look out of the window. The ground was crisp and clean, and the skies were wide open, flecked with sunlight.

Groaning, Libby turned over, drawing the clothes over her head. 'Go away!' came the muffled cry. The cry turned to laughter when he dived on top of her and began tugging at the clothes. 'Out, or I'll throw you out!' he threatened. 'I still haven't forgotten what you did to me the other morning, so what's good for me is good for you. I'll count to ten, then it's everyone for themselves.' He began to count.

Libby surrendered before he got to four. 'I'll be glad when you're back at work,' she lied. 'You wear me out.'

While Libby showered, he cooked breakfast, the fullest fry-up he could throw together: eggs, sausages, tomatoes, mushrooms, bacon. The alluring aroma brought the children crashing down the stairs. 'Two sausages for me,' Jamie decided, seating himself at the table. He ended up with two eggs as well, and a heap of mushrooms. He ate the lot and asked for more.

'Your eyes are bigger than your belly,' Dave chuckled.

'Finish your orange juice and find somebody else to nag.'

Daisy settled for an egg and two slices of toast.

'What's wrong?' Dave teased, half-serious. 'Don't you like my cooking?'

Going against everything Libby had taught her, she answered a question with a question. 'Daddy?'

'Mmm?' He felt that tingle down his spine again; the same, uneasy tingle he felt whenever he thought of the other one.

'When we've had our breakfast, will you take me to Miss Ledell's?'

Libby entered the kitchen, hair wet and a fresh, scrubbed look about her. 'Sorry, Daisy,' she intervened. 'According to your father, it's a perfect day for walking, so let's hold him to it. I thought we could walk right across the valley and back through the woods.' She giggled deliciously. 'That ought to curb his enthusiasm.'

Tucking into the tail end of a sausage, Dave shook his head. 'You wouldn't be able to make it,' he remarked wryly. 'We'd get as far as the woods then I'd have to carry you the rest of the way on my back.'

'A pound says you're wrong.' Making her way to the cooker, she tousled her thick mane of hair, a magnificent sight even when wet.

'You're on, but you'll be a pound poorer afterwards.'

'No, I won't. You drive everywhere and I walk whenever I can. That's why I know I'll be a pound richer.'

Daisy sat quietly through the banter, but now she made a suggestion. 'We could go the other way, through Barker's field and then we go right past Miss Ledell's.' Her eyes widened. '*Please.*'

Little by little, Dave's good mood was being eroded. 'Not today, sweetheart,' he told her. 'You'll be going for piano lessons in a few days. You'll see her then.'

Daisy began to cry. 'I don't want her to go away.'

Growing impatient, Libby almost threw her plate on to

the table. 'You heard what Daddy said. You're having a piano lesson in a few days. If she was going away she would have called up and cancelled it.'

Daisy brightened. 'I hadn't thought of that.'

Taking a chunk out of her toast, Libby smiled. 'So you can stop worrying.'

Half an hour later, all wrapped up against the cold, they set out down through the village and towards the lane that would take them straight into the valley. Conscious that Daisy still hadn't altogether given up hope of their going by way of Miss Ledell's, Dave deliberately steered them in the opposite direction.

For his own peace of mind he intended paying her a visit himself sometime. But not yet. These few days over Christmas and New Year were for him and his family.

They walked and ran, and played hide and seek in and out of the trees, and when they reached the top of the hill, the children rolled down the bank, laughing and squealing while Dave and Libby watched from the top, enjoying it almost as much. 'These past few days have been really lovely,' Libby admitted. 'It's been good for all of us.' She felt closer to Dave now than she had done for a long time – ever since he had taken her to the restaurant for her birthday treat, in fact. Funny that, she thought with a little shock. It should be a good memory, not one she would rather forget.

As daylight slowly turned to dusk, Dave suggested they should make their way home.

In the woods it was warm, almost sultry as they pushed on. 'Mummy, I don't like it.' Jamie had always been afraid of the dark, and suddenly it was closing in fast.

Dave hoisted him on his shoulders. 'Keep your head down, Jamie,' he warned, dipping and weaving as he went. 'Some of these branches are spiteful.' He cursed himself for not having started back earlier.

'I've never known it get dark so early,' Libby

remarked, peering up through the branches at a greyer sky. Taking a quick glance at her watch, she gasped with astonishment. 'It's only half past two!' Shaking her watch, she followed the second hand as it clicked round. No. It hadn't stopped.

'It's always shadowy in the thick of the woods,' Dave reflected. 'Once we're out, you'll see. There's a good two hours of daylight yet.'

Though the way through was clear enough, the shadows lengthened and the children grew restless. 'Are we lost, Daddy?' Jamie was close to tears.

'No, we're not lost,' he replied confidently. But in fact the possibility had already crossed his mind that he might have taken a wrong turn.

He pushed on, quickening his steps and keeping an eye on the gathering clouds. The air became oppressive, seeming to choke him. For no apparent reason, he felt threatened. Suddenly *she* was in his mind, threading her way into his senses, calling him, always calling him.

Frantic now but outwardly calm, he hurried them along, out of the woods and down towards the brook where the daylight still lingered. 'It's all right,' he told the children, and Libby too, because by now she was looking worried. 'We're almost home.' Dropping Jamie on to his feet, he held his hand. 'All the same, we'd better get a move on.' He studied the angry sky. 'Looks like the weather's changing.'

No sooner had he said this than the rain began falling, big, sploshy drops that soon had them soaked to the skin. 'You and your perfect day for walking.' Relieved to be within sight of the village, Libby managed a smile.

'Look at me,' Daisy laughed. As the rain ran down her face, she licked it with her tongue. 'I'm wet through but I don't care.' In fact she seemed to be enjoying the grown-ups' discomfort, and now that they were out of the dark woods, Jamie, too, was beginning to think it all a huge adventure.

Dave looked at Libby and they had to smile. 'Kids!' he moaned and their smiles turned to laughter.

Suddenly, the hairs on the back of his neck stood up. He turned and there, out of the corner of his eye, he saw her. Standing beside an oak tree, she looked exactly as she had looked on that night.

Shock turned to amazement when Libby called out, 'Who the devil's that?'

He stopped in his tracks. 'What did you say?'

'There.' For a split second Libby stared at him. When they looked again to where the figure had been, no one was there. 'She was just there!' Libby cried. 'You must have seen her.'

Before he could answer, Daisy said sadly, 'She was crying, Daddy. You have to help her.'

Angry and afraid, Dave felt himself being sucked into a darker abyss. 'We'd better get home.' *All he could think of was that Libby had seen her!* First him, then Daisy, and now Libby. With the exception of Jamie, his whole family were being drawn into something that was way beyond his comprehension.

Suddenly, it was as though someone had scraped back the clouds. One minute the sky was black, the rain driving down. The next minute it was clear, with the rain giving way to a cold, hazy sunshine. A gentle breeze stirred the trees, and with it came her voice, soft and haunting, like the voice of a child: '*D . . . a . . . v . . . e.*'

He froze. She knew his name. How could she know his name?

Her whisper enveloped him, sounding in his brain like an eerie echo. '*Tell him . . . I won't leave him.*'

The blood ran cold through his veins. 'Hurry!' Picking Jamie up, he threw him on to his shoulders. Libby had Daisy by the hand and he told her to get in front of him. 'Run!' he yelled. 'Before the heavens open again.'

CHAPTER EIGHT

Libby loaded the children into the car. 'We won't be long,' she told Dave. 'I don't feel like trudging round the shops but the New Year sales have started, and the kids need new clothes.' She gave him a disdainful look. 'And you need a new tie.'

Leaning in the window to kiss her goodbye, he groaned. 'I'm quite happy with the one I've got.'

She tutted. 'It's two years old and frayed at the edges. No, I'll get you a new one, and don't worry, it won't be gaudy. There won't be flowers on it or anything too raunchy, if that's what you're worried about.'

'The raunchy bit doesn't bother me,' he chuckled. 'It's the flowers that worry me.'

'Leave it to me,' she grinned. The horrors of that walk when they had come back like drowned rats were almost forgotten. 'I might treat myself to a new handbag,' she mused. 'My old one's falling apart at the seams.'

She looked up at his handsome face, thinking how very much she loved him, and how these past days had been wonderful, apart from that walk and the girl whose dark eyes held such profound sadness. Not for the first time she wondered fleetingly whether Dave knew her. Worse, she wondered whether he knew her intimately.

Panic gripped her. 'What will you do while we're gone?'

He kissed her, impatient for them to leave now, needing to be alone with his thoughts. 'I expect I'll find something to do.' He was saying one thing and thinking another, and because of it he felt guilty. 'There's a pile of paperwork to be gone through, ready for the office tomorrow.' Winking at the children in the back, he asked, 'Or would you rather I had a go at the leaking tap in the bathroom?'

Horror spread over her face. 'Don't you dare!' she exclaimed. 'The last time you had a go at a leaking tap, you flooded the whole house!'

'You ruined my action man,' Jamie yelled, 'and my trainers went squelchy.'

Daisy just sat back in the seat and giggled helplessly.

'I'd better be going,' Libby said. 'I promised to collect May at nine-thirty.' She glanced at the dashboard clock. 'It's nearly that now.'

''Bye, Daddy.' Jamie pressed his nose to the window as they drove away.

''Bye, Jamie!' He waved them out of sight, and returned to the house.

Once inside, he made straight for the telephone and dialled Jack's number. He let it ring for an age but there was no answer. Either Jack was out or he and Patsy were enjoying themselves too much to be disturbed. Dropping the receiver into its cradle, he cursed. 'Dammit, Jack. If I don't talk to someone soon, I think I'll go mad.'

A few moments later he threw on his coat, locked the house, and drove away at some speed, heading in the direction of Milton Keynes. He looked grim and determined as he came on to the open road. Pressing his foot hard to the floor, he swerved round the bend on two wheels, slowing when he realised how he might easily have lost control. 'It can't go on,' he said, his dark eyes burning. 'Somehow, I have to find a way to be rid of her.' He couldn't afford to waste time either. 'If Libby gets home before I do, she'll start getting suspicious again, and right now, that's the last thing we need.'

His first stop was the library, a huge, attractive building

on the outskirts of the city centre. After parking his car and obtaining a ticket from the parking meter, he went through the main doors and scanned the board inside. Running his finger down and along, he located directions for the reference section. 'That's as good a place as any to start,' he mused, running up the stairs two at a time. 'If they can't help me, they might be able to point me in the right direction.'

The librarian was both extremely attractive and quietly efficient. 'I'm afraid you'll have to wait a while,' she apologised, while at the same time stamping out books for several people. 'There are only four of us in, and we've been run off our feet this morning. Most of the staff aren't due to return from their holidays until tomorrow.'

'It's OK, I can wait.' Now that he was here, he had no intention of leaving. Besides, he was back at the office himself tomorrow. Once he was caught up in the rush of things, there was no saying when he'd have time to follow this through.

As it was, he only waited twenty minutes before she was beckoning him over. 'Sorry about that. What can I do to help?' She smiled sweetly, thinking what a good-looking man he was, and how she might have made a play for him if he hadn't been wearing that broad ring on his wedding finger. That kind of trouble she could well do without.

He decided to start where he had first seen the young woman. 'Bluebell Hill,' he ventured cautiously.

'Yes?'

'I want to know everything there is to know about that road,' he declared. 'How old is it? Have there been any reports of strange incidents along the lanes thereabouts?'

She was intrigued. 'What kind of strange incidents? You don't mean hauntings, do you? Because now I come to think of it, there *is* something.' She half-turned to look at the shelves, trying to recall. While she concentrated, she bit her fingernails so hard he heard them split. It made him cringe.

Surreptitiously removing the remnant of a nail from her lips, she suddenly smiled. 'I'll check the records,' she said, 'and bring over anything I find.' She tapped her fingers over the computer keyboard, made a few notes and took them with her to the shelves on the far side of the room.

It wasn't long before she returned with a number of books. There was also a microfiche, and even a video recording. 'Here you are.' With a triumphant smile, she dropped the pile of books before him. 'These should tell you what you want to know.' With that she returned to her counter and the long line of impatient people. 'I'm sorry about that,' she said coolly. Her smile put them at ease and soon she was too busy even to glance at him.

Bent over the books, Dave flipped through musty old pages, frowning when they revealed nothing. Laboriously he studied one book, laid it down and opened another. An hour passed, then two hours, and still the frown remained. When the last book was closed, he sat up in the chair and stretched his aching back, astonished to see he'd actually been there for two and a half hours.

'Have you found anything helpful?' The librarian was enjoying a quiet ten minutes.

He shook his head. 'Nothing.' Taking a deep breath, he held it for a while, then let it out with a weary smile. 'Maybe I'll have better luck with the microfiche and video.'

'I'll set it up for you if you like.' Against her better judgement, she was drawn to him. 'If you don't know your way about them, the machines can play havoc with you.'

The smile turned to a friendly grin. 'You'd better do it for me then,' he conceded. 'I'm not in the mood to be played havoc with.'

As it turned out, the machine behaved impeccably,

though it yielded nothing about the young woman or the lane where he had first seen her. 'This material refers to other roads, other counties,' he informed the librarian. 'I had no idea there were so many Bluebell Hills. Are you sure you haven't got any more information relating to Bluebell Hill in Bedfordshire?'

'This is all we have.' Rewinding the tape, she explained, 'I asked the computer to highlight everything on Bluebell Hill. It would have searched for every piece of information available.' She paused. 'But maybe it's under another heading.' Collecting the pile of books, she led him to the counter. 'What exactly is it you want to know?'

By this time he was desperate. 'I simply want to know if it's haunted.'

She took a moment to think about that. 'We'll try under "Haunted",' she said, going over the keyboard with lightning fingers. There was a pause while she waited for the machine to answer. When eventually it came up, she quickly ran her eyes over the screen. 'Nothing.' She sounded as disappointed as he was.

Dave had an idea. 'Try "Strange Happenings".'

'I doubt there'll be anything under that,' she said, but entered it all the same. 'Well, I never!' Her smile was like the dawn of a new day. 'Here it is. Bluebell Hill, Bedfordshire. Reference B/64397.' Clicking the button to 'Hold', she wrote the number down. 'Come with me.'

She went across the floor like a mother hen leading her chick. 'Shelf B,' she muttered, tapping the pencil against her teeth. 'Here we are.' Running a long finger along the shelf, she came to the slot where the documents should have been. 'That's funny.' The triumphant smile slid from her face. 'There's nothing here.'

Another voice intervened. 'They've gone missing.' It was the senior librarian. 'They disappeared off the shelves about a week ago. I know that because they were there when I did the stocktaking ten days ago, and they weren't there when I had a request for them yesterday.'

In his frustration, Dave asked who had requested them only yesterday.

'I'm sorry,' the senior librarian replied. 'I can't divulge confidential information. We have entered them as being stolen and we're taking the usual steps, but I'm afraid there are no guarantees that they'll be returned. Thousands of books go missing each year and less than half are recovered.' To her mind, it was the worst crime.

Not knowing what to say or do, Dave thanked them. 'I'll leave my name,' he said. 'If they turn up, please let me know.'

All three walked back to the desk, but it was the senior librarian who dealt with him. 'What was it you wanted to know?' she asked casually, while writing his name.

He shook his head. What was the point? 'It doesn't matter,' he answered dejectedly.

She peered up through her spectacles. 'We'll need your address, please.'

He gave her his address and phone number, intently watching while she keyed it into the computer. After all this, he was leaving nothing to chance.

'Strange,' she mused, looking up to study his face, 'we've had no requests on this particular reference for a long time, and suddenly, in a matter of weeks, you're the third person asking after Bluebell Hill near Ampthill. Mind you, I'm not surprised there's a lot of interest,' she went on. 'People do love a mystery, don't they?'

He stared at her. 'What mystery?' He hardly dared hope.

Her grey eyebrows rose in surprise. 'Oh, I'm sorry. I assumed you were like the others, interested in the paranormal – apparitions, that kind of thing.'

'Are you telling me the lane *is* haunted?' Excitement rose in him. Maybe it hadn't been a wasted morning after all.

Flustered for a moment, she collected her thoughts.

'Well, yes, or so they say. A young woman has been seen wandering the lanes, though of course there's no real reason to suppose she's a ghost.' She shook her head slowly from side to side. 'I'm afraid I don't believe in such things, but then it's just as well we're not all the same, don't you think?'

Dave was thrilled. 'This young woman, what else do they say about her?'

'That she wanders the lanes. That she seems to be searching . . . waiting.' She shrugged her shoulders. 'That's all I've ever heard, I think. I never take too much notice of such talk. Some people have over-active imaginations. Sorry I can't be more help, but if the missing material turns up, we'll be in touch.'

Dave drove away jubilant. 'I know for sure now, that young woman is real – or something. Whatever she is, I'm not the only one to have seen her, so at least I know I'm not going crazy.' It was remarkable how the knowledge lifted his spirit.

Suddenly, like a lead weight, his spirit fell. 'It still doesn't change the fact that she's attached herself to me. And for what reason? Who is she? Somebody must know.' He only had to tap beneath the surface of his mind to find the answer. 'The old lady . . . the painting. Of course!' Anger took hold of him. 'She knows something. I'm certain she does.'

He swung the car away from the roundabout. There was only one way to find out and that was to ask her, face to face.

Twenty minutes later he manoeuvred the car along the winding track. As he straightened up to approach the house, he couldn't believe his eyes.

The house was a blackened shell!

'God Almighty!' Slamming on the brakes, he sat there, unable to comprehend what he saw in front of him. That beautiful old house was reduced to rubble, window frames charred and crumbling, its roof open to the skies. He leaped out of the car and ran towards the house. The acrid smell of burning lingered all around. For one awful minute he wondered if the old lady was still inside. And where was Cliona Martin?

Peering through the remains of what had been a window, his horrified gaze took in the extent of the damage. Every stick of furniture had burned to cinders, the walls were black and scarred and the carpet was like a layer of ash on the ground. But as his eyes turned towards the spot where the piano had stood, he gasped with amazement.

The piano was undamaged.

Intrigued, he climbed in. Going to the piano, he touched it, feeling it sound and hard beneath his fingers. 'How could that be?' he wondered aloud. 'It isn't even scorched.' Something urged him to glance up, and when he did he was shaken to his roots. Staring down at him was the face of the young woman. Like the piano, the painting had been spared.

He stood for a time, just staring at the face, thinking how very beautiful she was. His every instinct told him to leave that place but his feet wouldn't do what his brain asked of him. *She* held him there, and he was powerless to move away.

After a while the inexplicable force that rooted him to the spot seemed to ease. Unsure of himself, he lowered his gaze, afraid to look on her face again, and made his way out, through the hallway to the front door which was now loose on its hinges. The house had a cold, hostile feeling, clinging to him, like many clawing fingers. And yet he could feel heat beneath his feet, burning through his shoes.

He heard her then. She was calling his name, over and over. Like an echo it bounced off the walls, ringing in his ears, deafening in its softness.

When, eager to get away, he tripped and stumbled, he

put out his hand to save himself, flattening it against the door. Pain seared through him. 'Jesus! The door's still burning!'

Outside, he stood staring at the ruined house. 'How did this happen? When?' He saw now that there were flames rising from the back of the house. Surely the fire brigade would have stayed to make sure the fire was properly out.

As he continued to stare, he felt cut off from everything he knew and loved. It was a chilling sensation.

Familiar sounds from the woods began to take on a different nature, playing on his mind and filling him with fear. The wind rose up in anguish from the treetops; the skies above grew black, and as flocks of birds blotted out the sun, the valley resounded with their plaintive cries. In the distance, soft at first, came a strange buzz. Even while he listened, fascinated, wanting to leave, not wanting to leave, the sound began to swell, crushing his eardrums, heavy and rhythmic, like the many feet of a marching army. And her voice, rising above it all, calling his name. Driving him to madness.

Suddenly he was running, a great weight pressing down on his back, as though in some strange way he was being pursued. He knew then. If he didn't make good his escape now, he never would.

In that moment before he climbed into the car, he looked back, and was so shocked he felt his knees go from under him.

Where only a moment ago he had seen a house reduced to a burnt shell, it now stood as it had always stood. Proud and lovely, it was bathed in bright sunshine, more reminiscent of a summer's day than a day in January. And there were people on the lawn. They were laughing, enjoying a picnic. Suddenly the child turned and opened her arms, and his heart turned over.

'Daisy!' He heard his voice call and yet it didn't sound like him. Filled with a terrible dread, he ran forward, arms outstretched, calling her name. There was a glance, a smile as she realised who it was, and then, before he could take her in his arms, she was gone.

For a long time he pounded on the door where only minutes before he had walked through the charred doorway, burning his hand as he fell. He looked at it. There was no blister. No pain. It was as though he had imagined it all.

Fired by rage, or madness, he broke down the back door and ran through the house. There was no sign of life. No sign of Daisy.

Some time later, when he was far enough away from the house to breathe easy, he went over the experience in his mind. 'What's happening to me?' he whispered. But he had no answers. All he knew was that he must find his family and make sure they were safe.

The rage was still on him, a rage he had never felt before, destructive, vengeful. 'It started that night at the restaurant,' he told himself. '*They* knew.' He was growing more convinced of it. 'He's gone now, but she's still there.' His mind was made up. 'It's time I paid a visit.'

He thought of Libby and the kids, how Libby had suspected he was having an affair, and he knew that whatever he said, she would not be easily convinced otherwise. Before he had taken her to that restaurant, everything was wonderful. Since that night there had been a sense of unease between them. And lately there had been arguments. It had been that way once before and had left his life in ruins. It must not be allowed to happen again. His family was all he had, and he would do whatever it took to keep and protect them.

He drove into town and found a space in the multi-storey car park. He ran through the shopping mall, peering in every window and round every corner. Anxious, he stood under the clock, his troubled eyes searching every passing face. After a time, he looked up at the clock, realising with a shock that it was already three thirty. 'Maybe she's on her way home,' he muttered, hoping he was wrong. But the mall was open until eight p.m. and with May along, Libby might not get home until soon after that.

Deciding to check the car park to see if her car was there, he made his way back through the crowds of people. Suddenly he heard a child's laughter. 'Daisy!'

He swung round and there they were, Libby and May, chatting together, and the children, teasing each other as usual. 'Thank God.' He didn't approach them or make his presence known. 'I've got things to do,' he muttered. 'See you all later.' He ran back to the car park. When he saw there was a queue for the lift, he went up the stairs at a run. There was no time to waste.

Collecting the car, he strapped in and was quickly away, relieved to have seen them. 'At least they're safe,' he muttered, following the spiral that would lead him to the exit. 'But for how long?' A cold hand squeezed his heart.

The rage still bubbled beneath the surface. It had not left him. Nor had the knowledge that until he was free, his family would remain in danger.

'Tony Fellowes knew, and so does his widow.' That was where he must go. That was his destination.

As he drove on, the rage grew cold and hard inside him.

The old man was asleep. 'Wake up, you!' Digging her bony fingers into his shoulder, Ida screeched in his ear, 'I've got something important to show you.'

Opening his eyes as though the lids weighed heavy, the old man turned his gaze on her. From the look on his aged face, he recognised who she was. Unblinking, he continued to stare at her, tasting her hatred yet not understanding it.

Taken aback by the brightness in those wise, searching eyes, she was momentarily mesmerised, unable to look away, yet finding it wounding to look on him. 'You bastard! Don't look at me like that.' Clenching her fist, she brought it down on his face again and again, stopping only when she had drawn blood.

The red, meandering rivulet wept down his cheeks and on to the bed, staining the sheet. 'Now look what you've done, you bad old man,' she said sweetly, her manner mellowing. 'I'll have to change the bed all over again. What a nuisance, and only because you can't do as you're told.'

He looked away, igniting her anger again.

'Look what I've got here.' Reaching down, she drew a tattered old suitcase on to the bed. 'It isn't really mine,' she confided. 'It belonged to someone I loved and I have to keep it safe. You see, there is no one else.' Tears blurred her vision. Impatient, she blinked them away. 'I expect you recognise it. Look.' She held it closer. 'It's very old, like you.' Affection trembled in her voice. 'In all these years I've never let it out of my sight. Even your son didn't know about it. He didn't know *anything*.'

Closing her eyes as though in pain, she hugged the suitcase to her breast, stroking her hands over its cracked leather surface. *'He didn't even know I was his own sister,'* she whispered hoarsely.

She watched him then, wondering how he might react. But he lay there, like he had lain there these many years. 'You didn't know either, did you?' she goaded. 'Oh, there were times when I was sorely tempted to tell you. Then I thought, no! Why should I? I'll tell him when I'm good and ready. When I know the time is right.' Cackling now, she ran her fingernails down his neck. 'I can do whatever I like to you,' she whispered, 'and you can't do a thing to stop me.'

Again, he turned his gaze on her. Pained, stricken eyes stripped her soul. He had seen all there was to see in this world and now he longed for the next.

Her manner changed abruptly. 'You can't hurt me, but you hurt her, didn't you, eh? You hurt her until she screamed for mercy!' Words became sobs and she was so choked with emotion she found it hard to go on. Dropping her head to the suitcase, she hid her face, taking a while to recover.

When next she looked at him, it was with a smile. 'I'll show you what's inside, shall I?' Excited now, she opened the lid of the case, her finger pointing to the wording there. 'Do you see that?' Grabbing him by the hair she jerked his head round, making him look. 'Do you see the name?' Running her finger along the letters, she said the name slowly, making certain there was no way he could mistake it: 'Julianne.' Releasing him, she went on, 'That's who it belonged to, Julianne. You haven't forgotten her, have you? Oh, dear me, no. We can't allow that, can we now?'

She lovingly caressed the suitcase. 'She gave this into my keeping, and I've guarded it ever since. It's all here. Things that have never seen the light of day since it came into my keeping.' Dipping into the suitcase, she took out a silver-backed hairbrush. 'Look at this.' She held it close to his face. 'Isn't it lovely? Oh, but she had such good taste.' She sniffed it then pressed it to the old man's nose. 'You can still smell her perfume. Julianne always wore the same, wonderful perfume. She was such a beautiful, sensitive woman. Feel it.' Taking his hand in hers, she wrapped his fingers tightly round the handle. 'I'm sure she wouldn't mind if you used it,' she whispered, making him brush his own wispy hair, and pressing it so hard into his scalp that the skin was soon red.

Feebly he tried to struggle free. 'Oh, I'm sorry, old man, does it hurt? I'm sure she wouldn't want you to be hurt, however bad you've been. She was too kind. But I'm not, you see. I'm a little bit wicked, like you.'

He gasped, as if fighting for breath.

'Oh no you don't!' Pushing the suitcase to the bottom of the bed, she hooked her hands beneath his armpits and sat him up as best she could. But she was older now, and her bones ached more these days. Slapping him gently on the back, she was relieved when his breathing eased. 'Don't you dare die on me,' she said crossly. 'We have so much more to talk about.'

Propping him against the pillow, she fussed and fretted. 'Comfortable now, are you?' she asked. 'Don't go slipping down the bed, will you, eh?' A crooked smile creased her worn features. 'Sometimes I wonder if you're more trouble than you're worth.'

The smile gave way to a frown. 'Now then, let me see.' Returning the hairbrush to the suitcase, she took out a sheaf of papers, her voice a thin wail as she accused, 'You thought it was all forgotten, didn't you? After all this time, you thought you had got away with it.' Shaking the papers under his nose, she taunted, 'Well, you reckoned without me, old man! Because I won't ever let you forget. It's all here, written down and kept safe in Julianne's suitcase.'

Shoving the papers back, she brought the lid down and turned the lock. 'There's nothing missing. It's all here, in her own beautiful hand, in every little detail. All the terrible, wicked things you did.'

He peeked at her, and in that peculiar way he had, one eyebrow went up and the side of his mouth gently twitched, as if he was trying to smile.

But this time she didn't lose her temper. Instead she laughed out loud. 'You can look at me any way you like, old man,' she told him. 'And you can wonder too. I *want* you to wonder. I want you to worry until your head feels as if it might explode.' Her voice quietened and her eyes grew dull. 'As long as you never forget,' she murmured. 'That's why I'm here, to make certain you never forget.'

Before she let herself out of his room, she leaned over him, her face close, her gaze melting into those confused, frightened eyes. 'When I'm done with you, and we're both in hell, don't think it ends there, old man, because it won't.' Her voice invaded his senses. 'When the time comes, this suitcase will be in the hands of the newspapers. It's all arranged. I've left no stone unturned.' She chuckled gleefully. 'They have to know, don't they? People have a right to know. The newspapers will see to that. When they print the truth, the whole world will know your shame!'

She fell back, breathless and spent. 'I can't even bear to be near you,' she rasped, 'but I gave my promise, and I'm bound by it.' Agony shaped her words. 'Day and night, every hour I must keep watch. Making sure you never forget. Keeping *the other one* away.' A deep, shivering sigh shook her whole body. 'It's good to see you suffer, old man. To know that *she's* suffering too.'

As the door closed behind her, the echo of her voice sent him back over the years, to when he was young. His dark, troubled gaze shifted to the door. He hadn't forgotten.

'Julianne.'

Oh, but that was a lifetime ago.

In her room, Ida checked that the suitcase was locked. 'Silly old fool,' she chuckled. 'Just like his son. All these years I've kept the evidence here, right under his nose, and he never knew.'

She was still chuckling when, without warning, a blow struck her from behind. Like a felled ox she crumpled to the ground. There was no groan, no sound of any kind. For a long moment the room was cloaked in a deadly silence. She lay twisted on the carpet, seemingly lifeless, her fingers clutching the handle of the suitcase as though it meant more to her than life itself.

The intruder stared down at her, bright, hateful eyes

boring into her face, taking time to witness her helplessness. Satisfied now, the eyes crinkled into a smile. There was a small sound, like a laugh, yet not like anything human, and the hands reached down, prising her fingers from the suitcase. Then, sighing deeply, like someone in despair, the intruder went away, suitcase in hand.

When first she opened her eyes, Ida couldn't remember. She tried to sit up but the pain was crippling. Rolling over, she stared round the room, at the open wardrobe. Suddenly she knew, and the knowledge gave her the strength of ten men.

Some distance away, in her pretty rose cottage, Eileen was just settling down to her tea. The scones were baked and warm on the table, and she had just finished making herself a cheese and pickle sandwich. The kettle was on the boil and, after a busy day – all morning at the Fellowes' house, then another two hours behind the post office counter – she was starving hungry. On top of that, her feet felt like two hot potatoes.

When the phone rang, she was in the middle of pouring boiling water into the teapot. Cursing under her breath, she quickly finished the task, put the lid on the teapot and covered it with the cosy.

Running into the hall, she grabbed up the phone. 'Eileen speaking.' Her gaze strayed to the kitchen table where her tea was set out and looking inviting. Her stomach rumbled so much she was certain they could hear it on the other end of the line. At first there was no answer. 'Hello. Who is this?' Anxiety coloured her voice. There had been so many mystery calls in this area lately.

Alone in her room, Ida struggled to speak. 'Ei . . . leen . . .' Gripped with pain, she forced herself to go on. 'Come quick . . . it's . . . Ida . . .'

In no time at all, Eileen had rushed to the house, dressed Ida's wound and checked the old man was safe in his bed. He was, though he seemed unusually agitated.

'He probably senses something wrong,' she told Ida, 'but he's all right. You're not to worry about him.'

After that, and in spite of Ida's protests, she called the police.

Ida saw them arrive. 'I don't want them here,' she grumbled, 'poking and prying.' But that wasn't the only reason she didn't want the police involved. There were other things here that the outside world must never suspect.

Frantic at the loss of her precious suitcase, she wondered about the identity of the thief. She had her own ideas, but they could wait. For now, she wanted her suitcase back. That was all. Nothing else mattered.

Dave remained hidden on the slip road. He waited until the police car was out of sight, then he drove out, on to the main road and away. 'That was a close thing,' he muttered. Then he turned the radio on and filled his mind with music.

CHAPTER NINE

Libby looked at him across the breakfast table. His head was down, his hands pushed into his hair; staring at the table, he hadn't heard a word she'd said.

'Dave!'

He jerked his head up, the beginnings of a grin on his mouth. 'Sorry, sweetheart. What did you say?'

Out of patience, she glared at him. 'What the devil's wrong with you?' she snapped. 'You've been edgy all weekend, and now you're miles away again. It's getting impossible to hold a conversation with you.' Scraping her chair back, she stormed out of the kitchen. 'Oh, forget it! I'd better get the children to school.' With that she slammed out of the house, to the car where the children were already waiting.

'What's the matter, Mummy?' Daisy had heard the arguments over the weekend and it worried her.

'Nothing,' Libby lied. 'We're late, that's all.' She started the engine, slammed the gear into first and drove off like someone demented.

At the junction she almost went through a red light; a car came hurtling from the other direction, with the driver shaking his fist and mouthing bad language at her. It was a sobering experience. After that she slowed down and was able to think more clearly.

In spite of his denials, she knew something bad was troubling Dave. Either he had another woman, in which case she would show him the door however much it hurt her and the kids, or there was something else on his mind. Something so worrying that he couldn't even talk to her about it.

She wondered if Jack might know and, with that in mind, she decided to take an hour off this morning, if May agreed.

'You take as long as you like,' May told her later. 'If he's got another woman, you need to know, and if he hasn't you need to know that as well.' Always a philosopher was May.

Smiling to herself, Libby dialled the agency number.

'I'll do that if you're worried about being recognised,' May offered.

Libby told her it was all right because so far she and the new secretary had not exchanged words. 'She won't know me from Adam,' she said confidently.

All the same, when someone answered at the other end, she tried to disguise her voice. 'I'd like to speak to Jack Arnold, please.'

'Of course. Who shall I say is calling?'

Libby thought the new secretary had an intriguing voice. 'It's a private matter.' Turning, she winked at May, who put her thumb up in a triumphant gesture.

When Jack came on the line, Libby waited a second or two in case the secretary might still be listening. 'Jack, don't say a word,' she pleaded, 'it's Libby. I need to see you, and I don't want Dave to know.'

There was a brief silence on the other end while Jack recovered from the shock. 'I'm sure I could manage that, sir,' he answered authoritatively. 'If you'll just give me the address.'

'Boots coffee shop in Milton Keynes,' she said. 'It's tucked away upstairs, so I think we'll be safe enough there.'

'I'm sure I'll find it, sir,' came the reply. 'What time were you thinking of?'

'Half an hour?'

'Yes, sir. Leave it with me.' At that moment Dave called him into the back office, so he put the receiver down hastily. 'That's another viewing,' Jack lied, thinking he was about to be questioned. 'But I wouldn't put much on it. As far as I can tell it's some rundown place on the far side of . . .' Realising Dave wasn't even listening, he paused. 'Dave?'

'What?'

'Why did you call me in here?'

Fumbling through the papers on his desk, Dave said without looking up, 'It's my drawer key. You haven't seen it, have you? Only I can't get into my drawer and there are some important papers I need to look at.'

'Sorry. Not guilty.' Shrugging his shoulders, Jack collected a folder from his desk, made his excuses and parted.

A moment later Dave found the key. But it wasn't where he had left it.

When she saw Jack emerge from the escalator, Libby gave a sigh of relief. She waved to him and he hurried over. 'I've only been here a few minutes myself,' she said. 'I took the liberty of getting you a pot of tea and a sandwich, if that's all right.'

'You're a girl after my own heart, sure yer are,' he laughed. Taking off his coat he laid it across the back of the chair. 'Now then, me beauty, what's bothering yer?'

Between tea and sandwiches, Libby told him. 'I don't know how to deal with it,' she confessed. 'We don't seem to talk any more, and when I do manage to get him into a conversation, his mind is elsewhere.' She blushed, but went on anyway. 'We used to make love regularly, but not any more. We get in bed and he turns his back on me. I can't get through to him, Jack, and I'm afraid.' She lowered her voice to an almost inaudible whisper. 'I don't want our marriage to fall apart, Jack.'

'Aw, come on now, Libby. You two are more in love than a newly married couple. How can it fall apart?'

'It did once before.'

'Yer joshing me!' He looked shocked.

'We kept it quiet for obvious reasons, but we went through a very bad patch.' She leaned closer. 'He was seeing another woman. At first I swore I'd never take him back, but I love him and, well, it wasn't all his fault. I have to take some of the blame.'

Jack stared at her. 'Dave was seeing another woman? I can't believe it. Why, the man has eyes for nobody but you. Anyone can see he's mad for yer.'

'Don't lie to me, Jack.'

'I'm not lying. He's head over heels in love with yer.' The tiny glimmer of a smile lit his eyes. 'Sure, it's disgusting, so it is.'

'Answer me truthfully, Jack. Is he cheating on me? And please, Jack, don't cover for him.'

Jack took a drink of his tea, then, with slow deliberation, he put his cup on the saucer. 'I swear to you, Libby, yer man has no time for any other woman. He loves yer like I've never seen a man love a woman before. Believe me, you and the young 'uns are his life.'

She believed him. 'Well, if there's no other woman, what's wrong with him?'

Jack thought about that. 'Now yer come to say, he is a bit absent-minded lately. Just now, he was frantically searching for his drawer key. I've never known him lose anything before. His desk is in a turmoil and, like yer say, yer can be talking to him and suddenly he's not listening any more.'

'Oh, Jack. Is he ill, do you think?'

Jack shook his head. 'No, I don't think he's ill. But he knows something we don't know, and I'll tell yer what, me beauty. I mean to find out what it is.'

'Follow him, Jack. Watch his every move. If he's in some kind of trouble, I want to know.'

It was decided. At home, Libby would try by every means she knew how to find out what was playing on his mind. At work, Jack would do the same.

CHAPTER TEN

The two women walked up the path together. 'I've worked here fifteen years,' remarked the older one, a stout person with flyaway hair and a big round face. 'I've brought my family up on the wages I've earned here, and I've made some good friends over the years, but I'm always glad to see the back of it. By! It's a grim-looking place and no mistake.' Shuddering, she averted her eyes from the building before them. 'Never a day goes by when I don't thank my lucky stars I'm shut inside for only ten hours a day. Not like them poor souls who, through no fault of their own, are bound to end their days here.'

Her companion had only been working here for the past month and was still learning the ropes. A small, pretty thing with short fair hair, her eyes roved over the building. 'I think it's got a grand look, and anyway, you can't blame the building for what's inside. It's *people* that cause misery in this world, not bricks and mortar. Besides, where would these sorry creatures go if there weren't places like Broadfields?'

The older woman regarded her with interest. 'I hadn't looked at it that way,' she admitted. 'Yes, I expect you're right when all's said and done. One way or another I suppose this place does keep the inmates safe from the outside world.'

'They are *patients*, Maggie,' the young woman reminded

her. 'Matron would blow her top if she heard you call them inmates.'

The older woman chuckled. 'You don't mince your words, do you, Sara?' she said. 'You young 'uns have more tongue than the cat licks its arse with.'

'Sorry.' She wasn't though.

'Aw, it's all right. You've every right to your opinion, but I still think the poor buggers are more inmates than patients. I mean, some of them don't have family to visit or take them out, do they? They don't have anybody but us, and all we've got time for is to ask if they've had their bowels open, or pass the time of day while we change their beds or wheel them to the toilet. You can't even do that with the ones who are bedridden or have lost their faculties.'

'I know.'

Maggie shook her head and sighed. 'It's a cruel world. We all do our best but in the end it's never enough. As for Matron not wanting us to call them inmates, all I can say is, some of them poor devils are shut away in there until the day they die, and if that's not being an inmate, I don't know what is.' She brought her gaze to the building. 'All the same, I do see what you mean,' she conceded. 'Now that I look at it, there is something about the place that makes you feel it'll be here for ever.'

The grey stone building was two storeys high, with fluted chimneys and many long narrow windows. The main entrance was high and arched, with the original solid oak door. Outside, there were lawns and flowerbeds, and walkways flanked with tall, bulbous-headed lamps. Here and there, the path led into small, paved nooks, with flowerpots and a bench where the more fortunate ones could sit and chat with their loved ones. In the winter, like now, it was a dead place. When summer came, the flowers opened, the birds returned, and it was a colourful, lovely place.

Over the years there had been much renovation, and only recently every stone and artefact had been meticulously cleaned. But, deep down, under the skin, the essential character of the place had not changed. Built in Victorian times to house lunatics and grave offenders, Broadfields was still used for treating the mentally sick. These included both those who had broken down under the stress of modern living but would one day probably be able to resume their lives and those who, for whatever reason, had lost their way and seemed destined never to live a normal life outside the walls of the institution.

Matron was there as usual, tapping her watch and scowling. 'Come along, there's work to be done.' She tutted and fussed, and when her bleeper sounded, she switched it off with a groan, turned on her heel and hurried away.

'Same sweet mood as ever,' Maggie laughed. 'Why does she always act as if we're late?' She looked at the wall clock. 'We've ten minutes yet.'

'Time for a fag.'

'Haven't you given them things up yet? What happened to your New Year resolution?'

'Went up in smoke.'

Maggie burst out laughing. 'You little sod!'

In the staff room they changed into their auxiliary uniforms. Taking a newspaper out of her bag, Sara laid it down on the table. 'There's been another attack at that place near Ampthill.'

'Oh?' Maggie picked up the newspaper and began flicking through it. 'I did hear something about it but I try not to listen. I'd rather not know about these things. Living on my own, it frightens me.'

Tying up her shoelaces, Sara went on regardless. 'First the restaurant owner was murdered, and now his wife's been attacked. Somebody tried to smash her skull in.'

'Dreadful!'

'That article says it might have been the same person who killed her husband.'

Her interest aroused, Maggie quickly scanned the article. 'Good God!'

'What's wrong?'

Dropping into a seat, Maggie seemed shocked to the core. 'I didn't realise.' She would have said more, but suddenly the door was flung open and there stood Matron. She didn't say a word. She didn't have to. Her face said it all.

Maggie leaped to her feet. 'Sorry, Matron,' she gasped. 'We're just on our way.' With that she rammed on her hat, pinned it into place and went through the door like the devil himself was after her.

The wards were busier than usual, with the nurses sending Maggie and Sara here and there. Two patients refused their breakfasts, and another tipped a bowl of water over herself. All in all, it was one of the worst mornings Maggie could remember. 'I'm knackered,' she told Sara as they rushed by each other in the corridor.

At twelve o'clock, the two of them made their way back to the staff room where Sara made tea while Maggie got her breath back. 'I'm getting too old for this,' she moaned. 'There's a job going at the garden centre. I think I'll apply.'

Sara laughed. 'You'll never stick it. You'll miss Matron's happy face – you'll even miss emptying the bedpans.'

'You little bugger, give us a cup of that tea before I die of thirst.'

Bringing the tea and biscuits to the table, Sara quizzed, 'What were you about to say when Matron opened the door this morning?'

Maggie's eyes went instinctively to the newspaper still lying where she'd dropped it on the table. 'It was that article.'

'What? The one where that woman was attacked?'

Maggie nodded.

'What about it?'

Frowning, Maggie sipped her tea, trying to organise the facts in her mind. 'The name struck a chord, that's all. Fellowes, Tony Fellowes.'

'The old man who's bedridden? The police said he was too ill to have heard or seen anything.'

'He was here.'

'The old man? Here, at Broadfields?'

Deep in thought, Maggie didn't answer right away. She vaguely recalled something else. But was it the same time? Or had he gone by then?

'Maggie!' Now that her interest was fired, Sara wouldn't let it go. 'What are you saying?'

'He was here, Tony Fellowes was an inmate.'

'Patient!'

'All right. He was a patient here.'

'When?'

'Some time back.' She shook her head. Her memory was not what it used to be. 'I can't recall exactly when, but it was some years ago. He was very ill. Apparently he'd been ill for a long time. His son had been caring for him but as he got older he couldn't manage any more.'

'And you say the old man was unbalanced?'

'I didn't say that but yes, I suppose you could call him unbalanced.'

'What made him that way?'

'Something that happened years before, when his son was barely out of his teens. I remember that, because I caught the old man crying one night and he told me he could remember his son's eighteenth birthday, but after that his mind was a blank. When I spoke to the son about it, he just said there had been an accident and his father had been badly affected by it.'

'What kind of accident?'

'I didn't ask, and he didn't say. The son wasn't the kind

of man you had a conversation with. He was a bad-tempered individual, with very little time for anyone but his father.' She recalled that much at least. 'He adored the old man, anyone could see that.'

'Did the old man get better?'

'He didn't want to. For some reason known only to himself, he just gave up.' She shook her head sadly. 'You know as well as I do, when that happens, there's nothing anyone can do, not even the doctors.'

'I've read somewhere that a tribe of Indians can will themselves to die. They sit with their arms and legs folded, and they just pass away.'

'Mind over matter. A powerful thing.'

'So what happened to old Mr Fellowes?'

'His son got married and his wife wanted to take care of him.'

'But she didn't even know him, did she?'

Smiling, Maggie reminded her, 'We don't really know any of these here, do we? But we care for them all the same.'

'It's our job. But she didn't have to do it, did she? If the old man was past all help, and he was being cared for well enough here, why would she want to take him away? Looking after an elderly man, especially if he's mentally ill, well, it's a hard, time-consuming job. And if she was only just married, it doesn't seem fair on her husband, does it?'

'No, I don't suppose it does. But he must have wanted the old man home. When all's said and done, it was his father.'

'And now he's dead. And the wife's been attacked. Doesn't seem fair after what they did for the old man.'

'Life is never fair.'

'What was he like, the old man?'

'He was a bit younger when he was here, of course, but if I remember rightly he was a fine-looking bloke. Tall, big-framed, with a back broad as an ox. He had the kind of face where you could still see the young man in him.'

'Good-looking, was he?'

'In his time, I should think.'

She kept thinking of that other matter. For some reason it worried her.

The door opened and a fat, middle-aged nurse waddled in. 'What a morning!' she groaned, taking off her hat and stuffing it in her pocket. Her eyes caught sight of their teacups. 'Any more in the pot?' she asked.

'Enough for one more.' Sara bit into her biscuit and for a while was quiet.

While the nurse busied herself at the sink, Maggie asked casually, 'Do you remember Tony Fellowes? He was here some years back. Never spoke. Slept most of the time. A fine figure of a man, he was.'

'Yes, I think so. A sad case, if I remember right. He was one of the few that the doctors couldn't help.' She added milk to her tea and turned round, cursing when she spilled some over her apron. 'Didn't the son take him away after he got married?'

'That's right.'

'I always thought the woman must have been some kind of an angel to take him on like that, especially when she was only just married.' Lowering her voice, she admitted, 'To tell you the truth, I'm not sure I'd have done it.'

Sara piped up, 'That's just what I said!'

'There was something else as well,' the fat nurse said. 'It all happened round the time the old man was taken away.' She glanced at Maggie. 'You must remember, all hell was let loose.'

Maggie nodded slowly. 'I was trying to remember whether it was before the old man left, or soon after.'

'I can't be certain either, but I know the incidents followed one another.'

Sara was so excited, she couldn't sit still. 'Tell me!' She

leaned forward, her face alight with anticipation. 'What happened?'

It was the fat nurse who replied. 'There was a murder. Right here in the hospital. One of the nurses, it was. A sweet young thing, only been here a few months.'

'Bloody hell!'

Maggie took up the story. 'That wasn't the end of it either. A few days later, two women patients disappeared. One of them was due to be discharged the following week. The other was a trusty. The place was crawling with police for weeks, but they never found the murderer of that poor nurse.'

'What about the other two?'

'Well now, there's another mystery. One of them was found three days later, drowned in the river. The other was never traced. The police did all they could but in the end they had to abandon the search. As far as I know, the case is still open. Unsolved.'

Sara was thrilled. 'Cor! It all happens here, eh?' Her curiosity grew morbid. 'How was that poor nurse murdered? Strangled, I suppose, that's usually how they do it.'

The fat nurse didn't approve of Sara's excitement but was caught up in it all the same. 'That wasn't the way she died.' Edging her fat little arms across the table, she leaned her head down, glancing furtively at the door, before confiding in a whisper, 'She was in the stockroom, reaching up into a cupboard, when somebody crept in and hit her on the back of the head with a heavy object.'

Sara leaped to her feet. 'That's just how Mrs Fellowes was attacked!' she cried. 'Somebody crept up behind *her* and hit her on the head. Blimey! If you ask me, she's lucky to be alive.'

'It just goes to show,' Maggie remarked apprehensively, 'nobody's safe. Not then. And not now.'

Dave was like a cat on hot bricks, pacing back and forth,

frantically running his hands through his hair, the way he did when troubled.

From the adjoining office, Jack anxiously watched him. 'Libby's wrong,' he mused, tapping his pencil on the desk while keeping an eye on Dave. 'Dave isn't having an affair. This is something far more serious.'

'I know what it could be.' Cliona's soft voice startled him.

'What did you say?' As he looked round, the dark eyes enveloped him. 'How would you know what's troubling him?' Cliona had been a real asset in Mandy's absence. She had a gentle, unassuming manner that kept the phone ringing, and she was devastatingly attractive; so much so that normally he would be chasing her at every opportunity. But he was wary of her. He couldn't make her out, couldn't get through somehow. There was something different about her and though it irked him to think it, she frightened him. Imagine that, he thought. Jack Arnold, being frightened of a woman.

She smiled, as though she knew what he was thinking. 'I just put a call through from the owner of the big house on Weathercock Lane. Mr Walters forgot the appointment and now the vendor's withdrawing his property from this agency.'

'Jaysus, Mary and Joseph!' Jack's gaze went to Dave. 'I'd better see if there's anything I can do.' Getting out of his chair, he hurried across the office and knocked on Dave's door. 'Got a minute?' Without waiting for an answer, he went inside, closing the door behind him.

Dave was adamant. 'I'll deal with it, Jack. Thanks all the same. Barclay is quick to temper, that's all. He's a difficult man, but this time it's entirely my fault. I'll go and see him. It's no good over the phone.'

Jack wasn't so easily dismissed. 'What's wrong, Dave?'

Alarmed, Dave answered cautiously, 'What makes you think there's anything wrong?'

'You've forgotten two appointments this last week. Fortunately the land deal is still going through but the house on Weathercock Lane was one you'd been after for some time. You fought off the competition to get it on the books, and now it seems you've blown it.'

'I've told you, I'll deal with it.' He didn't take kindly to being carpeted, and by Jack of all people. 'If that's all, you'd best get back to your work.'

Jack was persistent. 'I know you don't want me saying this, but I think we've known each other long enough for me to speak out when I see you going wrong.'

'I think you'd better go, Jack.' Dave could feel himself growing angry. He had more than enough on his mind without listening to Jack sounding like the echo of his own conscience.

Unabashed, Jack went on, 'You're hardly ever in the office lately, and just now I saw you pacing the floor as if you were haunted or something.'

'What's that supposed to mean?' Dave demanded frostily. He felt vulnerable. Jack couldn't know how close he'd come to the truth.

Taking the liberty of seating himself in the chair opposite, Jack gave him a direct, no-nonsense look. 'I thought we were more than just business colleagues. Am I wrong?'

Dave closed his eyes, his whole body sagging as though the life had ebbed from it. 'No, Jack, you're not wrong.'

'So confide in me. What is it that's driving you crazy?'

'Nothing I can't handle.'

'Is it a woman?'

'What?'

'Libby thinks you're cheating on her.'

'Dear God! You mean she's been talking to you about it?' He couldn't believe she would do such a thing, but then, when he thought about it, it was only natural. Jack was here and she wasn't. He could keep an eye out when she couldn't. 'If I was seeing another woman, would you tell her?'

'Yes.'

'You're a good friend, Jack. To both of us.'

'Libby spoke to me in confidence.'

Dave nodded. 'I understand. Don't worry.'

'And there isn't another woman?'

'No.' He smiled, thinking about the dark-eyed young woman who had invaded his every waking minute. She was at the root of all his troubles. But how could he explain it to Jack? Practical, down-to-earth Jack who believed only what he saw with his own eyes? 'It's not a woman,' he said firmly. 'Well, not in the way you might think.'

'Cliona thinks it might be money troubles.' He used her name purposefully. He felt uncomfortable with her in the office. Maybe if Dave knew she was talking about him, he would send her packing.

At first Dave seemed angry. 'She said that?' His handsome features gave way to a smile. 'She knows nothing, and no, it's not money troubles. You know as well as I do the business is on the up and up.' He frowned. 'Though I'm concerned we could have lost a big sale because of my neglect.'

'Want me to go and see him?'

'I've already said. My fault. My responsibility. I'll get it back.' He was confident.

Jack knew that look. 'I'm sure you will,' he laughed.

Just then the phone rang. Dave picked up the receiver. 'Dave Walters here. How can I help you?'

While he was talking, Jack departed, only partly reassured.

'I understand.' Dave had been chasing this solicitor for weeks to shift things along on a difficult purchase. 'No, I'm not prepared to lower the price. The vendor insists he won't go lower, and I agree. We've gone far enough on this one.' He listened patiently. 'If she backs out after signing the contract, she's liable, you know that as well as I do.' Again he listened, growing angrier by the minute. 'No, I won't go back to him yet again. Enough is enough. We complete the deal, or we sue.'

There the conversation ended, but he had a gut feeling it would go his way. 'Some people are never satisfied.'

Tackling his pile of overdue letters, he was interrupted by a knock on the door. When he looked up, it was to see Cliona enter with his coffee. 'Thought you might need this,' she said, setting it down before him.

For a moment their eyes met and, like some awful spectre, the image of Miss Ledell's house loomed large in his mind, blackened and charred, empty. Without being aware of it, he murmured, 'How did the fire happen?'

She looked at him for a while, her dark eyes smiling. 'There was no fire,' she answered softly. 'You must have imagined it.'

The spell was broken. He mentally shook himself and stared round the room. The door was closed, he was utterly alone.

At that moment, there came a knock on the door. 'Come!' The door opened and in came Cliona.

'I thought you might be ready for your coffee.' When he just stared at her, she entered, set the coffee cup on his desk and silently departed.

After she had gone, he sat motionless for a minute or two, gazing after her. He looked down at the desk, half expecting to see two cups of coffee. There was only one.

Numbed, he couldn't take his eyes off the cup. The bubbles of milk in the centre were still swirling, and he could see the steam rising, warming his face. 'Maybe I *am* going mad,' he whispered. If he wasn't losing his mind, what other explanation could there be?

He looked through the window into the adjoining office. Cliona and Jack were both engrossed in their work.

Nothing untoward. Everything normal. His eyes were drawn to Cliona. 'What is it about you?' he murmured. 'You and the woman in the rain. You and Miss Ledell.' He had been back to the house three times since that day. 'The old lady's gone now. The house is deserted and Daisy is distraught.' The obvious thing to do was to ask Cliona where Miss Ledell was, but he baulked at the idea. Cliona was somehow part of the mystery, he was certain, and if he was honest, the thought of confronting her frightened him.

He got to his feet. He began pacing, muttering to himself. 'My whole life is falling apart. Libby's convinced I'm seeing another woman. I can't sleep, can't eat. This morning I yelled at Daisy for nothing and now she won't even talk to me.' Anguish thickened his voice. 'I can't go on like this. I've got to confide in someone.'

'*D . . . a . . . v . . . e.*' The voice was like a hush falling over the room.

Startled, he swung round, his eyes drawn to the far corner. 'Who's that?' Imagining he saw someone there, he rushed over. No one was there and he laughed harshly. 'I'm seeing shadows now, for Chrissake!'

The shrill ringing of the phone brought him back. In two strides he was at the desk. 'Yes?' Impatience quickened his voice.

'Mr Walters?'

'Yes?'

'It's the library here.'

He visibly relaxed. 'Oh, hello.'

'I'm ringing about the documents you requested, the ones that went missing. That was odd in itself, but even odder is the fact that they have now been returned. They appeared on the shelves some time last evening, and no one seems to know who put them there.'

'Whatever you do, don't let them out of your sight.' Relief coursed through him.

'When shall I expect you?'

'I'll be there in fifteen minutes,' he said. 'I'm already on my way.'

That night, while Libby slept, Dave crept down to the study. Here he took out the thick wad of documents from the library. Excited by what he had already discovered, he resumed reading.

There were newspaper cuttings dating back to the 1930s. The car accident had been a bad one, killing the passenger and badly injuring the driver. There was a witness, a young woman who had been walking her dog. One of the smaller, more local newspapers had carried her account.

> It was just after nine o'clock in the evening. I was walking my dog when I saw the car. It was heading towards Ampthill. I took little notice of it. It was dark, and the rain was coming down in sheets. All I know is, suddenly the car went out of control and came across the pavement. I thought we were going to be killed.

Dave wondered if the woman was still alive. He felt instinctively that he ought to speak to her. According to the paper, her name was Rosemary Dwight, of Arrian Gardens, Ampthill, Bedfordshire. Eagerly, he made a note of this.

Turning the pages, he came across a national report. This time it was to do with events following the tragedy. Under the heading 'The Ghost of Bluebell Hill', there were detailed accounts of ghostly sightings on the road, of a woman, searching, lost, stopping the drivers as they travelled along that particular stretch of road, appearing out of nowhere, then disappearing.

He turned the page and the photograph of the dead woman stared up at him.

'My God!' It was her, the young woman in the rain. Dark-eyed and beautiful, she looked into his eyes, touching him deep inside, turning his heart over.

His fingers burned at the touch of the paper bearing her image. With a gasp of horror, he dropped the page and backed away. But then the strangest thing happened. As he continued to look into those dark, pleading eyes, a great, sweeping calmness came over him. The shock slid from his soul, and in its place came an overwhelming sadness. The eyes seemed to smile gently. She was watching him. Feeling what he felt inside. She was so real, so incredibly real, he felt her presence as though she was standing right beside him. Her nearness was overwhelming, like a warm, caressing vapour all around.

Her voice, silky, murmuring, filled the air. *'Help me.'*

He wasn't imagining it. This time he knew. She needed him. More importantly, he needed her. If he was to save his marriage, his life, he must let go, believe what his own eyes were telling him.

'What do you want of me?' He looked into her eyes. They were quiet now, a yellowing picture on a page. 'I want to help,' he whispered, 'if you'll only show me how.'

He wasn't mad. He knew that now, and it felt like the most natural thing in the world to be talking to her.

That night, Ida had a terrifying experience.

It was midnight when she finally got the old man settled. He was fretful, crying out in his sleep. 'What's wrong, you old fool!' Forcing the sedative down his throat, she cursed when he spat it out. 'Filthy old sod!' Wiping the mess from his chin, she continued to moan, 'You've given me no sleep for two nights now. What's the matter with you? If I didn't know better, I'd say you were up to something.'

Eventually he seemed to drift into a deep sleep, but she

didn't leave straightaway. Instead she sat by his bed, her eyes weighed down with lack of sleep.

'I often wondered if I looked like you,' she whispered, holding his hand with unusual tenderness. 'I never knew, you see. No one ever told me. When I was little, I used to dream about what you would be like, how you smiled, the way you walked.' She sighed deeply. 'Now you're just an old, old man, and I will never know these things. I had to imagine then and I still have to imagine.'

Anger sharpened her features. Only a moment ago she had been holding his hand with tenderness; now she began to squeeze. Squeeze and squeeze, until her bony knuckles were white. Even then she didn't let go, not until her fingers went into spasm and the pain was too much. She dropped his hand to the bedcovers, noting with satisfaction how her grip had left its mark on him – long, thin patterns of red and white where her fingers had dented his flesh.

'I'll see you in the morning,' she said, spitefully pinching his nose. 'Don't you dare wake me up till then.'

Only his deep snoring answered. 'Unconscious, eh? Well, it took you long enough to sink, you bugger.' Chuckling, she ambled away. 'Such willpower,' she muttered. In many ways they were too alike.

In her own room she held her aching back. 'I'm paying a hard price for what you did, old man,' she groaned. 'Curse and damn you to hell.'

She quickly undressed, not bothering to wash; these days she hardly saw any point. The bed was inviting, the night outside cold and penetrating. 'I'm better on my own,' she sighed, pottering about. 'I'm glad he's gone, that husband of mine. He served his purpose, now he's gone and good riddance to him.' She paused a moment, listening to her own heartbeat. *Thump, thump.* A solitary rhythm, sending echoes all over her body. She felt empty. The loneliness was overwhelming. 'Sometimes, though, it's not nice, being all on your own.' Dismissing such notions, she giggled like a child. 'Ah, but when you're on your own, there's nobody can tell you what to do, is there?'

She put on her pink flowered nightgown. It was her only one. Every other week she washed and dried it in the same day, and though it was growing frayed round the sleeves and the hem was falling down, she had no intention of replacing it. 'This old nightie has carried me through many a year, and it'll carry me to my grave.' Picking out a loose thread, she placed it carefully on the bedside cabinet. 'If that old bugger wakes me up in the night, he'll be sorry.'

She got into bed and was just beginning to dream when she thought she heard a sound. Irate but curious, she got up again. 'It isn't him,' she muttered, straining to hear. 'Sounds like it came from outside.'

On tiptoes, she went out on to the landing, her gaze going instinctively to the old man's room. His door was tightly shut, just as she had left it, and as far as she could tell the sound wasn't coming from there. 'There's somebody downstairs,' she croaked. 'It can't be *her*. She's never dared to come this far before.'

Apprehensive, she edged forward. 'I locked the doors, I know I did.' A spiral of fear shot through her. But she wasn't deterred. She had no intention of cowering in her room, waiting to be hit over the head again.

She searched the house, switching every light on and then off again as she went in and out of the rooms. They were just as she had left them. She checked the front and back doors. They were still tightly secured, no sign of a break-in there. She went to the kitchen window. It was partly open.

'I could have sworn I closed it,' she grumbled. But had she forgotten? Was she slipping? It was true that lately she had been feeling her age. Pressing her face to the windowpane, she stared into the night, drawing back with a gasp when she imagined she saw someone there. 'Who the devil's that?'

Panic-stricken, she snatched up the key and went to unlock the door, hopelessly fumbling until at last it sprang open. As the night flooded in, a shadow stole fleetingly across her path. With a shrill cry, 'Get away from here, you!' she ran into the night, across the lawn and on into the spinney, frantically slashing away the branches that scored her face. 'I know it's you!' she screeched. 'Go away!'

Half-crazed with fear, she ran on through the spinney like a wild thing, screaming abuse and striking out as if at some unseen attacker.

Some time later, dazed and hurt, she began her way back, all the while glancing behind as if afraid she might be followed. '*She* won't have him. Not yet. Not until one of us is rotting in the grave.' With every step she took, the hatred boiled over. And soon, the inevitable self-torture. What if somehow *she* had got through? What if one day the hatred wasn't enough to keep her out? If the day ever came when she was within reach of the old man, it would be the end.

Panicked by her own imaginings, she began running, her steps blind and faltering. Scratched and bleeding, she was frantic to get back. To him. To the burden that weighed her down.

When, only a few steps from the house, she felt someone touch her on the shoulder, her worst fears were realised. Screaming like a banshee, she lost her footing and fell face down into the undergrowth. When she managed to scramble up, she could see nothing but darkness all around. Strange, hollow sounds came at her from every direction. From behind she felt the brush of a hand and she ran like the wind. 'It's not her,' she gasped. '*It's not her!*' She had stalked the other one for so long, she knew her as well as she knew herself. But if it wasn't her, who was it?

She could see nothing, hear no one as she ran, and yet she knew they were only a few steps behind, bearing down on her with every minute. 'Help me,' she whispered. 'Mother! Help me.'

As she neared the house, she heard the softest sound, and then, before she could even turn, she felt the hand on her back, hard and square between her shoulder blades, pushing, forcing her forwards, downwards. Immensely powerful.

Terror made her bold. 'Leave me alone!' she screamed.

Seeing the back door, she made a mad dash towards it, twisting and struggling as she went. Falling through the doorway, she knew there was no time to waste. She ran into the kitchen and out again through the door at the far end, which led her straight back into the hallway. She crept into the understairs cupboard and closed the door behind her, and there she remained, crouched, hardly daring to breathe, eyes closed, and praying for the first time in her miserable life.

She heard the footsteps, and her heart stood still. They travelled up the hallway and paused right outside her hiding place. The suspense was unbearable. In her dark corner, she dared to wonder whether to go out and confront the intruder. But some deep instinct warned her this was no ordinary intruder. Whoever it was had already hurt her. Maybe they meant to kill her.

And still they waited outside, just an arm's reach away. She could hear the intermittent gasps of breath, much like that of an animal.

All her courage went, leaving a frightened little woman, scared to come out, afraid of what she might find there. Who would want to hurt her? And why? She remembered her husband. In her mind's eye she could see him so clearly. She wondered how he had felt in that moment just before he died. The same way she felt now, she thought, and her heart lurched with horror.

It seemed like an age before soft, hesitant footsteps carried the intruder away. Ida sighed with relief.

Her relief was short-lived as she realised that the footsteps were not leaving. Instead, they made their way deeper into the house and on up the stairs. She waited. Knowing it was not the old enemy. Feeling instinctively that the old man would not be harmed.

The footsteps returned, paused once more outside her hiding place – as if she was being challenged, taunted. It was almost as though the intruder knew she was there. The soft, whispering sound of laughter filtered in through the door. Any moment now, she thought, the intruder would burst in.

But no. Instead, the footsteps moved away but they trod so softly she couldn't be certain which way they had gone – outside, or back into the house.

'Why should they go back inside?' she breathed, trying to convince herself that the intruder had left for good. 'No. They've gone away now.'

She inched open the door and crept out. It seemed quiet enough.

Passing the mirror, she caught sight of herself in the moon's reflection. Reeling with shock, she backed away. It was like looking at some grotesque monster – clothes torn, lacerated face daubed with blood. Every bone in her body ached. She had been crouched in the cupboard for too long. But determination set in. 'I'm not beaten yet,' she muttered stubbornly. 'To hell with all of them.'

She searched the downstairs, trying every door and window as she went. 'All safe now,' she reasoned, misguidedly believing that, by locking doors and windows, she was keeping the evil out. Upstairs, she looked in on the old man. 'Out to the world,' she observed bitterly. 'The old fool. What would he know?'

When she went into her own room, her instincts were quickly alerted. Something was different here. Quickening her steps, she went to the wardrobe. It was open. She searched. 'Nothing!' Looking up, she noticed something brown protruding over the edge. Ignoring the pain that seared through her, she stretched up, gasping with astonishment when she felt her old suitcase hard and familiar beneath her touch. Refusing to believe what her fingers told her, she dragged the object down and threw it on to the bed. Flinging open the unlocked lid, she gazed at the contents. 'It's all here,' she muttered. 'Nothing missing!'

Puzzled, she sat hunched on the bed, pain and fatigue racking her frail form. Her mind was racing, chaotic. 'Why would someone take the suitcase and then return it intact?' She couldn't begin to understand. 'Who are you?' she called to the dark, and there was no answer. No answer from the dark. No answer in her own mind. She was not easily given to fear, but she knew it now. She could taste it like a poison.

Something different was happening.

Overcome with dizziness, she fell sideways against the pillow, her eyes fixed unblinking on the open suitcase.

Someone had terrorised her this night. Her mind fought to stay alert. Who? Why?

Her eyes closed, and she lapsed into unconsciousness.

CHAPTER ELEVEN

Detective Inspector Lowe had been on the police force a long time. Recruited as a young man, he had made the force his life. Having gained promotion early on, he knew about murders and, up until now, he thought he knew the mind of a person who could take a life without compassion.

Investigating a murder was a great challenge to him. He had been at the spearhead of eighty-five murder investigations and of these he had tracked down eighty-three killers. In spite of the two who had eluded capture, it was nevertheless a fine and distinguished record. Now, when he was heading for well-earned retirement, he didn't want to go out on an unsolved murder.

'I've no intention of giving up on it,' he snapped angrily. 'But the truth is, we've been down every avenue and they all lead nowhere. We've no real clues to go on, no motive, and despite a finger search of the immediate and surrounding areas, no sign of the weapon. All our enquiries have come to nothing, and the longer it takes us to track him down, the colder the trail.' Taking in a long deep gulp of air he blew it out the same way, long and hard, swelling his cheeks to plump round balloons. 'What do you make of it, Sergeant?'

Sergeant Coley was a younger man, an expert at computer language but less proficient when it came to hands-on policing. 'Well, sir . . .' He rolled his small blue eyes, as if it hurt to throw his mind back that far. 'You're right. The Fellowes murder was a difficult one, no weapon, no motive that we can pin down, and no clues of any kind. Truth is, I don't really see where we go from here.' He almost leaped out of his skin when the other man's fist came crashing on to the table.

'If it was up to you, we'd go nowhere at all!' Inspector Lowe stormed. 'Get your head away from that bloody computer and put your thinking cap on, man! Use the brain the good Lord gave you and go back over your notes. I want you to find anything and everything that might help.'

'Right, sir.' Sergeant Coley hadn't been assigned to Inspector Lowe all that long, and already he was thinking of asking for a transfer. Not that he didn't like the other man, but he felt hopelessly inadequate, not certain whether he was even cut out to be a detective. Lately he'd been wondering if he might be happier looking for a post in administration. 'Sir?'

'Mmm?'

'Am I looking for anything in particular?'

Suppressing his frustration, the inspector answered in a quiet controlled voice. 'Use your common sense, man. Sift all the information, like you were sifting for gold.'

'Yes, sir.' There were times when Coley wished the earth would open and swallow him whole.

Inspector Lowe got out of his chair and walked to the far side of the room. Here he stood, hands in pockets, staring at the men on the other side of the glass screen.

After a while he turned to look at his colleague, suggesting thoughtfully, 'I think it's time we paid Mrs Fellowes another visit, took a further look at the scene of the crime.'

The younger man shook his head. 'We went over that room with a fine-tooth comb, sir.'

The inspector was losing patience. 'Then we'll go over it again if necessary, Sergeant.' He smiled, an idea germinating in the back of his mind. 'A murderer nearly always returns to the scene of the crime, isn't that so, Coley?'

'Yes, sir.'

'Right. We have to think like the murderer would think, don't you agree?'

'In what way, sir?'

'I'm not sure, but I'll tell you what, Sergeant.'

'What's that, sir?'

'When we last searched that room, we missed something.' Turning round, he added thoughtfully, 'We *must* have or we'd have nailed the bugger by now!'

'Ouch!' Seated by the kitchen window, Ida snapped, 'Rip the skin off my face, why don't you?' Glowering at Eileen, who had been gently bathing her wounds, she began whimpering. 'It hurts. It bloody hurts.'

'I know, but the wounds are deep, Ida. I'm doing my best but you really should go to hospital.'

'No hospitals!'

Tenderly, Eileen dabbed at a long cut running from ear to throat. 'This one looks infected to me.'

'Infected or not, I'm going to no hospital, so you can stop trying to persuade me. All right?'

Dipping the swab into the TCP solution, Eileen shook her head. 'You're a stubborn woman, Ida Fellowes.'

'Always been that way. It's too late to change now.'

Satisfied she had done all she could, Eileen put away the cotton wool and emptied the liquid down the sink. Washing her hands, she told Ida, 'I still think you're mad not to call the police. You could have been killed, don't you realise that?'

Ida stood up and fastening her blouse said sharply, 'No hospital, and no police. I remember the last time, they were crawling all over this house, poking and prying, asking their damned questions.' She wagged a finger. 'I don't want them here again.'

Eileen had learned not to argue with Ida; she was too strong-minded. 'All right, don't get yourself into a state.'

Ida looked out of the window and saw two men approaching the house. 'It's them!' she cried. 'It's the bloody police!'

Surprised, Eileen ran to the window. 'You're right. Aren't those the same two who came here before?'

'How did they find out? Was it you, Eileen? Did you call them? Tell me the truth.'

'No, I didn't call them.' Eileen was indignant. 'I wanted to, but you wouldn't let me. Remember?'

'Who called them then? How did they know?'

'There's only one way to find out.' Eileen went to the door and opened it. 'Yes?' She recognised Inspector Lowe right away.

Taking his identity wallet out of his jacket pocket, he held it up. 'Is Mrs Fellowes at home?' When Eileen replied that she was, he went on, 'Good. I'd like a word with her. I won't take up much of her time.'

Suspecting from his manner that he had no idea there had been another attack, Eileen did her best to keep them out, for Ida's sake. 'Mrs Fellowes isn't well,' she told him. 'Perhaps you'd like to call back. Tomorrow maybe.'

'No. I'd like a word now, if you please. Like I say, I won't keep her too long.'

Inside the house, Ida listened. Hobbling to the door, she pushed her way through. 'You heard what she said. I'm not well. Clear off and leave me alone.'

The sergeant's eyes opened wide when he saw how cut and bruised she was. 'Been in a fight with a bear, have you?' he said, half smiling.

One cutting glance from the inspector and the smile vanished. 'Sorry to see you've injured yourself, Mrs Fellowes.' The older man's curiosity was heightened. 'Can I ask how you managed to do that?'

Before Ida could make some stinging retort, and since he was already here, Eileen thought he should know. 'She was attacked, that's how she was injured,' she announced. 'Right outside this house in the early hours of this morning.' Contemptuously she went on, 'It was probably the same man who murdered her husband – the one you should have arrested weeks ago.'

Ida glared at Eileen then turned her anger on the inspector. 'Is that why you're here?' she demanded. 'To tell me you've caught my husband's murderer at long last?'

'No such luck, I'm afraid, but we'll get him, don't you worry.' He looked at her mangled face, with the many superficial scratches and a few very nasty deep cuts, almost as though the tip of a knife had been zig-zagged along her skin. 'You were attacked, you say.'

Ida remained sullen.

'I think we'd better talk, don't you?'

With obvious ill will, Ida stepped back to let them in, exchanging glances with Eileen who anticipated a tongue-lashing and was already wishing she hadn't opened her big mouth.

The sergeant was firm but surprisingly gentle. 'Have you any idea who might have attacked you?' He had his notebook open but as yet the page was blank.

'No.' Ida was deliberately difficult. 'I've already told you,' she snapped, 'I heard a noise and went downstairs. I thought I saw someone prowling about outside and I went to investigate. After that I'm not sure. I felt something in my back, a fist, I think. I'm not sure. Whoever it was came after me, chased me into the house.' She paused, reliving the nightmare, before continuing in a quieter voice, 'I hid in the cupboard until they'd gone. That's all I can tell you.'

'Did they speak at all?'

'No.'

'And you didn't see their face?'

'I've already said.'

'Do you think it might have been the same person who attacked you before?'

'How should I know?' Ida retorted. She wasn't going to tell the police anything about the suitcase.

Frustrated, the sergeant put down his notebook.

At this point the inspector stepped forward. He wasn't as sympathetic. 'Look, Mrs Fellowes, you've been attacked twice now and not so long ago your husband was murdered.'

'Yes, and you still haven't caught the buggers who did it, have you, eh? So why should I think you can catch the bugger who frightened me very nearly to death last night?'

The inspector ignored her taunts. 'The point is, we don't want another murder on our hands, do we? If you can't help us, what about your father-in-law?' He recalled from the previous visit that the old man was barely conscious for most of the time.

'What about him?'

'I don't suppose he heard anything, did he?'

She laughed. 'He's ill, senile. The poor old bugger would sleep through an earthquake.'

'Would you mind if I had a word with him?'

'You can try.'

Confident that the old man would have nothing to contribute, she led the inspector to his bedroom. 'Don't distress him,' she warned. 'I've told you, he's very ill.'

The inspector nodded. 'I understand.'

He stood by the bed and spoke to the sleeping figure. At first there was no response. Then, just as he decided Ida had been right and he was wasting his time, the old man opened his eyes and looked at him. For a moment he was struck by the beauty of the old man's brown, shining eyes.

'Mr Fellowes,' he said softly, 'I'm sorry to disturb you, but I just wondered if there was anything you wanted to tell me. Anything unusual you might have heard last night.' It was difficult to question someone who just lay there, staring at you.

He waited a moment but there was no response. The eyes continued to look at him, sad and vacant. They made him feel uncomfortable. 'I'm sorry,' he muttered. 'Sorry to have disturbed you.' He turned away.

Ida ushered him from the room. 'You should be ashamed,' she said. And he was.

Downstairs, Ida refused to answer any more questions, though she did agree to their having another look at the room where her husband was murdered. 'After that, I want you out of my house.' Upstairs just now, she had seen something in the old man's face that had frightened her.

When the police left, with Eileen following soon after, Ida returned to the old man's bedroom. 'That was the police,' she told him, 'come to look at the room where your son was killed.' She waited for him to open his eyes but he didn't. 'Are you asleep, old man?' She prodded him with the tip of her finger. 'Or are you pretending?' She sat a while, watching him, and wondering. 'I gave you a sedative last night,' she said softly, 'so you couldn't have heard anything, and even if you did, it wouldn't have meant anything to you, would it, eh?'

He lay there, unmoving. Very still. Silent as always.

'That man, the inspector.' She leaned closer. 'Did you recognise him? Just now, when he spoke to you and you opened your eyes, I thought you recognised him.'

No response.

'Because if you did, that means you're not as dumb as you'd like me to believe.'

Still no response.

'You loved your son, didn't you, eh?' She was gazing out of the window now, her mind drifting. 'He looked after you all those years, gave up everything for you, but you were too much for him and he had to put you in a hospital.' She prodded him again. 'It nearly broke his heart, did you know that? When I came along and seduced him into marrying me, he thought I was in love. He didn't know I was doing it for my own purpose.' She giggled softly. 'I'd seen the article about the young woman roaming the lanes. "The Seeker", that's what the newspapers called her.' Her smile froze. 'But I knew straightaway who she was. You can understand how I couldn't let her get to you before I did.'

She reached out and took hold of his hand. It was cold to the touch. 'I never wanted your son,' she said, bringing her sorry gaze back to the old man's face. 'It was you I wanted. I put up with his hands all over me and I lay there always uncomplaining while he satisfied himself, using me like a man might use a whore.' Her features stiffened. 'I hated it. I always hated it!'

Her voice breaking with emotion, she went on, 'I had to be near you. That's why I had you removed from that hospital, so I could keep you here, safe with me. I promised her, you see. You know why, don't you, eh? We both know why.'

There was a span of silence while she caressed his hand, her eyes drawn back to the skies outside, and her old heart aching to be free. A tear fell from her eyes, trickled down her face and fell on the back of his hand. She wiped it away. 'I loved you so much,' she whispered. 'I missed you . . . all those years, and you never came back. I learned to hate you, just like she did.'

With that she laid his hand beneath the covers and made him comfortable. She didn't speak again and quietly left the room.

Behind her, the old man opened his eyes and stared after her.

He was crying. Her words had struck deep.

As the inspector climbed into the car, he paused, looking back at the house, his brow furrowing in puzzlement. 'I wonder.' Tapping his fingers on the side of the car, he cast his mind back to a day many years before. The pictures were blurred. Time had eroded his memory.

Sergeant Coley put the car into gear and moved away. They drove along the lanes and out on to the open road, and still the inspector was silent, obviously deep in thought. Another few miles and Coley had to ask, 'Is everything all right, sir?'

'Hmm?'

'Sir?'

Jerking his head round, Inspector Lowe seemed irritated. 'What is it?'

'Is there something wrong?'

The older man replied hesitantly, still thinking, still trying to remember. 'I'm not sure.'

'About what?'

He jerked his thumb back towards the lanes. 'Just now, when you were questioning Ida Fellowes.'

'It didn't do us much good, did it, sir? I mean, she told us nothing we couldn't have worked out for ourselves.'

'No, it's not that.'

'What then?'

'I can't be sure but I've got a gut feeling I've seen that woman before. Something was niggling at me the last time we came here, but now I can't get it out of my mind.' He had to be sure, though. In this game there was no room for doubt. 'Years ago,' he said. 'A bad case, one that got away, if you like.'

'What do you mean?' Coley was curious. 'What kind of case?'

Inspector Lowe stared straight ahead, his thoughts back there, in that house. 'One of the unsolved,' he murmured. 'To this day, it still haunts me.' He turned then, informing the sergeant in hushed tones, 'It was one of the worst murder cases I've ever been involved in.'

CHAPTER TWELVE

'Two customers since opening. I'm not likely to get rich this way, am I?' May had her backside on a chair and her feet on another. There was a steaming mug of coffee in front of her and the radio on in the background. 'Hear that?' she said, turning up the volume. ' "Single currencies and federal Europe". I always thought it was just going to be a big open, friendly trading market. It's all changed now though.' She tutted, turning down the volume again. 'Honestly, I sometimes wonder if the politicians know what they're doing.'

'They're all the same.' Having finished stacking the towels on the shelves, Libby joined her. 'You pays your money and you takes your pick, isn't that what they say?'

May laughed. 'Are we talking about towels or politicians?'

Libby smiled, thinking what good company May was. 'Whatever fits,' she said, and fell into a chair, thankful to take the weight off her feet.

They drank their coffee, and the conversation drifted to men. 'I'm past all that now,' May sighed, 'but there was a time, oh, many years ago, when a certain man could have made an honest woman of me.' Her eyes clouded over and she lapsed into silence.

Libby was intrigued. 'I've never seen you look so serious.' In fact, just then May seemed almost like a stranger.

'It was a serious love affair. The nearest I've ever come to getting married.'

'You never told me that, May,' Libby said cautiously. 'Who was he?'

'Just a man.'

'Was he in love with you?'

'Oh, yes.'

'And did you love him?'

'Like I've never loved anyone before or since.'

'So why did you never marry?'

May sipped her coffee, seeming not to have heard.

Reluctant to press the point, Libby discreetly observed May's face, thinking how she had always thought of her like a sister. Now, suddenly, she hardly knew her at all. There was a cruel hardness in May's face that she didn't recognise.

Quiet now, Libby averted her eyes, sipping her coffee and wondering what could have happened to May all those years ago to make her so bitter.

After a while, May answered. 'Men are best left alone. They worm their way into a woman's heart until she's like putty in his hands, ready to do *anything* to keep him.' She smiled, a pitiful expression, betraying a deeper emotion. 'Life makes cowards of us all, don't you think, Libby?'

Libby didn't know what to think. 'It can be difficult,' she answered cagily. 'I mean, look at me. Dave assures me he isn't having an affair but I still don't know whether to believe him or not.'

'Follow him.'

Astounded, Libby retorted, 'I can't do that!'

'Why not?'

'Well, it's not right, is it? I mean, *following* him. It would be as if I didn't trust him.'

'You just said you don't.'

Exasperated, Libby shrugged. 'I didn't mean it like that. Not really.'

'What did you mean then?'

'Well, I'm not sure. I feel, oh, I don't know, left out, somehow. It's as though he's got something, or someone, on his mind.'

'Do you want to know if he's having an affair or not?'

Lost for words, Libby nodded.

'There you are then. Follow him, and you might find out.'

'But it seems such a sly thing to do to your own husband.'

'I told you, Libby. That's what men do to you. They make you do cruel things that go against your nature.' She had an odd, faraway look in her eyes.

Unsure of herself, and feeling unusually nervous, Libby stood up. 'Dave assured me he wasn't having an affair, and I have to trust him. If I can't do that, our marriage counts for nothing.'

'You're too naive, Libby.'

'I won't follow him, and that's that.'

'Because you're afraid of what you'll find out?'

'Maybe. Maybe not.'

The phone rang. May was the nearest, so she snatched up the receiver. 'Draper's shop.'

While she listened she looked at Libby, beckoning with her finger as she spoke. 'Yes, she is. Just a minute.' Holding out the receiver, she told Libby, 'It's Jack Arnold. He wants a word with you.'

'Hello, Jack.' Turning her back on May, Libby bent her head to the phone. 'Is anything the matter?' She suspected he wouldn't be ringing her unless it was something to do with their illicit meeting the other day.

While Jack explained his reason for calling, Libby's whole body seemed to sag. 'Are you sure? Couldn't he just be out with a client? Or maybe he's got a viewing some miles away.' Dropping herself into the chair, she glanced up. May saw at once that the colour had drained from her face.

'All right, Jack. Thanks for letting me know. You will ring if he comes back to the office, won't you?' She listened again, her eyes appealing to May as she told him, 'Don't be silly, Jack. No, honestly, I'm grateful. Besides, you're only doing what we both agreed.' Slowly, she returned the receiver to its cradle.

May was quickly at her side. 'What's wrong?'

Getting out of the chair, Libby walked about, her arms up and her hands behind her neck while she mentally ran over what Jack had told her. 'He says Dave wasn't there when he got to the office this morning. Apparently there was a note on his desk to say Dave would be out for the day, and could Jack either take over his appointments or, if he was too busy for that, would he phone the clients and make new appointments.'

May stood by the towel rack. 'Where's he gone?'

'According to Jack, he didn't say, but soon after he got the note, Jack thought he might have gone out on a new viewing. He looked through the secretary's notes and he listened to the answerphone. He even rummaged through Dave's desk, but there was nothing to suggest that Dave had gone to meet a client.'

Stopping in her tracks, she swung round, telling May in a sombre voice, 'Jack contacted all the clients in Dave's appointment book and, according to them, Dave had given no indication that he might not be able to make the meetings. As far as they were concerned, he would be turning up today, as arranged.' She racked her brains for an answer. 'It seems he just took off on a whim.' She daren't think of the alternative.

May did though, and it was in her eyes when she remarked meaningfully, 'If you ask me, it's all very strange.'

'You're sure he's having an affair, aren't you?'

'It doesn't matter what I think, Libby,' May answered diplomatically. 'It's what *you* think that counts.'

Libby's face fell. 'Honestly, May, I don't know what he could be up to.' Ashamed and unhappy, she looked away. 'There is *something* going on, though, I'm sure of it now.' She bowed her head and seemed close to tears.

Moving closer, May urged kindly, 'There's something else, isn't there?'

Composing herself, Libby revealed calmly, 'These past weeks he hasn't been sleeping too well. Remember? I told you.'

May nodded.

Libby went on, 'He had a bad night last night. I heard him downstairs moving about for, oh, hours, it was. I didn't go down because I don't know what to say to him any more.' She smiled sadly. 'I've said it all before. I ask him if there's anything on his mind and he says it's business, and that's as far as we get. It's been that way for some time. It gets better, then it gets worse. I don't know where I am any more.'

'Go on.'

'It was almost three o'clock when he finally came to bed. I asked him if he was all right and he said he was, that I should go to sleep, and he was sorry if he'd woken me. We talked for a while, about everything and nothing. In the end I must have fallen asleep. When I woke up, I could hear the kids downstairs, and Dave was not in bed. I went down and they were all in the kitchen. Dave was cooking breakfast.'

'And?' May knew that wasn't all.

'He'd had hardly any sleep and there he was, up with the larks and getting the kids their breakfast. He was full of himself. Then, at half past seven, he got ready to leave. I told him it was still early, and he said how he had a lot of paperwork to get through before he started his appointments.' She paused, going back over the morning's events in her mind. 'He doesn't normally leave home until about eight thirty, sometimes eight o'clock if he has urgent appointments.'

'And you accepted that?'

'Well, yes. I know how busy he's been lately, and I was beginning to think it really was work that was playing on his mind. When he left as early as that this morning, I didn't really give it a second thought.' She gave a wry little smile. 'Until now.'

'So now you suspect it was something other than work.' May went through it with her. 'Last night he had something on his mind, so urgent that he couldn't sleep. And this morning he couldn't wait to get out of the house. He went to the office, left a note, with no explanation, and now he's gone off, nobody knows where. So . . .'

Angry now, Libby finished the sentence for her. 'So where the hell is he? More to the point, who is he with? And what could be so important that he would neglect his work for it?' Her heart sank. 'I'm beginning to think you're right, May. It *has* to be a woman.'

'You'll have to ask him,' May said. 'He'll tell you unless he's got something to hide.'

Libby shook her head. 'I have asked him, time and again, and he keeps shutting me out. Something tells me it isn't another woman, but I can't be sure, that's the awful thing, and if he doesn't want to confide in me, there's no trust. And if there's no trust, there's no point in going on.' She never dreamed she would be saying it, and it hurt like hell, but Dave had left her little choice.

'You really do love him, don't you?' May had not realised just how devoted Libby was to him.

'I've always loved him, and I can't imagine a life without him, but I've been through this before with him,' she said regretfully, 'and I don't mean to go through it again. I *will* ask him, just once more. I hope, for the sake of the kids and our marriage, that he'll be honest with me. Because, however much I love him, if I go this time, I go for good.'

★ ★ ★

Dave had been driving for almost three hours when he spotted his petrol was running low. About another hour before he ran out altogether, he calculated. That was the last thing he needed. As he came out of Swindon, he kept one eye on the road and the other looking for a garage along the way.

Six miles or so on, he saw a Little Chef sign high up on the hill. 'Hopefully, there'll be a garage there. I ought to look at the map too. I need to be sure I'm heading in the right direction.'

He sighed with relief as he neared the Little Chef and saw there was a garage alongside. Thankfully, he pulled in. Climbing out of the car, he glanced at his watch. 'Jesus! It's almost midday.' His stomach rumbled with hunger, and his mouth felt dry as sandpaper. 'I'd die for a cuppa,' he groaned, 'but I have to get on. I don't want to be late home, or Libby will be getting all the wrong ideas.'

He filled the tank and checked the water. That done, he went to pay. At the counter a middle-aged man with a kindly face tapped the computer. 'Thirty-two pounds, if you please.'

After passing over the notes, Dave asked, 'How far to the West Bay?'

'An hour if you're on a good run,' came the reply. 'Sometimes it takes me twice that if the traffic's heavy.'

'You live there, do you?'

'Born there, and raised three children the same. No lovelier place, as far as I'm concerned, and I've travelled most of the world. I was in the Royal Navy, d'you see? But West Bay is home and always will be.' He was a man with few regrets. 'Three generations of my family lived in the house I'm in now,' he explained. 'God willing, when I leave there, it'll be feet first in a box.'

Outside, Dave checked the map. 'Say it takes me an hour and a half by the time I've found the nursing home. Maybe an hour there, and then back on the road . . .' He totted up the time it would take before he was back home with Libby. 'With a bit of luck and a following wind I should be home before six, and nobody any the wiser.' He knew he'd have to tell Libby what he was up to some time, but not yet. Not until he'd got to the bottom of it all.

Turning the car round, he looked up at the sign depicting a steaming cup of coffee and a hearty breakfast. 'I'm hungry enough to eat the bloody sign!' he groaned. 'Oh, to hell with it, I can spare twenty minutes for a cuppa, if nothing else.'

Luckily the cafe was nearly empty. He ordered tea and a bacon roll, and was satisfied that would hold him until evening.

Half an hour later he was on his way again. The traffic was thinner now, so the half-hour stop had been fully worthwhile. All the same, he speeded along the dual carriageway, the speedometer pointing above the limit. 'Hope there aren't any traffic cops on my tail.' He glanced in the mirror. There weren't, so he quickly used up the empty carriageway.

Just outside West Bay a lorry had overturned, spewing its entire cargo of wooden pallets and causing the following traffic to jam up for some five miles.

'This is all I need!' Dave looked at the map. There was no other way in. He had no choice but to sit and inch his way along with the others. Turning on the radio, he monitored the intermittent reports on the traffic news.

Precious time passed. He checked his watch. 'Ten past two. Come on! Come on!' Other drivers, frustrated, were turning round, making dangerous manoeuvres to get out of the hold-up. 'Silly buggers,' Dave grumbled. 'But at least they have a choice. Not me, though. I need to get through. I've come all this way and I'm not turning back without doing what I came here to do.'

Another half-hour passed before slowly but surely the traffic began to move on. As he passed the scene of the accident, Dave was appalled at the damage. It looked as if the whole load had shifted sideways and taken the lorry with it; the tail end of it had smashed into the side of a van, which was now being loaded on to a breakdown vehicle. Most of the pallets were matchwood on the road, with the remainder piled across the pavement. The lorry was still belly up, but cordoned off until it could be righted and taken away.

To Dave's dismay, it was almost three o'clock by the time he located Fairleigh Nursing Home.

Taking out the slip of paper given to him by Rosemary Dwight's old neighbour, he checked the name and address written there. 'Yes,' he popped the paper back in his pocket, 'this is the place all right.' A large, modern building, surrounded by beautiful old oak trees and with a great expanse of lawn either side, Fairleigh Nursing Home was a pleasant-looking place.

Not without some trepidation, Dave rang the bell. He felt like an intruder, afraid he might be caught and turned away.

After a few moments, a rather large and puffy-faced woman opened the door. She just stood there, not saying anything, obviously expecting Dave to explain himself, which he did, with the utmost charm.

'Rosemary Dwight,' she repeated, looking him over with her little eyes and thinking what a catch he must be for some woman. 'Are you a relative?'

'Not exactly, but I was given this address by Mrs Goodson, an old neighbour of hers from Ampthill. I need to talk to Rosemary, and she said I would be welcome. She also said to send her love.'

'So you're a friend.'

'Yes.' He hated lying but felt it was excusable in this instance.

'You'd better come in then.'

As they made their way to the conservatory, the woman

made up for her previous silence. Chatting all the way, she told him, 'It's such a pity Mrs Goodson can't come any more. Rosemary does miss her. But then of course Mrs Goodson must be in her late eighties now. She's some three or four years older than Rosemary, I believe. Anyway, she used to visit regularly – her son brought her, you know, had this wonderful old car. Still, I'm sure Rosemary will be glad to have news of her old friend.'

As they neared the conservatory, she confided softly, 'Of course Rosemary had that bad stroke last year, but I'm sure you already know that. Only she can't seem to concentrate as well as she could, and sometimes her mind wanders. No staying power, if you know what I mean.' She smiled winsomely. 'Try not to tire her.'

'Of course.' He was a little apprehensive, hoping against hope that Rosemary Dwight would be able to throw some light on what happened on the night of the accident. She would need to tap into her memory and then convey the information to him, and from what this woman was saying, that might be asking too much.

With his heart in his boots, Dave followed the fat woman into the conservatory.

Two people were in there, a strange, sombre-faced man of middle years, who was hunched in a chair with his legs tucked beneath him. He brought his gaze to Dave as he walked in and from then on watched him like a hawk.

In the far corner, seated on a high-backed chair, sat an old woman, a small, pretty thing with silver, wavy hair and legs so short her feet barely touched the ground. Dave thought she looked like one of Daisy's dolls.

As they approached, she looked up, surprising Dave with her startling blue eyes. 'Hello,' she squeaked, sounding comically like a polly parrot. 'Who are you?'

The fat woman sat down beside her. 'This is a friend of Mrs Goodson. You remember Mrs Goodson, don't you, dear?'

Rosemary was still observing Dave. 'Who are you?' she insisted, as though having forgotten she'd already asked that.

'I'm Dave Walters,' he answered. 'I've come a long way to see you, Rosemary.'

She smiled, a soft and very pretty smile that made Dave feel humble. 'Come a long way . . . come a long way.' She sang-song it several times before the fat lady stopped her.

'Mr Walters wants to talk to you, Rosemary. Be a good girl and I'll fetch you a glass of milk.' Turning to Dave she asked, 'Tea or coffee?'

'Coffee, please. Black and strong. Two sugars.'

Dave waited until the fat woman had gone out of earshot before he spoke to Rosemary. 'I went to the house in Ampthill where you used to live,' he told her. 'I began to think I would never track you down, but Mrs Goodson kindly told me where I might find you.' He didn't go into the detail of how he had had to work very hard to convince that good woman he meant Rosemary no harm.

The blue eyes stared at him. 'Mrs Goodson,' she murmured. 'My friend.' The eyes filled with tears. 'Oh dear, I've lost her.'

'No.' Dave was at odds with himself. He needed to talk about the accident, to find out what Rosemary saw that night, and here the poor thing was, visibly distressed about her friend not coming to see her any more. 'You haven't lost her,' he said. 'She hasn't been able to come and visit because she had a bad fall, but I'm sure she'll find a way to visit you when summer comes.'

'What did you say?' The eyes were vague. So pretty.

'I need to ask you about something that happened a long time ago.' He spoke slowly, letting each word sink in. 'When you lived in Ampthill. You were out walking your dog. There was an accident and someone was killed.'

A light dawned. 'The young woman, so lovely.' Raising her hands, she brushed them down her hair and over her shoulders. 'Long hair. Oh, she did have such long, thick hair.'

'What colour was it, Rosemary?' In his mind's eye he saw the young woman in the rain, in the woods, in his heart and soul.

'Mrs Goodson doesn't visit any more.'

'Rosemary.' Taking her hand in his, he gently urged, 'The young woman who was killed. You saw her, didn't you? She was lovely, that's what you said, and she had long, thick hair. Tell me what else you remember, Rosemary. What colour was her hair?'

'I touched her hair.'

'What colour was it?' He felt he was so close. He wanted her to describe the dead young woman in every small detail. Her hair. Her clothes. Even the smell of her, for whenever she appeared to him, the fragrance of fresh roses came like a cloud to fog his brain. 'You must tell me,' he pleaded. 'Please, Rosemary, tell me what you remember.'

The desperation in his voice seemed to jolt her. She turned to stare at him, and there was such fear in her face that he thought for one awful minute she was about to scream. 'Ssh,' he whispered. 'It's all right. Take your time. It's all right.'

Suddenly her mood changed. Holding out her hands, she rubbed thumbs and fingers together, a look of disgust on her face. 'Wet.' She closed her eyes, the fingers madly working together. 'Sticky.'

'I understand, Rosemary.' Though he didn't understand at all. 'Tell me everything.'

'Blood!' Wide-eyed, she put out her arms and gestured all round the room. 'Everywhere.'

'What was she like?' He felt excited. She was remembering. Thank God, she was remembering!

Rosemary didn't heed his question. Instead she frantically hugged herself, her face suffused with horror. 'Blood everywhere!' She began screaming, pointing at the wall as if she was talking to someone there. 'Go away. Don't you touch her!'

'Rosemary?'

'I told him. I *did*!'

'Who, Rosemary? Who did you tell?'

She was sobbing loudly now. 'The man!' She was frantic. 'I don't know if he heard.' Appealing to Dave, she pleaded, 'Did he hear? Did I do it right?'

'Tell me what you said, and I'll be able to decide if you did it right.'

Suspicious now, she hunched her shoulders and stared round the room. In a voice that shook him rigid, she rasped harshly, 'Go away. Leave her alone!'

'Listen to me, Rosemary.' He felt out of his depth. 'I promise you, no one is going to be hurt.'

His assurances seemed to comfort her. With round, wet eyes, she whispered, 'I held her. In my arms.' Cradling her arms together, she rocked them back and forth. 'She told me a secret. I never told the others. Only him. "Tell him," she said, and then she closed her eyes.' She began whimpering. 'Blood everywhere.'

Dave persevered. 'What was the secret, Rosemary?'

'Can't tell.'

'Why can't you tell?'

'The other one!' Fearfully glancing about the room, she held on to his coat lapels. 'Watching me.'

He was taken aback by the things Rosemary was saying. He wondered how much of it was real and how much the product of an over-fertile imagination. 'The young woman who died. The one you said you held. What did she say to you?'

'Black hair. She had black hair, like midnight.'

He sat bolt upright. 'What did she say, Rosemary?'

'The other one . . . watching.' She began wailing, like a soul in torment. 'Don't let her hurt me.' She was looking beyond him now, at someone else. 'I don't want her to hurt me!'

When Dave turned, it was to see the fat lady, red with anger. 'Whatever have you been saying to her?' She rushed in and put down the tray. 'What is it, Rosemary dear?' she purred, hugging the old woman and scowling at Dave as if he was some kind of monster. 'You'd better go,' she snapped. 'Now!'

Apologising but desperately sorry he had learned only half-truths, Dave found his way through the rooms and out into the cold, biting air. He leaned against the wall, fists clenched. 'I almost had it!' he groaned, banging his fist against the wall. 'Another minute and I know she would have told me.'

A thin, unpleasant voice broke his chain of thought. 'I haven't got a watch.'

Dave looked round and there stood the sombre-faced man who had been in the room when he was talking to Rosemary. 'What did you say?'

'If you give me your watch, I'll tell you something.'

'What can you tell me?'

'The watch first.'

'No.'

'Then I won't tell about the dead woman. I know, 'cause Rosemary told me.' He grinned and there wasn't a straight tooth in his head. 'When I first came here, she used to sit with me in the kitchen. She told me everything. She's forgotten now, though. She's too old.'

Dave ripped off his watch and held it out. 'What did she tell you?' When the other man made a grab for the watch, he snatched it back. 'Tell me first, then you can have it.' He suspected this strange fellow might be lying but he had nowhere else to turn.

'The woman's hair was black, her eyes too. Rosemary said she cried for her because she was too beautiful to die like that.'

'All of it. Tell me everything or the deal's off.'

'Rosemary cuddled her, and the woman told her things.' He looked down to the ground, as if afraid to go on.

'What things?' Grabbing him by the shoulders, Dave held him there. 'The watch is yours if you tell me the truth. I'll know if you're lying,' he bluffed. 'One lie, that's all, and I'm taking the watch with me.'

With a lopsided grin on his face, the fellow put his hand over the watch, laying claim. 'She asked about the man. When Rosemary told her he was badly hurt but wasn't dead, she said, "Tell him I'll come back for him. *Tell him I will never leave him.*" '

'God Almighty!' An icy chill ran down his back.

The other man tugged at the watch. 'That's what she said and now I want my watch.'

'Who was the other one . . . the one who "watched"?'

'Don't know.'

'Why is Rosemary so afraid?'

'She never told me that.'

'Remember what I said? One lie and I take the watch with me.'

'Lenny!' The fat woman raced out of the building and caught him by the scruff of the neck. 'What are you doing here, you bad boy?' After ordering Dave off, she marched Lenny to the front door.

Dave got into his car and was about to pull away when she tapped on the window. 'I believe this is yours,' she said, showing him the watch.

Thinking he had made a reasonable swap, Dave shook his head. 'I don't think so. Who said it was mine?'

'Lenny did.' Thrusting the watch through the open window, she snapped, 'He may be a bit soft in the head but he's not a liar. You can always rely on Lenny to tell the absolute truth, even if it gets him into hot water.'

'That's very commendable.' Relief ebbed through him.

'Not really. He just isn't cunning enough to lie, that's

all.' With that she departed, while Lenny waited sullenly in the doorway, his eyes fixed on Dave, whom he believed had cheated him.

As the fat woman retreated, Dave opened the window wide and showed Lenny the watch. With Lenny's eyes following his every move, he drove towards the shrubbery where he raised the watch once more, before dropping it where it wasn't easily seen. Lenny saw, and his bright, crooked smile was something Dave would never forget.

Giving a short wave, he turned out of the drive and headed home. He thought about Libby. After a while he'd phone her, but for now he needed time to think.

And what he thought about was 'the other one'. The one Rosemary had been so afraid of.

Libby had been to the window umpteen times. It was now seven o'clock and there was still no sign of him.

For the second time that evening, she called Jack at his home. 'Are you absolutely certain he didn't leave word with someone?' she asked. 'Did you check with the secretary? Was there anything on his desk that might have showed where he was going?'

Jack was anxious too. 'You know I did all that,' he reminded her. 'We have to face it, Libby. Wherever Dave has gone, he didn't want anyone to know, but I'm convinced it's not a woman. Dave worships the ground you walk on, and I don't care what happened in the past, I just know he isn't fooling around now.'

'Then where is he? And why hasn't he called?'

'Well, we know he left his mobile on his desk, so that tells us two things. First, he was in such a hurry and so preoccupied that he didn't have his mind on what he was doing. And secondly, he can't call from his car.'

'He can call from a phone box though, can't he? That's if he really wants to.' Her blood was beginning to boil. 'I'll tell you this, Jack, he'd better have a good explanation or there'll be sparks flying when he gets back, I can promise you.'

'Give him a chance to explain, Libby.'

'I'll think about it!'

In a mood as dark as the night outside, Libby made the children clear up their toys. 'Upstairs to bed,' she ordered, needing to be on her own.

They moaned and groaned about how it wasn't eight o'clock yet and anyway they wanted to wait up for Daddy. 'You'll do as you're told,' she snapped. 'Wash and bed. Now!'

When Jamie started crying and Daisy looked as though the world was about to end, she relented. 'All right. Wash and get into your nightclothes, then you can come back down for half an hour. After that it's upstairs and into bed, and no arguments.' It was wrong of her to send them packing early just because she was angry, she reasoned.

While the children ran upstairs, she went once more to the window where she looked out on a cold, wild night. 'Where the hell are you, Dave?' she muttered.

Through her anger there spiralled a worm of anxiety. He had been so moody of late. Preoccupied and secretive. What else was she supposed to think other than that he was seeing another woman? And yet, like Jack, she didn't think so. But if it wasn't another woman, what was wrong with him? Where was he? And why wouldn't he confide in her?

She rang May. 'I just don't know what to think,' she said. 'Maybe I should call the police. Maybe he's hurt somewhere.'

May calmed her down. 'He's stayed out late on business before, hasn't he?'

'Well, yes, but this is different.'

'Why? I mean, does he always tell Jack where he's going? And when he's out until this time, does he usually call you?'

'Not always,' Libby had to admit, 'but if he knows he'll be late, he usually tells me before he goes out in the morning.'

'Maybe he forgot. Or maybe he didn't think he'd be late.'

'That's not good enough, May. What about the message he left for Jack? He *knew* he'd be out all day. So why didn't he tell me?'

'Think about it, Libby. Why should he? He probably thought he'd be back at his usual time, that's why.'

'You still think he's seeing another woman, don't you?'

'I shouldn't have worried you like that, Libby, and I'm sorry. Maybe I jumped to the wrong conclusion but, like I said, if you're still worried, the only way is to ask him when he gets in. Right now you should make yourself a cuppa, play with the kids for a while and wind down. Sounds to me like you've got yourself into a right state, my girl.'

'If he is seeing another woman, he'll swing for it, the bastard!'

'Look, I can come round if you like.'

'What? You think I'm in a mood to commit murder, do you?'

'Are you?'

'At this minute, yes.' She laughed. 'Don't worry. When he walks through that door, I'll be calm and collected.'

'Good.'

'But he'd better have a damned good tale to tell.'

That very thought was in Dave's mind as he came along the lanes. 'I'd better be prepared for fireworks,' he mused grimly. The clock on the dashboard said twenty minutes past eight. 'I've been home later than this,' he muttered, 'but I never told her, that's the trouble.' He cursed himself for not trying harder to find a phone box. 'If only I hadn't left my mobile behind. There's never a bloody phone box in sight when you want one.' But then he had travelled on the motorway whenever possible, and it would have wasted too much time to stop at the services on the way back.

With his heart in his mouth, he parked the car and went into the house. His mind was still alive with what Rosemary Dwight had said. He had given it a great deal of thought on the way back and was very close to telling Libby everything. But even now he held back, particularly since his visit today, because he honestly believed it would be too dangerous for her to know.

Libby was in the kitchen. Just as she had promised May, she remained calm and collected in spite of feeling the urge to bounce all the pots and pans off the walls. 'No lies,' she said, looking up from her place at the table. 'And no excuses. I want to know exactly where you've been and who you've been with.' She paused, regarding him with such a hard expression he knew it was make or break time. 'Or I swear to God, Dave, I'll have my case packed and be out of here with the kids before you've even taken your coat off.'

He had a choice. Either he risked losing his family for a second time or he came clean and told her everything. Neither was what he wanted. 'It's not what you think.'

'Then it's up to you to put me right.'

'Don't put me on the spot like this, Libby. Please. There is no other woman.'

'What then?' Seeing how worried he was, she began to soften. 'Are you in some kind of trouble?'

'You could say that, yes. But it's not the kind of trouble I've ever faced before. It's something I need to sort out for myself.' His mouth felt dry and uncomfortable. Licking his lips, he sat down, holding her gaze with serious eyes. 'I'm asking you to trust me, Libby. Later, maybe, I can tell you about it. But not now.'

'Why not now?' Anger simmered beneath her calm

exterior. 'Aren't we supposed to confide in each other? Didn't we promise we'd never have secrets from each other ever again?'

Dave walked across the room, where he stood with his back to the sink and his eyes on Libby. 'Yes, you're right,' he conceded. 'I want to tell you but it might be dangerous. Besides, I'm not all that sure you'll believe me.'

Libby settled back in her chair. 'Try me.'

'Where are the kids?' What he had to say was not for their ears.

'In bed. They fell asleep waiting for you.'

Without another word, he went out of the house and collected the folder of papers from his car. Returning to the kitchen, he threw it down on the table. 'Read that.'

While she read the cuttings, he took off his coat and hung it over the back of a chair. Then he went into the lounge and poured himself a good measure of whisky. He was hunched on the sofa, deep in thought, when she came in, her face white and puzzled. 'This stuff doesn't make sense,' she said, sitting down beside him. 'It's all about a *ghost* – haunting and suchlike.'

'And you don't believe in things like that, do you, Libby?'

'No, I don't.' She stared into the fire, her mind in a whirl. 'What's all this got to do with us, anyway?'

'Look at me, Libby.' When she did as he asked, he spoke to her softly, deliberately. 'You saw her. That day in the woods, you saw her too, didn't you?'

She knew what he meant and didn't dare admit it. 'That was just a woman who'd lost her way.'

'No, sweetheart. That was the same woman who sat in the car with Daisy. She spoke to Daisy and I didn't even know she was there. It's the same woman I saw that day we were driving back from the restaurant, and it's the same woman as the one in Daisy's drawing. Remember how Daisy took that drawing with her to the restaurant when we went to fetch your scarf? She followed the kitten to the old man's bedroom and she said he was very upset when she showed him the painting.'

'We only have Daisy's word for that.'

'But you didn't think she was lying, did you?'

'I can't remember what she said exactly.' In truth, she remembered every word.

'When she showed the old man the painting, he was "upset". That's what Daisy said. She also said how Mrs Fellowes came in and ran her out.'

'I remember.' She had never forgotten.

'There's something very weird going on and whether we like it or not, we're caught up in it. You have to believe me. The evidence is there, in those documents. That woman was killed in an accident on the very lane where I first saw her. Her husband was badly injured but he survived. From that day on, he was like a cabbage, unable to communicate.' Falling to his knees, Dave grabbed Libby by the arms and shook her. 'It's the old man, Libby. The old man!'

'I don't know what you mean.' Against all her instincts, she was being made to see what he could see, and it terrified her.

'The reports say the woman was in her early thirties when she was killed in that accident. I've worked it out. The old man could well be her husband.'

'But you don't know that, do you?'

He struggled for the right words. 'I don't know for certain,' he admitted, 'but I honestly believe that old man Fellowes is the same man who was badly injured in that accident all those years ago. He survived but his young wife was killed.'

'What are you saying?' She couldn't believe she was even discussing it.

'I believe she's searching for him.'

'Why on earth should you think such a thing?'

'I went to visit an old woman called Rosemary Dwight today. She was there when the accident happened and the dying woman told her that she would never leave her husband.' Dave emphasised every word. 'Before she died in Rosemary's arms, the woman begged Rosemary to tell her injured husband that she would come back for him.'

Libby made no sound. She sat very still, visibly shaking.

'Don't you see, sweetheart? That's why she haunts the lane. She's searching for him. She can't rest until she finds him.'

Pushing him away, Libby laughed nervously. 'If that's true, why was she in the woods? Why did she get in the car with Daisy? Assuming she really did and it wasn't Daisy's vivid imagination.'

'You might well ask. And you might well ask why she's chosen to haunt me in particular. Because that's what she's doing, Libby. That's why I've been almost out of my mind. She appears out of nowhere. She talks to me. She wants me to help her, she's *pleaded* with me to help her, and she's said other things too – "The lane. The old man." She told me if I looked there, I would find the answer.'

'That's enough, Dave.'

'I didn't want you involved but you asked and now I'm telling you. It all begins to add up. Everything leads back to that night – that restaurant and the Fellowes.' Grabbing the papers, he shuffled through them until he found one right at the bottom of the pile. 'Look there, Libby.' Handing her the page, he watched her face drain of colour.

'My God!' Her eyes wide with disbelief, she looked up. 'It's uncanny!'

'Now do you see? That's a photograph of her husband when he was a young man.' Going to the mantelpiece he took down a photograph of himself and Libby and placed it alongside the cutting. 'We could be brothers,' he said. 'I believe that's why she chose me. Because she saw *him* in me. She trusts me and, for whatever reason, she believes I can bring him to her.'

'Dave, stop and think what you're saying.' She was very

frightened. He seemed so convinced. She had never believed in the supernatural, and yet deep inside her there lurked a whisper of belief in what he was saying. Suddenly she understood why he had been so distant lately. Something like this could drive a person crazy.

'I wish I hadn't told you.' He was regretting it already, although at the same time he felt a tremendous sense of relief. 'I don't want you to worry.'

'How can I not worry?'

'At least you know what's been on my mind.'

She smiled. 'I was right though.'

'In what way?'

'It *was* another woman, though not of the usual kind.' Reaching up, she wound her arms round his neck. 'You've frightened me. I want you to leave it be now.'

The clock on the mantelpiece chimed the tenth hour. 'I'm ready for my bed,' he murmured in her ear. 'What about you?'

'Didn't you hear what I said?' Leaning back in his arms, she looked seriously into his eyes. 'I want you to leave it be. Please!'

Dave was thankful that the phone rang just then. He hurried to answer it. After a few moments' conversation he was back beside Libby. 'Jack says he thought I'd emigrated.'

'He wasn't the only one. Don't you ever do that to me again.'

'I won't.'

The phone rang again. This time it was Barclay, the man who had threatened to take his valuable properties out of the agency's hands. Libby listened to Dave's side of the conversation. 'Of course you can rely on me, Mr Barclay. Nine thirty in the morning, yes. That's fine. Yes, I'll be there.' With an angry flick of the wrist, Dave dropped the receiver into its cradle. 'Damn!'

'What's wrong?'

'It's just that I planned to go and see Ida Fellowes in the

morning, and now I've been pinned down by this fellow Barclay. I can't not go, because it took me long enough to court him back after I missed our last appointment. Now there are other properties involved, and a handsome profit to be made if I can swing a good deal.' He grimaced. 'There's also the reputation of the agency at stake. Barclay is an influential man. We don't want any more skirmishes with him, not now we've got a chance to redeem ourselves. It shouldn't take me above a couple of hours though. I'll go and see Ida Fellowes after that.'

'I don't want you to go anywhere near that awful place.' Libby caught his gaze and held it. 'Promise me, Dave. Promise me you won't go.'

Before he could answer, the phone rang yet again. 'Popular tonight, aren't we?' Once more, he was deeply grateful for the timely intervention. 'Hello? Yes, she's right here.' He called Libby to the phone. 'It's the dreaded May,' he said with a disarming smile. 'I suspect she's checking up on me.'

While Libby was talking, he slipped off to bed.

When she came into the room, he pretended to be asleep. *She had asked for a promise he could not give.*

When Libby woke in the morning, he was gone. A note was propped against the kettle; he knew this was the first place she'd make for.

> Don't worry, sweetheart, I haven't gone missing again. It's just that I have a lot of paperwork to get ready before I team up with Barclay. Meet me in the pub at one and I'll treat you to lunch.
>
> See you then.
>
> P.S. Bet you look gorgeous!

There was no mention of Ida Fellowes or whether he'd do

as she asked and keep away from that bloody awful place. 'The cunning bugger! He knew I'd raise the issue again this morning, so he got out from under while the going was good.'

In the cold light of day, the conversation last night seemed unreal. But the apprehension she felt was very real.

Later, after dropping the children off at school, she relayed the entire conversation to May, who was not in the least taken aback. 'It doesn't sound as if he could have made it all up,' she said. 'Men aren't all that inventive.'

'You mean you actually believe it?' May never ceased to amaze her.

'Don't you?'

'I'm afraid to.'

'Sounds to me like you already do.' Astute as ever, May went on, 'If you didn't believe it, you'd have no cause to be afraid.'

The idea had been swimming in Libby's mind all morning. Now she made up her mind. 'I'm going there.'

'Going where?'

'To see Ida Fellowes.'

'Is that sensible?'

'Maybe not, but she seems to be involved and if I can prove to Dave that he's wrong, it will be worthwhile.'

'I'll shut up shop and come with you.'

'No need for that. I can handle Ida Fellowes.'

'Dave won't like you going out there.'

'He won't know.' Giving May a meaningful look she added, 'Unless, of course, somebody tells him.'

'I hope you don't mean me.' May opened her eyes wide with indignation. ' "Safe as houses", that's what they used to call me at school because I never broke a confidence.'

'All right then, "Safe as houses", can I have an hour or so off?' She studied the wall clock. 'It's quarter past ten now. If I leave straightaway, I should be back by one. Did I tell you, I've been invited out to lunch by a handsome man?'

'No, but I can always take your place if you're not back in time.'

'I wouldn't miss this date for anything,' Libby said with a grin, 'especially if I can put his mind at rest over this other business.'

'Off you go then, and remember, I'll dock the time from your wages.'

'You wouldn't!'

'Make it up then.'

'I will.'

CHAPTER THIRTEEN

Barclay was a big man in business circles. He was also a well-respected magistrate and refereed the youth football team. He was a clever entrepreneur; there was little he had not dabbled in. His pet love was buying tired houses, modernising them and selling them on at a profit. His latest acquisition was an old disused water mill near Stoke Hammond. Attached to a rundown cottage and surrounded by two acres of land, he had picked it up for a song only twelve months ago. His plan was to renovate and make a profit as usual, but something else had taken precedence, on both his capital and his time.

'I've decided to move abroad,' he explained as he and Dave strolled the area. 'I invested in a property development outside Marbella and it's exceeded my wildest dreams.' Pleased with himself, he puffed out his chest. 'I've always been fairly well off but now it seems I'm a very rich man. I can afford to take things easier. At my time of life – I'm sixty-four next year, you know – I ought to slow down. My wife is always urging me to spend more time with her and the grandkids. Well, now I think it's time to put a smile on her face and do as she asks.'

'I don't blame you.' Dave looked forward to the time when he might be in the same position.

'Now then, Walters,' Barclay paused in his stride, 'I have a proposition to put to you.' Leaning back on the gate, he looked for all the world like a barrow boy, with his mop of curly grey hair and weather-beaten face. 'I reckon I'm worth a couple of million, in property alone.'

Dave gave a soft whistle. 'I'm impressed.' What he really felt was frustrated and impatient. He needed to get away. He had to see Ida Fellowes. The questions he meant to ask her whirled round his brain until he could think of little else.

'Impressed, eh?' To Barclay's mind, Dave had said the right thing. With him, flattery went a long way. 'And so you should be,' he said, smirking. 'And so you should be. I'd like you to handle the sale of all my UK property.'

'All of it?' Dave's impatience vanished. Barclay now had his full attention.

'That's right, all of it.'

Dave was thrilled, mentally calculating that if he was to achieve such substantial sales, he could settle all his debts, expand his business and still have a healthy bank balance. It was the chance of a lifetime. 'You can rest assured the agency will get the best prices for your property. On top of that, we'll charge a lower commission, but not so low it doesn't make it worthwhile for me. I have to earn a living too, as I'm sure you appreciate.'

Barclay nodded. 'We're both men of the world,' he said. 'I'm not out to fleece you, as I'm sure you're not out to fleece me.'

Dave held out his hand. 'I'll shake on that.'

Compared to Barclay, Dave was slim and lithe, weighing some twelve pounds less. Even so, it was Barclay who found his hand being so strongly shaken that he flexed his fingers afterwards. 'I reckon we understand each other,' he said.

'Right.' Dave began leading the way back. 'We've a great deal to work out, so we'll need to meet up again.' They were standing on top of a hill, with the heightening wind lifting the collars of their coats and a spattering of rain pecking at their faces. Though the sun was shining, it had no warmth and, having come out without his overcoat, Dave felt chilled to the bone. 'We need to meet somewhere more comfortable, where we can get down to business and talk through the details.'

The older man's face crinkled into a leathery grin. 'Over a drink, you mean?'

'Why not?'

'I know just the place.' Taking Dave by the elbow, Barclay propelled him over the stony ground and on towards the cars. 'There's a lovely old inn not far from here,' he said. 'I spotted it on the way.' His smile widened. 'I bet they've even got a log fire.' Dave was persuaded to go along with the idea. This was the biggest deal of his life, the one he and Libby had hoped for.

Libby knocked on the door, and waited.

No answer.

She knocked again.

The silence was eerie.

'Hello?' She lifted the letterbox and called through, 'Mrs Fellowes? It's Daisy's mother. I need to talk to you. I won't take up much of your time.' She thought she heard a noise. 'Hello?'

Nothing.

Dropping the letter flap, she wondered what to do next. 'The old bat is either deaf as a doorpost or deliberately ignoring me.' This looked like being a wasted trip but she couldn't just leave, not after coming all this way, and especially when she suspected Ida Fellowes was inside, probably spying through a window at her right now.

Lifting the flap once more, she called out, 'I know you're in there! I have no intention of leaving until you've seen me. I'm not here to cause trouble, even if you did frighten my daughter so much she had nightmares for a week. But I'm not here to talk about that, and I'm not here to be a nuisance. I just want to talk about . . .' Should she tell? No. 'Something else,' she finished. 'Like I say, it'll only take a minute or two of your time, then I'll be away.'

Cocking her head to one side she was able to peer through one eye into the hallway. 'Please, Mrs Fellowes!'

Again, the most uneasy silence.

'Right.' Squaring her shoulders, she muttered indignantly, 'Round the back, my girl. She'll see me or my name isn't Libby Walters.'

She made her way through the neglected garden and reached the back door. She hammered on it until, to her astonishment, the door sprang open.

Gingerly, she stepped inside. The rank smell of damp and dust assailed her nostrils, and some other aroma she couldn't quite recognise. 'Mrs Fellowes?'

The silence seemed to thicken and she had half a mind to turn tail and run. But she didn't want Dave coming here again. If only she could clear things up and show him there was nothing in what he was thinking, everything would be all right.

'It's Daisy's mother,' she called again. 'Please, I just need to talk.'

She went through the house. Satisfied there was no one downstairs, she went up the stairs, wondering if this was the same way Daisy had come when she followed the kitten. At the top of the stairs she saw an open doorway. Having come this far, she decided she might as well go on, though her limbs were trembling and her heart was thudding uncomfortably. She approached the doorway.

She saw him then, an odd, bulky shape lying in the bed. She couldn't see his face. Curious, she went closer. 'Mr Fellowes?' Her voice was soft. 'Are you asleep?' The clothes were drawn so high over him, she wondered how he could breathe.

She was halfway across the room when she thought she heard a sound behind her. She turned. No, it was only her imagination, but what was that smell? Sweet, thick. Where had she smelled it before?

As she neared the bed, something moved, but it wasn't the shape on the bed. Not him. Her gaze fell to the floor. There! *Oh my God!*

Her eyes grew big and round, her mouth opened to scream and suddenly she was falling . . . falling. The hands round her neck were like iron. No! Please, no!

Something rough and strangely pleasant smothered her cry.

And all was dark.

The whiskered old sergeant who kept the files was growing angrier by the minute. Just five minutes, that's how long he'd been gone, and now, he'd returned to find Inspector Lowe rummaging about in his files.

All these years he had kept his records meticulous, neatly labelled, carefully put away and entered into the ledger. Next to his family, they were his pride and joy. He knew every file, every corner and drawer in his room, *his* room, *his* work. 'If you tell me what it is you're looking for, I might be able to help!'

He felt the urge to grab the inspector by the hair and throw him out, but rank had privilege and he had to make do with standing aside, while his precious papers were frantically shifted from one pile to another.

Head down, the inspector was too intent on his goal to be disturbed now. Silent and sullen he ploughed into the paperwork, scanning, shifting . . . scanning, shifting. He knew it was here. He felt it in his bones.

But 'feeling it in his bones' would not get him listened to. He needed proof. He needed records.

Suddenly he snatched up the file and his face lit up like a beacon. 'GOT IT!' With trembling fingers he opened the file and peered inside, taking a few moments to reassure himself, that his suspicions were right.

In the next moment he was heading for the door, the precious file clutched tightly in his fist.

'Look at the mess you've left!' The old sergeant was furious. 'It'll take me forever to clear this up.'

With a chuckle, the inspector called over his shoulder, 'Then you'll be a rich man from the overtime, won't you?'

He could afford to laugh. If his hunches were right, and he had every reason to believe they were . . . he would end his career in a blaze of glory!

Dave couldn't believe it had taken so long.

At the end of the meeting, where he and Barclay had thrashed out a mutually beneficial deal, he waved the other man off and got into his car. Here he switched on the mobile and dialled the office number. 'Jack? Look, I've just done one hell of a deal with Barclay . . . I'll tell you all about it when I get back to the office.'

He didn't stop to listen to what Jack was trying to tell him. He didn't let Jack get a word in edgewise. 'I've got another appointment, and I'm already late,' he went on. He consulted the dashboard clock. 'I should be back at the office before two thirty. Talk to me then.'

Cutting Jack off, he dialled again. 'Hello, May. I'm running a bit late, is Libby still there?'

'You'd better get back here now, Dave,' May told him. 'I'm worried sick about Libby. She went out ages ago and hasn't got back yet. I should have stopped her. She said you'd be furious, but she was so worried about you. She said if she could find out the truth, it would put your mind at rest.'

'Calm down, May. What are you saying . . . that Libby went to the Fellowes' place, is that what you're trying to tell me?'

'I'm sorry, I really am. I know I should have stopped her, but I thought it would be all right. I thought you'd told her all that stuff to hide the fact that you were having an affair. Oh, Dave, I'm so sorry.'

Anxiety covered the anger. 'Shut up, May, and listen!' He suddenly realised it was May who had been putting the ideas of an 'affair' into Libby's head. 'What time did she leave?'

'Early . . . some time before ten, I can't be sure.'

'Stay by the phone, and, if we're not back before the kids finish school, will you collect them . . . keep them with you?'

'Of course. You don't have to ask, you know that.'

'Thanks for that, anyway.' He'd have a few strong words to say to her when he saw her again. 'I'm going after her,' he said. 'Ring me if she turns up. Jack's got my mobile number.'

Turning the car round, he headed east. As he drove, he wondered why Libby had gone out there. 'Doesn't she understand the risk she's taking?' he mumbled. 'After I told her my suspicions?' He was terrified she might be in danger. He wanted her safe. He wanted her home.

He told himself to calm down. After all, the ghost of Bluebell Hill had never bothered Libby before, so why should she bother her now? But it wasn't that lost soul who worried him so much as Ida Fellowes. The woman gave him the creeps, and there were things going on in that house; weird things. First the restaurant was fired, then Larry Fellowes met a violent end, and soon after that Ida Fellowes herself was viciously attacked. None of it made any sense, but there was a definite link between the old man and the young woman who haunted the lane.

He feared for Libby. 'Be safe, sweetheart,' he murmured. 'Don't do or say anything to antagonise her.'

CHAPTER FOURTEEN

It was dark. Waking from a deep, unsettled sleep, Libby struggled to sit up. The air was bitingly cold. The sticky, pungent dampness clogged her throat. For a minute she didn't know what was happening. Slowly, agonisingly, it dawned on her. 'The bedroom.' In her mind's eye she saw herself going into the old man's bedroom, but after that, everything was hazy. She shivered. The knot of fear in the pit of her stomach tightened.

She began to realise why she couldn't sit up. Her hands and feet were tightly bound; her arms drawn behind her back and her legs bent up beneath her. Every bone in her body was stretched to breaking point. The pain was too intense for her to think clearly.

'The old man . . . in the bed.' She dug deep into her memory. Was he really there? She had seen a long shape like that of a body, but she hadn't seen his face, it was covered by the bedclothes. 'It could have been anyone. Or it could have been no one.' The sound of her own voice, soft and unsteady, was oddly comforting.

Another voice intervened, whispering, cold and harsh. 'Talking to yourself? They say you're mad if you talk to yourself.'

Shocked, Libby instinctively scuttled back, nearer to the wall; it was sheer agony even to move that little way.

'What do you want here? Who sent you?' the voice rasped.

Looking about, Libby could see only blackness. The voice was strange, disguised in a frightening, hissing whisper that seemed to come from the walls. She couldn't tell whether it was a man or a woman.

'No one sent me,' she answered tremulously.

'You're lying.'

'No, I'm not lying. Let me go. I mean you no harm.'

'I'm sorry. I can't do that.'

'Please! I came here to talk about something my husband said. I need to set his mind at rest. I didn't mean to come into the house. Please believe me.'

'Too late!' The laughter was like nothing Libby had ever heard before. Like someone whose mind had snapped.

Libby screamed out, 'Let me go! What harm can I do you?'

The laughter cut through the darkness. It was followed by a series of little sounds, as though a door or hatch was being shifted into place. Then all was quiet.

Leaning back against the damp, cold wall in the awful silence, Libby closed her eyes and prayed.

Suddenly she had the feeling there was someone close. 'Who's there?' Her skin crawled. 'Someone's there. Who is it?'

There was no reply. Libby gritted her teeth. 'Get a grip, Libby,' she told herself sternly, 'or you'll end up as mad as whoever put you here.'

She set about trying to break free but after a while she realised it was a hopeless task. Her arms felt as though they'd been stretched on the rack, and her spine was in such pain that she hardly dared move. Exhausted, she fell back to the wall, tears rolling down her face. 'Find me, Dave,' she whispered. 'Don't let me die here.'

Outside, the police took up strategic positions. 'No lights, no sound, and for God's sake don't make a move until I say so.'

Inspector Lowe knew the dangers. 'This is a devious, clever killer who has managed to elude us for years. One wrong move and it's all for nothing.' Keeping low, he crept through the perimeter of the trees, where the chief was despatching men to the house. 'We're ready, sir,' Lowe said. 'The men have their orders.'

The chief was tall and carried an air of authority, in direct contrast to Lowe's portly, rather shabby figure. He didn't waste words. 'Right. Get on with it,' he ordered.

In the cellar, Libby had no idea what was going on outside. When she heard scratching sounds, she thought it must be rats. Horrified, she shuffled away.

'It's me!' The voice was a mere whisper, but not like before. This time it was familiar, and Libby thought she really must be going mad.

'Daisy?'

'Ssh, Mummy. Don't make a noise.'

Disorientated and losing the battle against hysteria, Libby shouted, 'Go away! You're not Daisy!'

Suddenly a small, warm body fell against her. 'Ssh! They'll hear you. I saw them just now, creeping about in the woods.'

With that wonderful little face pressed close, Libby wept with relief. 'I thought I was being tricked,' she sobbed. 'Oh, Daisy! What's happening? How did you get here?' A terrible thought occurred to her. 'Are you all right? Did they hurt you?' Instinctively, she kept her voice low.

'I'm all right.' Tugging at the ropes that held Libby right, she explained, 'I heard you and Daddy arguing. I knew you'd come here, so I didn't go to school. I sneaked out of the gates and followed you to work. I hid in your car.'

Libby was amazed. 'I ought to scold you for that,' she murmured, 'but I'm so glad you did.' In the darkness she smiled. 'It will teach me to leave my doors unlocked, won't it?' Dave was always telling her off about that. 'But what made you think I would come here? Even Daddy didn't know. Did you hear me telling May?'

'No.' Daisy had got one rope loose and now Libby was able to help. 'I was in the car, squashed down right under the back seat. It wasn't very comfortable.'

Libby asked again, 'If you didn't hear me tell May about coming here, how did you know?'

'*She* told me.' Both hands were free now.

'Who?'

Daisy chose not to answer.

At last Libby was free. 'You have to climb up these steps, over the coal and everything.' Daisy led the way. 'Careful, Mummy. Don't tumble back down.'

'I'm right behind you, sweetheart.' She had hold of Daisy, surprised that there could be so much strength in such a tiny hand.

Daisy drew herself against the wall and Libby went with her. 'Someone's there,' Daisy whispered. 'See the shadow?'

Now that they were higher up, Libby caught a glimpse of the sliver of light round the hatch and, sure enough, there was a shadow, as though someone was prowling about.

Pressing themselves against the wall, the two of them waited. 'I think it's all right now,' Libby said. She was feeling stronger, more able to move her limbs without wanting to cry out.

Daisy climbed out first, then helped Libby. It was still very dark. The hatch led out into a small confined area. There was a door, slightly ajar, with light shining through. They listened for a moment and then went cautiously towards the door.

'We have to go along the passageway and up the back stairway, then across the landing.' Daisy said confidently. Libby wondered how she knew her way around so well but before she could ask, Daisy went on, 'I have to make sure the old man is all right.'

Libby was horrified. 'You can't,' she gasped. 'We've got to get out of here.'

Daisy was adamant. 'I promised,' she said, and darted through the door and down the passageway. Libby had no choice but to follow.

Swiftly they made their way up to the landing and paused outside the old man's bedroom. Nothing disturbed the silence. Cautiously, Daisy opened the door and then stepped into the room.

The door closed behind them with a sharp click. 'I knew you'd make your way here.' The voice was the same one that had taunted Libby in the cellar. She whirled to see a woman standing there, holding a long, sinister-looking knife.

The woman turned the key in the lock and dropped the key into her pocket. 'I'm glad you're here,' she said, smiling at Daisy. The smile slid away as she brought her gaze to Libby. 'I can't let you leave. I can't let you spoil it now.' *Eileen's face was like a hard, cruel mask.* 'You see, there are things that have to be done, things you don't know about.' Her evil gaze went to Daisy. '*She* knows though.' The hard, twinkling eyes smiled wickedly. 'The girl knows everything.'

Growling at Libby again, she said, 'We didn't want *you* here. People like you don't understand.' She glanced to the floor, under the bed. 'Ida doesn't understand either. I had to put her to sleep, you see.' The eyes glistened. 'I may have to kill her.'

Libby followed her gaze, gasping when she caught sight of a woman's skirt peeping from beneath the bed. Suddenly she realised what that sweet, thick smell was that she had encountered earlier. 'Chloroform!'

Eileen laughed. 'How clever of you.' She moved away from the door and her arm snaked out and plucked Daisy away.

'No!' Libby ran forward but Daisy's voice stopped her.

'It's all right, Mummy. She won't hurt me.'

Delighted, Eileen giggled. 'See? I told you she knows everything.' Suddenly the voice trembled with rage. 'If I do hurt her, it will be your fault. Stay where you are and don't interfere.'

Libby did as she was told.

Addressing Daisy now, the deranged woman said softly, 'Look, Daisy.' She gestured to the old man whose soft brown eyes were trained on Daisy's face. 'He knows you're here. See how he looks at you? Tell him, Daisy. Tell him about *her*.'

Libby couldn't be sure, but she thought the old man was crying.

Stepping forward, Daisy took hold of the old man's hand.

'Go on. Tell him you've seen her,' Eileen urged. 'Tell him about her.'

Daisy stroked the old man's brow. 'She's very beautiful,' she murmured. 'She loves you so much, and she will never go away. She wants me to tell you that. *She will never go away*.'

Seeming to understand, he smiled at Daisy, then looked up at Eileen and nodded, a slow, accepting kind of nod.

Eileen's face softened and she bent to kiss him. Then, pushing Daisy to one side, she slowly, deliberately, raised the knife.

Libby screamed. Her scream mingled with another, and suddenly all hell broke loose.

From out of nowhere, Ida threw herself at Eileen and they tumbled to the floor, the knife skidding across the room, coming to rest at Libby's feet. Grabbing it up, she caught hold of Daisy and together they ran to the door. Libby used the knife to force it open. 'Please God,' she muttered, her hands trembling so much she couldn't get the blade through the gap. 'Hold on to me, Daisy,' she cried. 'Don't let go!'

★ ★ ★

Dave was travelling fast as he approached the house. Slowing down, he swung the car through the gates and was immediately pounced on.

'Sorry, sir,' the grim-faced officer threw open the car door. 'No one goes in or out.' He bundled Dave away from the car.

Vehemently protesting, Dave was delivered to Inspector Lowe. Here he was made to produce evidence of identity, while his car number was relayed to the station where it was checked out. Once his credentials were confirmed, he was informed of the reason for the police presence.

When Dave explained that his wife was in there and he had no intention of just standing by, he was sharply informed that if he posed a threat, they would have no choice but to escort him away. 'We have the situation under control, sir,' Lowe emphasised. 'We will get your wife out safely.'

Realising he would get nowhere by crossing them, Dave decided to play along. The moment they began to relax their vigilance of him, their attention now focused on the lighted bedroom window, he seized his opportunity.

The two women fought like wild things. Libby struggled to force the door open but it wouldn't budge. Suddenly, there was a cry. Eileen fell hard against the window ledge, the blow momentarily stunning her. In a flash, Ida turned on Libby and wrestled the knife out of her hands, cutting them both in the process.

By this time Eileen had recovered her senses, and as Ida turned away from Libby, Eileen punched her in the head with all her might. Ida crumpled to the floor, out cold.

Sergeant Coley could hardly believe his eyes. 'Look there!' Pointing to the higher reaches of the house, he brought Inspector Lowe's attention to the figure climbing up a drainpipe towards the lighted bedroom window. 'It's Walters!'

'The bloody fool! Doesn't he know we have men closing in? Who the hell was supposed to be keeping an eye on him?'

Sergeant Coley thought it best to retreat. There was little they could do about Walters now, except watch, and hope.

Libby sat hunched in the corner, blood pouring from the wounds in her hands and a deep gash down one shoulder. 'Don't move,' she told Daisy in a soft, low voice. 'Don't make a sound.'

Across the other side of the room, Eileen raised the knife once more over the old man's throat. Libby would have fought like a tiger to save that old man's life, but she couldn't move. She felt as if she was pinned there by some unseen hand.

Covering Daisy's face, she said, 'Look away, sweetheart. There's nothing we can—'

There was a loud thump at the door and then the window shattered and Dave was scrambling over the ledge.

In the seconds before Dave ran to take Libby in his arms and the room was swarming with police, Eileen rushed across and grabbed Daisy by the hair. Pulling her out of Libby's reach, she stood with her back to the wall and Daisy in front of her. 'Come nearer and I swear I'll kill her.' Pressing the blade to Daisy's throat, she drew blood. 'I mean it!'

Everyone froze where they were. All but Dave. 'Let her go.' Raising himself to his full height, he took one tentative step forward. 'She means you no harm,' he said. 'You must know that.'

'Stay away!'

Libby pulled at him. 'Please, Dave,' she moaned. 'Do as she says.'

Into the ensuing silence came another voice. Recovering from the blow, Ida inched herself up to the end of the bed where she leaned heavily against it. 'I thought you were my friend,' she said, looking at Eileen through a veil of pain. 'You killed Larry, didn't you?'

Eileen was quiet for a moment. The tension in the room was like a physical presence. 'He was nothing. He deserved to die.' Loathing shaped her words.

'And what about me? Do I deserve to die?'

'I didn't want you dead. I loved you. I didn't know.'

'What didn't you know?'

'You . . . his daughter!'

'Yes, Eileen. Tony Fellowes is my father and, knowing it, I married his son, my own half-brother.' Trembling, she hissed, 'Have you any idea how vile it is to be touched by a man of your own blood? To lie there while he satisfies himself on you? But I'd do it again, just to be near this old man. To keep him alive, not out of love, but loathing. I had to make him suffer like he made my mother suffer.'

'I stole the suitcase,' Eileen said. 'I read the things inside. Until then, I didn't know.' Her voice softened. *'Your mother lied to you.'*

'My mother never lied to me!' Ida's face was livid. She scuttled to the head of the bed and grabbed the old man's hair, jerking his head towards her. She stared into his open eyes and, twisting out every word as though it caused her agony, she said, 'Years ago he promised my mother they would be married. But then he made her pregnant with me, and he didn't want her – he didn't want either of us. She pleaded with him but he was heartless. He went away, and she never saw him again. To give me a name, she married a monster. Her life was hell from that day on, and all because of this man!' Twisting his hair, she delighted in his pain. 'Her life was miserable, and when she'd had enough, she ended it.' Her mouth twisted with pain.

'After he rid himself of my mother, he married someone

else. But I found out, and I decided I had to make him miserable, like my mother had been miserable. So I followed him one night, drove him off the road. I thought I'd killed them both. I should have waited but I had to get away. Someone saw me, a woman. I warned her off, frightened her so much she never dared tell that I was there. I went far away. When I came back, I discovered he wasn't dead after all but put away in some hospital.' She smiled. 'I read about the woman walking the lane. I knew she was searching for him. I couldn't let them be together, could I? How could I?' She seemed to be asking herself, as if she wasn't sure. 'No! I had to keep them apart. My hatred was like a barrier between them.'

Before she had learned Ida's true feelings towards the old man, Eileen had come to love her like a mother. That love was in her voice now when she said softly, 'Listen to me, Ida. You have to understand why I can't let you keep them apart any longer.'

Encouraged by Ida's silence, she stepped forward. She held on to the knife, and Daisy too. From the other side of the room, Dave watched for his chance.

'I know the truth,' she said, moving nearer. 'We have to let him go.' She looked up suddenly and stared from Dave to the police officers. It was a cold, calculating look. A look that said, 'I know what's on your mind.'

The police had already inched forward, but now Lowe shook his head and they stayed put. The risk was too great to the girl. Besides, he wanted these two to keep talking. It could defuse a very delicate situation. What's more, little by little the truth was emerging.

'What could *you* know?' Ida spat out.

'I was in the hospital when you came to get him. I was ill, just like him. My mind was sick. The other patients laughed at me, hurt me, but he didn't.' Her gaze went to the old man. 'He was my friend. Before he lost his speech, he told me things.'

In spite of herself, Ida was caught up in what Eileen had to say. 'Did he tell you about my mother?' she demanded. 'Did he tell you how he ran away after he made her pregnant with me? He never wanted us, either of us!' Her voice trembled with emotion. She would have given anything for things to be different.

'You're wrong. He wanted you both.'

'Then why didn't he stay?'

'Because your mother didn't want him to stay.'

'You're lying!'

'It was your mother who found someone else, not him. He loved her so much, Ida, and she sent him away. She deprived you of a father.'

'No!'

'Ask him, Ida. Go on, ask him if he ever wanted you.'

Slowly, Ida shifted her gaze to the old man's face. To her surprise, he was crying. Those wise brown eyes were looking at her like a father at his child, and in that moment all the years and the doubt rolled away. She knew then. 'She's telling the truth, isn't she?'

When he nodded, her voice broke and the awful grief, which had lain dormant for so long, broke free.

With a strength born of happiness, he raised his arms to her. Gratefully, she nestled into his embrace. 'I'm sorry,' she sobbed. She thought of all the years she had tortured him; all those times when she had felt an overwhelming tenderness towards him, as though his love had ignited the truth inside her. 'I love you, Daddy.' She was a little girl again, only this time her father was there. The agony was over for them both.

Suddenly, everyone moved at once. Dave snatched Daisy safely away, two officers took hold of Eileen, and Inspector Lowe rounded the bed to release the old man from Ida's embrace. As he pulled her away, the pillow fell from her grasp, and the old man rolled back on the bed, his eyes wide open.

Just then the curtain blew through the broken window, the wind sounding like a sigh. At peace now, Ida looked across the room at Eileen, their smiles mingling, knowing.

'Look! She's come to get him,' Daisy cried.

'I think you're right, sweetheart.' Libby looked towards the window with a sense of wonder. She had heard and seen things this day that she would remember for the rest of her life.

CHAPTER FIFTEEN

The events of that night became the talk of the country. News spread of how Ida had killed the old man. Some people thought they understood why she had done such a thing – guilt, remorse, love for her father. Others believed she was a cold-blooded murderer who should be strung up by the neck and shown no mercy.

Opinion about Eileen, too, was divided, but most thought she was a hard and calculating woman who had murdered not just once but many times, and all for the love of that old man.

The old man was buried a week later, in a little church in the village of Marston where as a young man he had lived with his wife for many happy years; it was here they had raised their son Larry and known their greatest joy.

The only mourners at the church were a scattering of strangers, brought there by morbid curiosity, two photographers, and, out of sympathy for what had happened to him in his later years, Dave and Libby. Daisy, too, came to pay her respects, for she would not be left behind.

The service was short and comforting, and when Tony Fellowes was laid to rest in the old churchyard, Dave took his family home.

On the following day, a beautiful Sunday morning more reminiscent of June than February, the whole family strolled through the woods and along by way of Miss Ledell's house.

'Such a lovely old house,' Libby said. 'Such a pity.'

The four of them stood, hand in hand, looking at the charred ruins of that delightful dwelling. 'No one seems to know how it was burned down,' Dave murmured. He had seen the burnt-out house before, as though he had been allowed a peep forward, into another time. He had looked on the same scene and been saddened by it. Now he felt a great surge of joy. There was something beautiful here still, though it was not tangible. The air was filled with a sense of happiness, and he felt it deep inside. Daisy had said the old man was happy now, and he believed it with every fibre of his being.

He thought about the young woman who had taken Mandy's place. And the old lady, Miss Ledell. Neither of them had been seen since the day of the old man's death. He smiled inwardly. For the love of her man, Cliona Ledell had taken on many guises.

They walked on, closer to the house. Dave wondered if the piano was still as before, untouched by the flames. As they came into the garden, the children ran ahead.

'Be careful, you two,' Dave called. 'Stay well away from the house.' He turned to Libby. 'All right, sweetheart?' This past week she had recovered well from her ordeal. Her hands were healing, but the deep gash on her shoulder would probably leave a permanent reminder of the horrors that had unfolded around her.

'I'm fine,' she assured him. 'It's such a lovely day, let's not be in too much of a hurry to go home.' Lately she had come to appreciate more than ever the beauties of a world she had almost lost. 'I do love you,' she murmured, looking up at Dave. 'Don't ever doubt that.'

He held her tight, kissing her long and tenderly. 'I'm a lucky man,' he whispered in her ear, smiling a little. 'We still haven't had our weekend away.'

'Soon.' Returning his smile, she said, 'But I think we might have to take the children along.'

He laughed. 'If we didn't, we'd probably find Daisy curled up in the boot of the car when we got to the hotel.'

Daisy and Jamie ran towards them.

'Daisy?' There was something he'd been meaning to ask her.

'What, Daddy?'

'Before you hid in Mummy's car, outside the shop that day, how did you know where she was going?'

Smiling, Daisy pointed towards the house. '*She* told me.'

They followed her gaze. For a moment they could see nothing. The sun was suddenly blinding.

'Look!' Libby cried. 'By the shrubbery.'

Dave stretched his neck to see, and there, hand in hand, a couple strolled down the path, away from the house, away from all things earthly. The woman was young, very beautiful, with long dark hair and a spring to her step. The man was old, grey-haired, but as they went away, the mark of time began to fade. He became younger, his hair darkened, and soon they were laughing and running, happy in each other's company.

'They want us to know,' Dave murmured, folding his arms about his family. 'They want us to see.'

'They're together at last,' Libby whispered. Leaning into Dave's arms, her eyes filled with tears. 'Let's go home, sweetheart,' she said.

As they made their way back, they were lost in wonder, knowing they were privileged to have seen another time. Another world.

It was good to know that, somehow, somewhere, life went on.

After that day, and to Dave and Libby's undying gratitude, neither of the children appeared to have any recollection of what had taken place. It was almost as though it had never happened.

Dave and Libby knew differently.

★ ★ ★

Convicted of causing the accident that killed Cliona, Ida was given a ten-year prison sentence. On her release it was rumoured that with the proceeds from the sale of the house and restaurant, she bought a small cottage in rural Wales, where she lived contentedly until the age of eighty.

Eileen confessed to three murders. The first was a nurse at the hospital where she and the old man had been patients. When Ida came and took Tony Fellowes away, Eileen was beside herself. Days later, on discovering one of the nurses had applied for the post of looking after him, she killed the nurse and took her place.

Escaping from the hospital, she took along another patient, a woman with the mind of a child. When she threatened to tell what Eileen had done, in a fit of rage Eileen drowned her in the river. This was her second victim. The third was Larry Fellowes.

Eileen was committed to a secure asylum for the rest of her life, and to this day she sits in her room, talking, apparently to thin air.

But is there really no one there?